The View from Mrs. Wilkins's Bedroom.
After a Water-Colour Drawing by the Hon. Lady Mallet.

Frontispiece

THE ENCHANTED APRIL

Elizabeth von Arnim

DOVER PUBLICATIONS, INC.
MINEOLA, NEW YORK

DOVER THRIFT EDITIONS

GENERAL EDITOR: SUSAN L. RATTINER
EDITOR OF THIS VOLUME: TERRI ANN GEUS

Bibliographical Note

This Dover edition, first published in 2017, is a republication of the edition published by Macmillan and Co., Limited, London, in 1922. The original color frontispiece has been reprinted here in black and white.

Library of Congress Cataloging-in-Publication Data

Names: Von Arnim, Elizabeth, 1866–1941, author.
Title: The enchanted April / Elizabeth von Arnim.
Description: Dover edition. | Mineola, New York : Dover Publications, Inc.,
  2017. | Series: Dover thrift editions
Identifiers: LCCN 2016041328| ISBN 9780486813417 (paperback) | ISBN
  048681341X (paperback)
Subjects: | BISAC: FICTION / Classics. | FICTION / Historical. | FICTION /
  Literary.
Classification: LCC PR6035.U8 E62 2017 | DDC 823/.914—dc23 LC record
available at https://lccn.loc.gov/2016041328

Manufactured in the United States by LSC Communications
81341X02   2017
www.doverpublications.com

THE ENCHANTED APRIL

I

I⊤ began in a woman's club in London on a February afternoon,—an uncomfortable club, and a miserable afternoon—when Mrs. Wilkins, who had come down from Hampstead to shop and had lunched at her club, took up *The Times* from the table in the smoking-room, and running her listless eye down the Agony Column saw this :

> To Those who Appreciate Wistaria and Sunshine. Small mediaeval Italian Castle on the shores of the Mediterranean to be Let Furnished for the month of April. Necessary servants remain. Z, Box 1000, *The Times*.

That was its conception ; yet, as in the case of many another, the conceiver was unaware of it at the moment.

So entirely unaware was Mrs. Wilkins that her April for that year had then and there been settled for her that she dropped the newspaper with a gesture that was both irritated and resigned, and went over to the window and stared drearily out at the dripping street.

1

Not for her were mediaeval castles, even those that are specially described as small. Not for her the shores in April of the Mediterranean, and the wistaria and sunshine. Such delights were only for the rich. Yet the advertisement had been addressed to persons who appreciate these things, so that it had been, anyhow, addressed too to her, for she certainly appreciated them ; more than anybody knew ; more than she had ever told. But she was poor. In the whole world she possessed of her very own only ninety pounds, saved from year to year, put by carefully pound by pound, out of her dress allowance. She had scraped this sum together at the suggestion of her husband as a shield and refuge against a rainy day. Her dress allowance, given her by her father, was £100 a year, so that Mrs. Wilkins's clothes were what her husband, urging her to save, called modest and becoming, and her acquaintance to each other, when they spoke of her at all, which was seldom for she was very negligible, called a perfect sight.

Mr. Wilkins, a solicitor, encouraged thrift, except that branch of it which got into his food. He did not call that thrift, he called it bad housekeeping. But for the thrift which, like moth, penetrated into Mrs. Wilkins's clothes and spoilt them, he had much praise. 'You never know,' he said, ' when there will be a rainy day, and you may be very glad to find you have a nest-egg. Indeed we both may.'

Looking out of the club window into Shaftesbury Avenue—hers was an economical club, but convenient for Hampstead, where she lived, and for Shoolbred's, where she shopped,—Mrs. Wilkins, having stood there some time very drearily, her mind's eye on the Mediterranean in April, and the wistaria, and the enviable opportunities of the rich, while her bodily eye watched the really extremely horrible sooty rain falling steadily on the hurrying umbrellas and splashing omnibuses, suddenly wondered whether perhaps this was not the rainy day Mellersh—Mellersh was Mr. Wilkins—had so often encouraged her to prepare for, and whether to get out of such a climate and into the small mediaeval castle wasn't perhaps what Providence had all along intended her to do with her savings. Part of her savings, of course ; perhaps quite a small part. The castle, being mediaeval, might also be dilapidated, and dilapidations were surely cheap. She wouldn't in the least mind a few of them, because you didn't pay for dilapidations which were already there ; on the contrary,—by reducing the price you had to pay they really paid you. But what nonsense to think of it. . . .

She turned away from the window with the same gesture of mingled irritation and resignation with which she had laid down *The Times*, and crossed the room towards the door with the intention of getting her mackintosh and umbrella and fighting her way into one of the overcrowded omnibuses and going to Shoolbred's on her way home and buying some soles for Mellersh's dinner—Mellersh was difficult with fish and liked only soles, except salmon—when she beheld Mrs. Arbuthnot, a woman she knew by sight as also living in Hampstead and belonging to the club, sitting at the table in the middle of the room on which the newspapers and magazines were kept, absorbed, in her turn, in the first page of *The Times*.

Mrs. Wilkins had never yet spoken to Mrs. Arbuthnot, who belonged to one of the various church sets, and who analysed, classified, divided and registered the poor ; whereas she and Mellersh, when they did go out, went to the parties of impressionist painters, of whom in Hampstead there were many. Mellersh had a sister who had married one of them and lived up on the Heath, and because of this alliance Mrs. Wilkins was drawn into a circle which was highly unnatural to her, and she had learned to dread pictures. She had to say things about them, and she didn't know what to say. She used to murmur, ' Marvellous,' and feel that it was not enough. But nobody minded. Nobody listened. Nobody took any notice of Mrs. Wilkins. She was the kind of person

who is not noticed at parties. Her clothes, infested by
thrift, made her practically invisible ; her face was non-
arresting ; her conversation was reluctant ; she was
shy. And if one's clothes and face and conversation are
all negligible, thought Mrs. Wilkins, who recognised her
disabilities, what, at parties, is there left of one ?

Also she was always with Wilkins, that clean-shaven,
fine-looking man, who gave a party, merely by coming
to it, a great air. Wilkins was very respectable. He
was known to be highly thought of by his senior partners.
His sister's circle admired him. He pronounced ade-
quately intelligent judgments on art and artists. He
was pithy ; he was prudent ; he never said a word too
much, nor, on the other hand, did he ever say a word
too little. He produced the impression of keeping copies
of everything he said ; and he was so obviously reliable
that it often happened that people who met him at these
parties became discontented with their own solicitors,
and after a period of restlessness extricated themselves
and went to Wilkins.

Naturally Mrs. Wilkins was blotted out. ' She,' said
his sister, with something herself of the judicial, the
digested, and the final in her manner, ' should stay at
home.' But Wilkins could not leave his wife at home.
He was a family solicitor, and all such have wives and
show them. With his in the week he went to parties, and

with his on Sundays he went to church. Being still fairly young—he was thirty-nine—and ambitious of old ladies, of whom he had not yet acquired in his practice a sufficient number, he could not afford to miss church, and it was there that Mrs. Wilkins became familiar, though never through words, with Mrs. Arbuthnot.

She saw her marshalling the children of the poor into pews. She would come in at the head of the procession from the Sunday School exactly five minutes before the choir, and get her boys and girls neatly fitted into their allotted seats, and down on their little knees in their preliminary prayer, and up again on their feet just as, to the swelling organ, the vestry door opened, and the choir and clergy, big with the litanies and command-ments they were presently to roll out, emerged. She had a sad face, yet she was evidently efficient. The combination used to make Mrs. Wilkins wonder, for she had been told by Mellersh, on days when she had only been able to get plaice, that if one were efficient one wouldn't be depressed, and that if one does one's job well one becomes automatically bright and brisk.

About Mrs. Arbuthnot there was nothing bright and brisk, though much in her way with the Sunday School children that was automatic ; but when Mrs. Wilkins, turning from the window, caught sight of her in the club she was not being automatic at all, but was looking

fixedly at one portion of the first page of *The Times,*
holding the paper quite still, her eyes not moving. She
was just staring ; and her face, as usual, was the face of
a patient and disappointed Madonna.

Obeying an impulse she wondered at even while
obeying it, Mrs. Wilkins, the shy and the reluctant,
instead of proceeding as she had intended to the cloakroom and from thence to Shoolbred's in search of
Mellersh's fish, stopped at the table and sat down exactly
opposite Mrs. Arbuthnot, to whom she had never yet
spoken in her life.

It was one of those long, narrow refectory tables, so
that they were quite close to each other.

Mrs. Arbuthnot, however, did not look up. She
continued to gaze, with eyes that seemed to be dreaming,
at one spot only of *The Times.*

Mrs. Wilkins watched her a minute, trying to screw
up courage to speak to her. She wanted to ask her if
she had seen the advertisement. She did not know why
she wanted to ask her this, but she wanted to. How
stupid not to be able to speak to her. She looked so
kind. She looked so unhappy. Why couldn't two
unhappy people refresh each other on their way through
this dusty business of life by a little talk,—real, natural
talk, about what they felt, what they would have liked,
what they still tried to hope ? And she could not help

thinking that Mrs. Arbuthnot, too, was reading that very same advertisement. Her eyes were on the very part of the paper.   Was she, too, picturing what it would be like,—the colour, the fragrance, the light, the soft lapping of the sea among little hot rocks ?   Colour, fragrance, light, sea ; instead of Shaftesbury Avenue, and the wet omnibuses, and the fish department at Shoolbred's, and the Tube to Hampstead, and dinner, and to-morrow the same and the day after the same and always the same. . . .

Suddenly Mrs. Wilkins found herself leaning across the table.   ' Are you reading about the mediaeval castle and the wistaria ? ' she heard herself asking.

Naturally Mrs. Arbuthnot was surprised ; but she was not half so much surprised as Mrs. Wilkins was at herself for asking.

Mrs. Arbuthnot had not yet to her knowledge set eyes on the shabby, lank, loosely-put-together figure sitting opposite her, with its small freckled face and big grey eyes almost disappearing under a smashed-down wet-weather hat, and she gazed at her a moment without answering.   She *was* reading about the mediaeval castle and the wistaria, or rather had read about it ten minutes before, and since then had been lost in dreams, —of light, of colour, of fragrance, of the soft lapping of the sea among little hot rocks. . . .

'Why do you ask me that?' she said in her grave voice, for her training of and by the poor had made her grave and patient.

Mrs. Wilkins flushed and looked excessively shy and frightened. 'Oh, only because I saw it too, and I thought perhaps—I thought somehow——' she stammered.

Whereupon Mrs. Arbuthnot, her mind being used to getting people into lists and divisions, from habit considered, as she gazed thoughtfully at Mrs. Wilkins, under what heading, supposing she had to classify her, she could most properly be put.

'And I know you by sight,' went on Mrs. Wilkins, who, like all the shy, once she was started plunged on, frightening herself to more and more speech by the sheer sound of what she had said last in her ears. 'Every Sunday—I see you every Sunday in church——'

'In church?' echoed Mrs. Arbuthnot.

'And this seems such a wonderful thing—this advertisement about the wistaria—and——'

Mrs. Wilkins, who must have been at least thirty, broke off and wriggled in her chair with the movement of an awkward and embarrassed schoolgirl.

'It seems *so* wonderful,' she went on in a kind of burst, ' and—it *is* such a miserable day. . . .'

And then she sat looking at Mrs. Arbuthnot with the eyes of an imprisoned dog.

'This poor thing,' thought Mrs. Arbuthnot, whose life was spent in helping and alleviating, 'needs advice.'

She accordingly prepared herself patiently to give it.

'If you see me in church,' she said, kindly and attentively, 'I suppose you live in Hampstead too ? '

'Oh yes,' said Mrs. Wilkins. And she repeated, her head on its long thin neck drooping a little as if the recollection of Hampstead bowed her, 'Oh yes.'

'Where ? ' asked Mrs. Arbuthnot, who, when advice was needed, naturally first proceeded to collect the facts.

But Mrs. Wilkins, laying her hand softly and caressingly on the part of *The Times* where the advertisement was, as though the mere printed words of it were precious, only said, 'Perhaps that's why *this* seems so wonderful.'

'No—I think *that's* wonderful anyhow,' said Mrs. Arbuthnot, forgetting facts and faintly sighing.

'Then you *were* reading it ? '

'Yes,' said Mrs. Arbuthnot, her eyes going dreamy again.

'Wouldn't it be wonderful ? ' murmured Mrs. Wilkins.

'Wonderful,' said Mrs. Arbuthnot. Her face, which had lit up, faded into patience again. 'Very wonderful,' she said. 'But it's no use wasting one's time thinking of such things.'

' Oh, but it *is*,' was Mrs. Wilkins's quick, surprising reply; surprising because it was so much unlike the rest of her, — the characterless coat and skirt, the crumpled hat, the undecided wisp of hair straggling out. ' And just the considering of them is worth while in itself—such a change from Hampstead—and sometimes I believe—I really do believe—if one considers hard enough one gets things.'

Mrs. Arbuthnot observed her patiently. In what category would she, supposing she had to, put her ?

' Perhaps,' she said, leaning forward a little, ' you will tell me your name. If we are to be friends '—she smiled her grave smile—' as I hope we are, we had better begin at the beginning.'

' Oh yes—how kind of you. I'm Mrs. Wilkins,' said Mrs. Wilkins. ' I don't expect,' she added, flushing, as Mrs. Arbuthnot said nothing, ' that it conveys anything to you. Sometimes it—it doesn't seem to convey anything to me either. But '—she looked round with a movement of seeking help—' I *am* Mrs. Wilkins.'

She did not like her name. It was a mean, small name, with a kind of facetious twist, she thought, about its end like the upward curve of a pugdog's tail. There it was, however. There was no doing anything with it. Wilkins she was and Wilkins she would remain ; and though her husband encouraged her to give it on all occasions as Mrs. Mellersh-Wilkins she only did that when he was within earshot, for she thought Mellersh made Wilkins worse, emphasising it in the way Chatsworth on the gate-posts of a villa emphasises the villa.

When first he suggested she should add Mellersh she had objected for the above reason, and after a pause,—Mellersh was much too prudent to speak except after a pause, during which presumably he was taking a careful mental copy of his coming observation—he said, much displeased, ' But I am not a villa,' and looked at her as he looks who hopes, for perhaps the hundredth time, that he may not have married a fool.

Of course he was not a villa, Mrs. Wilkins assured him ; she had never supposed he was ; she had not dreamed of meaning . . . she was only just thinking. . . .

The more she explained the more earnest became Mellersh's hope, familiar to him by this time, for he had then been a husband for two years, that he might not by any chance have married a fool ; and they had a prolonged quarrel, if that can be called a quarrel which is conducted with dignified silence on one side and earnest apology on the other, as to whether or no Mrs. Wilkins had intended to suggest that Mr. Wilkins was a villa.

' I believe,' she had thought when it was at last over

—it took a long while—' that *anybody* would quarrel about *anything* when they've not left off being together for a single day for two whole years. What we both need is a holiday.'

' My husband,' went on Mrs. Wilkins to Mrs. Arbuthnot, trying to throw some light on herself, ' is a solicitor. He——' She cast about for something she could say elucidatory of Mellersh, and found : ' He's very handsome.'

' Well,' said Mrs. Arbuthnot kindly, ' that must be a great pleasure to you.'

' Why ? ' asked Mrs. Wilkins.

' Because,' said Mrs. Arbuthnot, a little taken aback, for constant intercourse with the poor had accustomed her to have her pronouncements accepted without question, ' because beauty—handsomeness—is a gift like any other, and if it is properly used——'

She trailed off into silence. Mrs. Wilkins's great grey eyes were fixed on her, and it seemed suddenly to Mrs. Arbuthnot that perhaps she was becoming crystallised into a habit of exposition, and of exposition after the manner of nursemaids, through having an audience that couldn't but agree, that would be afraid, if it wished, to interrupt, that didn't know, that was, in fact, at her mercy.

But Mrs. Wilkins was not listening ; for just then,

absurd as it seemed, a picture had flashed across her brain, and there were two figures in it sitting together under a great trailing wistaria that stretched across the branches of a tree she didn't know, and it was herself and Mrs. Arbuthnot—she saw them—she saw them. And behind them, bright in sunshine, were old grey walls— the mediaeval castle—she saw it—they were there. . . .

She therefore stared at Mrs. Arbuthnot and did not hear a word she said. And Mrs. Arbuthnot stared too at Mrs. Wilkins, arrested by the expression on her face, which was swept by the excitement of what she saw, and was as luminous and tremulous under it as water in sunlight when it is ruffled by a gust of wind. At this moment, if she had been at a party, Mrs. Wilkins would have been looked at with interest.

They stared at each other; Mrs. Arbuthnot surprised, inquiringly, Mrs. Wilkins with the eyes of some one who has had a revelation. Of course. That was how it could be done. She herself, she by herself, couldn't afford it, and wouldn't be able, even if she could afford it, to go there all alone; but she and Mrs. Arbuthnot together. . . .

She leaned across the table. 'Why don't we try and get it?' she whispered.

Mrs. Arbuthnot became even more wide-eyed. 'Get it?' she repeated.

'Yes,' said Mrs. Wilkins, still as though she were afraid of being overheard. 'Not just sit here and say How wonderful, and then go home to Hampstead without having put out a finger—go home just as usual and see about the dinner and the fish just as we've been doing for years and years and will go on doing for years and years. In fact,' said Mrs. Wilkins, flushing to the roots of her hair, for the sound of what she was saying, of what was coming pouring out, frightened her, and yet she couldn't stop, 'I see no end to it. There *is* no end to it. So that there ought to be a break, there ought to be intervals—in everybody's interests. Why, it would really be being unselfish to go away and be happy for a little, because we would come back so much nicer. You see, after a bit everybody needs a holiday.'

'But—how do you mean, get it ? ' asked Mrs. Arbuthnot.

'Take it,' said Mrs. Wilkins.

'Take it ? '

'Rent it.   Hire it.   Have it.'

'But—do you mean you and I ? '

'Yes. Between us. Share. Then it would only cost half, and you look so—you look exactly as if you wanted it just as much as I do—as if you ought to have a rest—have something happy happen to you.'

'Why, but we don't know each other.'

'But just think how well we would if we went away together for a month ! And I've saved for a rainy day, and I expect so have you, and this *is* the rainy day—look at it——'

'She is unbalanced,' thought Mrs. Arbuthnot; yet she felt strangely stirred.

'Think of getting away for a whole month—from everything—to heaven——'

'She shouldn't say things like that,' thought Mrs. Arbuthnot. 'The vicar——' Yet she felt strangely stirred. It would indeed be wonderful to have a rest, a cessation.

Habit, however, steadied her again; and years of intercourse with the poor made her say, with the slight though sympathetic superiority of the explainer, 'But then, you see, heaven isn't somewhere else. It is here and now. We are told so.'

She became very earnest, just as she did when trying patiently to help and enlighten the poor. 'Heaven is within us,' she said in her gentle low voice. 'We are told that on the very highest authority. And you know the lines about the kindred points, don't you——'

'Oh yes, I know *them*,' interrupted Mrs. Wilkins impatiently.

'The kindred points of heaven and home,' continued

Mrs. Arbuthnot, who was used to finishing her sentences. 'Heaven is in our home.'

'It isn't,' said Mrs. Wilkins, again surprisingly.

Mrs. Arbuthnot was taken aback. Then she said gently, 'Oh, but it is. It is there if we choose, if we make it.'

'I do choose, and I do make it, and it isn't,' said Mrs. Wilkins.

Then Mrs. Arbuthnot was silent, for she too sometimes had doubts about homes. She sat and looked uneasily at Mrs. Wilkins, feeling more and more the urgent need of getting her classified. If she could only classify Mrs. Wilkins, get her safely under her proper heading, she felt that she herself would regain her balance, which did seem very strangely to be slipping all to one side. For neither had she had a holiday for years, and the advertisement when she saw it had set her dreaming, and Mrs. Wilkins's excitement about it was infectious, and she had the sensation, as she listened to her impetuous, odd talk and watched her lit-up face, that she was being stirred out of sleep.

Clearly Mrs. Wilkins was unbalanced, but Mrs. Arbuthnot had met the unbalanced before—indeed she was always meeting them—and they had no effect on her own stability at all ; whereas this one was making her feel quite wobbly, quite as though to be off and away, away from her compass points of God, Husband, Home and Duty—she didn't feel as if Mrs. Wilkins intended Mr. Wilkins to come too—and just for once be happy, would be both good and desirable. Which of course it wasn't; which certainly of course it wasn't. She, also, had a nest-egg, invested gradually in the Post Office Savings Bank, but to suppose that she would ever forget her duty to the extent of drawing it out and spending it on herself was surely absurd. Surely she couldn't, she wouldn't ever do such a thing? Surely she wouldn't, she couldn't ever forget her poor, forget misery and sickness as completely as that? No doubt a trip to Italy would be extraordinarily delightful, but there were many delightful things one would like to do, and what was strength given to one for except to help one not to do them?

Steadfast as the points of the compass to Mrs. Arbuthnot were the great four facts of life : God, Husband, Home, Duty. She had gone to sleep on these facts years ago, after a period of much misery, her head resting on them as on a pillow; and she had a great dread of being awakened out of so simple and untroublesome a condition. Therefore it was that she searched with earnestness for a heading under which to put Mrs. Wilkins, and in this way illumine and steady her own mind; and sitting there looking at her uneasily after her last remark, and feeling herself becoming more and more unbalanced and infected, she decided *pro tem*, as the vicar said at meetings, to put her under the heading Nerves. It was just possible that she ought to go straight into the category Hysteria, which was often only the antechamber to Lunacy, but Mrs. Arbuthnot had learned not to hurry people into their final categories, having on more than one occasion discovered with dismay that she had made a mistake; and how difficult it had been to get them out again, and how crushed she had been with the most terrible remorse.

Yes. Nerves. Probably she had no regular work for others, thought Mrs. Arbuthnot; no work that would take her outside herself. Evidently she was rudderless,—blown about by gusts, by impulses. Nerves was almost certainly her category, or would be quite soon if no one helped her. Poor little thing, thought Mrs. Arbuthnot, her own balance returning hand in hand with her compassion, and unable, because of the table, to see the length of Mrs. Wilkins's legs. All she saw was her small, eager, shy face, and her thin shoulders, and the look of childish longing in her eyes for something that she was sure was going to make her happy. No; such things didn't make people happy, such fleeting things. Mrs. Arbuthnot had learned in her long life with Frederick—he was her husband, and she had

married him at twenty and was now thirty-three—
where alone true joys are to be found. They are to be
found, she now knew, only in daily, in hourly, living
for others ; they are to be found only—hadn't she over
and over again taken her disappointments and discouragements there, and come away comforted ?—at
the feet of God.

Frederick had been the kind of husband whose wife
betakes herself early to the feet of God. From him to
them had been a short though painful step. It seemed
short to her in retrospect, but it had really taken the
whole of the first year of their marriage, and every inch
of the way had been a struggle, and every inch of it
was stained, she felt at the time, with her heart's blood.
All that was over now. She had long since found
peace. And Frederick, from her passionately loved
bridegroom, from her worshipped young husband, had
become second only to God on her list of duties and
forbearances. There he hung, the second in importance,
a bloodless thing bled white by her prayers. For years
she had been able to be happy only by forgetting happiness. She wanted to stay like that. She wanted to
shut out everything that would remind her of beautiful
things, that might set her off again longing, desiring. . . .

' I'd like so much to be friends,' she said earnestly.
' Won't you come and see me, or let me come to you

sometimes ? Whenever you feel as if you wanted to talk. I'll give you my address '—she searched in her handbag—' and then you won't forget.' And she found a card and held it out.

Mrs. Wilkins ignored the card.

' It's so funny,' said Mrs. Wilkins, just as if she had not heard her, ' but I *see* us both—you and me—this April in the mediaeval castle.'

Mrs. Arbuthnot relapsed into uneasiness. ' Do you ? ' she said, making an effort to stay balanced under the visionary gaze of the shining grey eyes. ' Do you ? '

' Don't you ever see things in a kind of flash before they happen ? ' asked Mrs. Wilkins.

' Never,' said Mrs. Arbuthnot.

She tried to smile ; she tried to smile the sympathetic yet wise and tolerant smile with which she was accustomed to listen to the necessarily biassed and incomplete views of the poor. She didn't succeed. The smile trembled out.

' Of course,' she said in a low voice, almost as if she were afraid the vicar and the Savings Bank were listening, ' it would be most beautiful—most beautiful——'

' Even if it were wrong,' said Mrs. Wilkins, ' it would only be for a month.'

' That——' began Mrs. Arbuthnot, quite clear as to

the reprehensibleness of such a point of view ; but Mrs.
Wilkins stopped her before she could finish.

'Anyhow,' said Mrs. Wilkins, stopping her, 'I'm sure
it's wrong to go on being good for too long, till one gets
miserable. And I can see you've been good for years
and years, because you look so unhappy '—Mrs. Arbuthnot opened her mouth to protest—'and I—I've done
nothing but duties, things for other people, ever since I
was a girl, and I don't believe anybody loves me a bit
—a bit—the b-better—and I long—oh, I long—for
something else—something else——'

Was she going to cry ? Mrs. Arbuthnot became
acutely uncomfortable and sympathetic. She hoped
she wasn't going to cry. Not there. Not in that
unfriendly room, with strangers coming and going.

But Mrs. Wilkins, after tugging agitatedly at a hand-
kerchief that wouldn't come out of her pocket, did
succeed at last in merely apparently blowing her nose
with it, and then, blinking her eyes very quickly once
or twice, looked at Mrs. Arbuthnot with a quivering air
of half humble, half frightened apology, and smiled.

'Will you believe,' she whispered, trying to steady
her mouth, evidently dreadfully ashamed of herself,
'that I've never spoken to any one before in my life
like this ? I can't think, I simply don't know, what
has come over me.'

'It's the advertisement,' said Mrs. Arbuthnot, nodding gravely.

'Yes,' said Mrs. Wilkins, dabbing furtively at her eyes, 'and us both being so—'—she blew her nose again a little—'miserable.'

Of course Mrs. Arbuthnot was not miserable—how could she be, she asked herself, when God was taking care of her?—but she let that pass for the moment unrepudiated, because of her conviction that here was another fellow-creature in urgent need of her help; and not just boots and blankets and better sanitary arrangements this time, but the more delicate help of comprehension, of finding the exact right words.

The exact right words, she presently discovered, after trying various ones about living for others, and prayer, and the peace to be found in placing oneself unreservedly in God's hands,—to meet all these words Mrs. Wilkins had other words, incoherent and yet, for the moment at least, till one had had more time, difficult to answer—the exact right words were a suggestion that it would do no harm to answer the advertisement. Non-committal. Mere inquiry. And what disturbed Mrs. Arbuthnot about this suggestion was that she did not make it solely to comfort Mrs. Wilkins; she made it because of her own strange longing for the mediaeval castle.

This was very disturbing. There she was, accustomed to direct, to lead, to advise, to support—except Frederick ; she long since had learned to leave Frederick to God—being led herself, being influenced and thrown off her feet, by just an advertisement, by just an incoherent stranger. It was indeed disturbing. She failed to understand her sudden longing for what was, after all, self-indulgence, when for years no such desire had entered her heart.

'There's no harm in simply *asking*,' she said in a low voice, as if the vicar and the Savings Bank and all her waiting and dependent poor were listening and condemning.

'It isn't as if it *committed* us to anything,' said Mrs. Wilkins, also in a low voice, but her voice shook.

They got up simultaneously—Mrs. Arbuthnot had a sensation of surprise that Mrs. Wilkins should be so tall—and went to a writing-table, and Mrs. Arbuthnot wrote to Z, Box 1000, *The Times*, for particulars. She asked for all particulars, but the only one they really wanted was the one about the rent. They both felt that it was Mrs. Arbuthnot who ought to write the letter and do the business part. Not only was she used to organising and being practical, but she also was older,

and certainly calmer ; and she herself had no doubt too
that she was wiser. Neither had Mrs. Wilkins any doubt
of this ; the very way Mrs. Arbuthnot parted her hair
suggested a great calm that could only proceed from
wisdom.

But if she was wiser, older and calmer, Mrs.
Arbuthnot's new friend nevertheless seemed to her to be
the one who impelled. Incoherent, she yet impelled.
She appeared to have, apart from her need of help, an
upsetting kind of character. She had a curious infec-
tiousness. She led one on. And the way her unsteady
mind leaped at conclusions—wrong ones, of course ;
witness the one that she, Mrs. Arbuthnot, was miserable
—the way she leaped at conclusions was disconcerting.

Whatever she was, however, and whatever her un-
steadiness, Mrs. Arbuthnot found herself sharing her
excitement and her longing ; and when the letter had
been posted in the letter-box in the hall and actually
was beyond getting back again, both she and Mrs.
Wilkins felt the same sense of guilt.

'It only shows,' said Mrs. Wilkins in a whisper, as
they turned away from the letter-box, 'how immaculately good we've been all our lives. The very first time
we do anything our husbands don't know about we feel
guilty.'

'I'm afraid I can't say I've been immaculately good,'

gently protested Mrs. Arbuthnot, a little uncomfortable
at this fresh example of successful leaping at conclusions,
for she had not said a word about her feeling of guilt.

' Oh, but I'm sure you have—I *see* you being good—
and that's why you're not happy.'

' She shouldn't say things like that,' thought Mrs.
Arbuthnot. ' I must try and help her not to.'

Aloud she said gravely, ' I don't know why you insist
that I'm not happy. When you know me better I think
you'll find that I am. And I'm sure you don't mean
really that goodness, if one could attain it, makes one
unhappy.'

' Yes, I do,' said Mrs. Wilkins. ' Our sort of goodness
does. We have attained it, and we are unhappy. There
are miserable sorts of goodness and happy sorts—the
sort we'll have at the mediaeval castle, for instance, is
the happy sort.'

' That is, supposing we go there,' said Mrs. Arbuthnot
restrainingly. She felt that Mrs. Wilkins needed holding
on to. ' After all, we've only written just to ask. Anybody may do that. I think it quite likely we shall find
the conditions impossible, and even if they were not,
probably by to-morrow we shall not want to go.'

' I *see* us there,' was Mrs. Wilkins's answer to that.

All this was very unbalancing. Mrs. Arbuthnot, as
she presently splashed through the dripping streets on

her way to a meeting she was to speak at, was in an unusually disturbed condition of mind. She had, she hoped, shown herself very calm to Mrs. Wilkins, very practical and sober, concealing her own excitement. But she was really extraordinarily moved, and she felt happy, and she felt guilty, and she felt afraid, and she had all the feelings, though this she did not know, of a woman who has come away from a secret meeting with her lover. That, indeed, was what she looked like when she arrived late on her platform ; she, the open-browed, looked almost furtive as her eyes fell on the staring wooden faces waiting to hear her try and persuade them to contribute to the alleviation of the urgent needs of the Hampstead poor, each one convinced that they needed contributions themselves. She looked as though she were hiding something discreditable but delightful. Certainly her customary clear expression of candour was not there, and its place was taken by a kind of suppressed and frightened pleasedness, which would have led a more worldly-minded audience to the instant conviction of recent and probably impassioned lovemaking.

Beauty, beauty, beauty . . . the words kept ring-ing in her ears as she stood on the platform talking of sad things to the sparsely attended meeting. She had never been to Italy. Was that really what her nest-egg was to be spent on after all ? Though she couldn't approve of the way Mrs. Wilkins was introducing the idea of predestination into her immediate future, just as if she had no choice, just as if to struggle, or even to reflect, were useless, it yet influenced her. Mrs. Wilkins's eyes had been the eyes of a seer. Some people were like that, Mrs. Arbuthnot knew; and if Mrs. Wilkins had actually seen her at the mediaeval castle it did seem probable that struggling would be waste of time. Still, to spend her nest-egg on self-indulgence—— The origin of this egg had been corrupt, but she had at least supposed its end was to be creditable. Was she to deflect it from its intended destination, which alone had appeared to justify her keeping it, and spend it on giving herself pleasure?

Mrs. Arbuthnot spoke on and on, so much practised in the kind of speech that she could have said it all in her sleep, and at the end of the meeting, her eyes dazzled by her secret visions, she hardly noticed that nobody was moved in any way whatever, least of all in the way of contributions.

But the vicar noticed. The vicar was disappointed. Usually his good friend and supporter Mrs. Arbuthnot succeeded better than this. And, what was even more unusual, she appeared, he observed, not even to mind.

'I can't imagine,' he said to her as they parted, speaking irritably, for he was irritated both by the audience and by her, ' what these people are coming to. *Nothing* seems to move them.'

' Perhaps they need a holiday,' suggested Mrs. Arbuthnot ; an unsatisfactory, a queer reply, the vicar thought.

' In February ? ' he called after her sarcastically.

' Oh no—not till April,' said Mrs. Arbuthnot over her shoulder.

' Very odd,' thought the vicar. ' Very odd indeed.' And he went home and was not perhaps quite christian to his wife.

That night in her prayers Mrs. Arbuthnot asked for guidance. She felt she ought really to ask, straight out and roundly, that the mediaeval castle should already have been taken by some one else and the whole thing thus be settled, but her courage failed her. Suppose her prayer were to be answered ? No ; she couldn't ask it ; she couldn't risk it. And after all—she almost pointed this out to God—if she spent her present nest-egg on a holiday she could quite soon accumulate another. Frederick pressed money on her ; and it would only mean, while she rolled up a second egg, that for a time her contributions to the parish charities would be less. And then it could be the next nest-egg whose original corruption would be purged away by the use to which it was finally put.

For Mrs. Arbuthnot, who had no money of her own, was obliged to live on the proceeds of Frederick's activities, and her very nest-egg was the fruit, posthumously ripened, of ancient sin. The way Frederick made his living was one of the standing distresses of her life. He wrote immensely popular memoirs, regularly, every year, of the mistresses of kings. There were in history numerous kings who had had mistresses, and there were still more numerous mistresses who had had kings ; so that he had been able to publish a book of memoirs during each year of his married life, and even so there were great further piles of these ladies waiting to be dealt with. Mrs. Arbuthnot was helpless. Whether she liked it or not, she was obliged to live on the proceeds. He gave her a dreadful sofa once, after the success of his Du Barri memoir, with swollen cushions and soft, receptive lap, and it seemed to her a miserable thing that there, in her very home, should flaunt this re-incarnation of a dead old French sinner.

Simply good, convinced that morality is the basis of happiness, the fact that she and Frederick should draw their sustenance from guilt, however much purged by the passage of centuries, was one of the secret reasons of her sadness. The more the memoired lady had forgotten herself, the more his book about her was read and the more free-handed he was to his wife ; and all that he gave her was spent, after adding slightly to her nest-egg—for she did hope and believe that some day people would cease to want to read of wickedness, and then Frederick would need supporting—on helping the poor. The parish flourished because, to take a handful at random, of the ill-behaviour of the ladies Du Barri, Montespan, Pompadour, Ninon de l'Enclos, and even of learned Maintenon. The poor were the filter through which the money was passed, to come out, Mrs. Arbuthnot hoped, purified. She could do no more. She had tried in days gone by to think the situation out, to discover the exact right course for her to take, but had found it, as she had found Frederick, too difficult, and had left it, as she had left Frederick, to God. Nothing of this money was spent on her house or dress ; those remained, except for the great soft sofa, austere. It was the poor who profited. Their very boots were stout with sins. But how difficult it had been. Mrs. Arbuthnot, groping for guidance, prayed about it to exhaustion. Ought she perhaps to refuse to touch the money, to avoid it as she would have avoided the sins which were its source ? But then what about the parish's boots ? She asked the vicar what he thought, and, through much delicate language, evasive and cautious, it did finally appear that he was for the boots.

At least she had persuaded Frederick, when first he

began his terrible successful career—he only began it
after their marriage ; when she married him he had been
a blameless official attached to the library of the British
Museum—to publish the memoirs under another name,
so that she was not publicly branded. Hampstead read
the books with glee, and had no idea that their writer
lived in its midst. Frederick was almost unknown, even
by sight, in Hampstead. He never went to any of its
gatherings. Whatever it was he did in the way of
recreation was done in London, but he never spoke of
what he did or whom he saw ; he might have been perfectly friendless for any mention he ever made of friends
to his wife. Only the vicar knew where the money for
the parish came from, and he regarded it, he told Mrs.
Arbuthnot, as a matter of honour not to mention it.

And at least her little house was not haunted by the
loose-lived ladies, for Frederick did his work away from
home. He had two rooms near the British Museum,
which was the scene of his exhumations, and there he
went every morning, and he came back long after his
wife was asleep. Sometimes he did not come back at
all. Sometimes she did not see him for several days
together. Then he would suddenly appear at breakfast,
having let himself in with his latchkey the night before,
very jovial and good-natured and free-handed and glad
if she would allow him to give her something,—a well-fed

man, contented with the world; a jolly, full-blooded, satisfied man. And she was always gentle, and anxious that his coffee should be as he liked it.

He seemed very happy. Life, she often thought, however much one tabulated was yet a mystery. There were always some people it was impossible to place. Frederick was one of them. He didn't seem to bear the remotest resemblance to the original Frederick. He didn't seem to have the least need of any of the things he used to say were so important and beautiful,—love, home, complete communion of thoughts, complete immersion in each other's interests. After those early painful attempts to hold him up to the point from which they had hand in hand so splendidly started, attempts in which she herself had got terribly hurt and the Frederick she supposed she had married was mangled out of recognition, she hung him up finally by her bedside as the chief subject of her prayers, and left him, except for those, entirely to God. She had loved Frederick too deeply to be able now to do anything but pray for him. He had no idea that he never went out of the house without her blessing going with him too, hovering, like a little echo of finished love, round that once dear head. She didn't dare think of him as he used to be, as he had seemed to her to be in those marvellous first days of their love-making, of their marriage. Her child had died;

she had nothing, nobody of her own to lavish herself on. The poor became her children, and God the object of her love. What could be happier than such a life, she sometimes asked herself ; but her face, and particularly her eyes, continued sad.

'Perhaps when we're old . . . perhaps when we are both quite old . . .' she would think wistfully.

THE owner of the mediaeval castle was an Englishman, a Mr. Briggs, who was in London at the moment and wrote that it had beds enough for eight people, exclusive of servants, three sitting-rooms, battlements, dungeons, and electric light. The rent was £60 for the month, the servants' wages were extra, and he wanted references, —he wanted assurances that the second half of his rent would be paid, the first half being paid in advance, and he wanted assurances of respectability from a solicitor, or a doctor, or a clergyman. He was very polite in his letter, explaining that his desire for references was what was usual and should be regarded as a mere formality.

Mrs. Arbuthnot and Mrs. Wilkins had not thought of references, and they had not dreamed a rent could be so high. In their minds had floated sums like three guineas a week; or less, seeing that the place was small and old.

Sixty pounds for a single month.

It staggered them.

Before Mrs. Arbuthnot's eyes rose up boots : endless vistas, all the stout boots that sixty pounds would buy ; and besides the rent there would be the servants' wages, and the food, and the railway journeys out and home. While as for references, these did indeed seem a stumbling-block ; it did seem impossible to give any without making their plan more public than they had intended.

They had both—even Mrs. Arbuthnot, lured for once away from perfect candour by the realisation of the great saving of trouble and criticism an imperfect explanation would produce—they had both thought it would be a good plan to give out, each to her own circle, their circles being luckily distinct, that each was going to stay with a friend who had a house in Italy. It would be true as far as it went,—Mrs. Wilkins asserted that it would be quite true, but Mrs. Arbuthnot thought it wouldn't be quite—and it was the only way, Mrs. Wilkins said, to keep Mellersh even approximately quiet. To spend any of her money just on the mere getting to Italy would cause him indignation ; what he would say if he knew she was renting part of a mediaeval castle on her own account Mrs. Wilkins preferred not to think. It would take him days to say it all ; and this although it was her very own money, and not a penny of it had ever been his.

'But I expect,' she said, 'your husband is just the same. I expect all husbands are alike in the long run.'

Mrs. Arbuthnot said nothing, because her reason for not wanting Frederick to know was the exactly opposite one,—Frederick would be only too pleased for her to go, he would not mind it in the very least; indeed, he would hail such a manifestation of self-indulgence and worldliness with an amusement that would hurt, and urge her to have a good time and not to hurry home with a crushing detachment. Far better, she thought, to be missed by Mellersh than to be sped by Frederick. To be missed, to be needed, from whatever motive, was, she thought, better than the complete loneliness of not being missed or needed at all.

She therefore said nothing, and allowed Mrs. Wilkins to leap at her conclusions unchecked. But they did, both of them, for a whole day feel that the only thing to be done was to renounce the mediaeval castle; and it was in arriving at this bitter decision that they really realised how acute had been their longing for it.

Then Mrs. Arbuthnot, whose mind was trained in the finding of ways out of difficulties, found a way out of the reference difficulty; and simultaneously Mrs. Wilkins had a vision revealing to her how to reduce the rent.

Mrs. Arbuthnot's plan was simple, and completely successful. She took the whole of the rent in person

to the owner, drawing it out of her Savings Bank—
again she looked furtive and apologetic, as if the clerk
must know the money was wanted for purposes of self-
indulgence—and, going up with the six ten pound notes
in her hand-bag to the address near the Brompton
Oratory where the owner lived, presented them to him,
waiving her right to pay only half. And when he saw
her, and her parted hair and soft dark eyes and sober
apparel, and heard her grave voice, he told her not to
bother about writing round for those references.

'It'll be all right,' he said, scribbling a receipt for
the rent. 'Do sit down, won't you ? Nasty day, isn't
it ? You'll find the old castle has lots of sunshine,
whatever else it hasn't got. Husband going ? '

Mrs. Arbuthnot, unused to anything but candour,
looked troubled at this question and began to murmur
inarticulately, and the owner at once concluded that she
was a widow—a war one, of course, for other widows
were old—and that he had been a fool not to guess it.

'Oh, I'm sorry,' he said, turning red right up to his
fair hair. 'I didn't mean—h'm, h'm, h'm——'

He ran his eye over the receipt he had written.
'Yes, I think that's all right,' he said, getting up and
giving it to her. 'Now,' he added, taking the six notes
she held out and smiling, for Mrs. Arbuthnot was agreeable to look at, 'I'm richer, and you're happier. I've

got money, and you've got San Salvatore. I wonder which is best.'

'I think you know,' said Mrs. Arbuthnot with her sweet smile.

He laughed and opened the door for her. It was a pity the interview was over. He would have liked to ask her to lunch with him. She made him think of his mother, of his nurse, of all things kind and comforting, besides having the attraction of not being his mother or his nurse.

'I hope you'll like the old place,' he said, holding her hand a minute at the door. The very feel of her hand, even through its glove, was reassuring; it was the sort of hand, he thought, that children would like to hold in the dark. 'In April, you know, it's simply a mass of flowers. And then there's the sea. You must wear white. You'll fit in very well. There are several portraits of you there.'

'Portraits ? '

'Madonnas, you know. There's one on the stairs really exactly like you.'

Mrs. Arbuthnot smiled and said good-bye and thanked him. Without the least trouble and at once she had got him placed in his proper category : he was an artist and of an effervescent temperament.

She shook hands and left, and he wished she hadn't.

After she was gone he supposed that he ought to have asked for those references, if only because she would think him so unbusiness-like not to, but he could as soon have insisted on references from a saint in a nimbus as from that grave, sweet lady.

Rose Arbuthnot.

Her letter, making the appointment, lay on the table. Pretty name.

That difficulty, then, was overcome. But there still remained the other one, the really annihilating effect of the expense on the nest-eggs, and especially on Mrs. Wilkins's, which was in size, compared with Mrs. Arbuthnot's, as the egg of the plover to that of the duck; and this in its turn was overcome by the vision vouchsafed to Mrs. Wilkins, revealing to her the steps to be taken for its overcoming. Having got San Salvatore—the beautiful, the religious name, fascinated them—they in their turn would advertise in the Agony Column of *The Times*, and they would inquire after two more ladies, of similar desires to their own, to join them and share the expenses.

At once the strain of the nest-eggs would be reduced from half to a quarter. Mrs. Wilkins was prepared to fling her entire egg into the adventure, but she realised that if it were to cost even sixpence over her ninety pounds her position would be terrible. Imagine going to Mellersh and saying, 'I owe.' It would be awful enough if some day circumstances forced her to say, 'I have no nest-egg,' but at least she would be supported in such a case by the knowledge that the egg had been her own. She therefore, though prepared to fling her last penny into the adventure, was not prepared to fling into it a single farthing that was not demonstrably her own; and she felt that if her share of the rent was reduced to fifteen pounds only, she would have a safe margin for the other expenses. Also they might economise very much on food,—gather olives off their own trees and eat them, for instance, and perhaps catch fish.

Of course, as they pointed out to each other, they could reduce the rent to an almost negligible sum by increasing the number of sharers; they could have six more ladies instead of two if they wanted to, seeing that there were eight beds. But supposing the eight beds were distributed in couples in four rooms, it would not be altogether what they wanted, to find themselves shut up at night with a stranger. Besides, they thought that perhaps having so many would not be quite so peaceful. After all, they were going to San Salvatore for peace and rest and joy, and six more ladies, especially if they got into one's bedroom, might a little interfere with that.

However, there seemed to be only two ladies in

England at that moment who had any wish to join them, for they had only two answers to their advertisement.

'Well, we only want two,' said Mrs. Wilkins, quickly recovering, for she had imagined a great rush.

'I think a choice would have been a good thing,' said Mrs. Arbuthnot.

'You mean because then we needn't have had Lady Caroline Dester.'

'I didn't say that,' gently protested Mrs. Arbuthnot.

'We needn't have her,' said Mrs. Wilkins. 'Just one more person would help us a great deal with the rent. We're not obliged to have two.'

'But why should we not have her? She seems really quite what we want.'

'Yes—she does from her letter,' said Mrs. Wilkins doubtfully.

She felt she would be terribly shy of Lady Caroline. Incredible as it may seem, seeing how they get into everything, Mrs. Wilkins had never come across any members of the aristocracy.

They interviewed Lady Caroline, and they interviewed the other applicant, a Mrs. Fisher.

Lady Caroline came to the club in Shaftesbury Avenue, and appeared to be wholly taken up by one great longing, a longing to get away from everybody she had ever known. When she saw the club, and Mrs. Arbuthnot, and Mrs. Wilkins, she was sure that here was exactly what she wanted. She would be in Italy,—a place she adored; she would not be in hotels,—places she loathed; she would not be staying with friends,—persons she disliked; and she would be in the company of strangers who would never mention a single person she knew, for the simple reason that they had not, could not have, and would not come across them. She asked a few questions about the fourth woman, and was satisfied with the answers. Mrs. Fisher, of Prince of Wales Terrace. A widow. She too would be unacquainted with any of her friends. Lady Caroline did not even know where Prince of Wales Terrace was.

' It's in London,' said Mrs. Arbuthnot.

' Is it ? ' said Lady Caroline.

It all seemed most restful.

Mrs. Fisher was unable to come to the club because, she explained by letter, she could not walk without a stick; therefore Mrs. Arbuthnot and Mrs. Wilkins went to her.

' But if she can't come to the club how can she go to Italy ? ' wondered Mrs. Wilkins, aloud.

' We shall hear that from her own lips,' said Mrs. Arbuthnot.

From Mrs. Fisher's lips they merely heard, in reply

to delicate questioning, that sitting in trains was not
walking about; and they knew that already. Except
for the stick, however, she appeared to be a most desirable fourth,—quiet, educated, elderly. She was much
older than they or Lady Caroline—Lady Caroline had
informed them she was twenty-eight—but not so old
as to have ceased to be active-minded. She was very
respectable indeed, and still wore a complete suit of
black though her husband had died, she told them,
eleven years before. Her house was full of signed
photographs of illustrious Victorian dead, all of whom
she said she had known when she was little. Her father
had been an eminent critic, and in his house she had seen
practically everybody who was anybody in letters and
art. Carlyle had scowled at her; Matthew Arnold
had held her on his knee; Tennyson had sonorously
rallied her on the length of her pig-tail. She animatedly
showed them the photographs, hung everywhere on her
walls, pointing out the signatures with her stick, and
she neither gave any information about her own husband
nor asked for any about the husbands of her visitors;
which was the greatest comfort. Indeed, she seemed
to think that they also were widows, for on inquiring
who the fourth lady was to be, and being told it was a
Lady Caroline Dester, she said, ' Is she a widow too ? '
And on their explaining that she was not, because she

had not yet been married, observed with abstracted amiability, ' All in good time.'

But Mrs. Fisher's very abstractedness—and she seemed to be absorbed chiefly in the interesting people she used to know and in their memorial photographs, and quite a good part of the interview was taken up by reminiscent anecdote of Carlyle, Meredith, Matthew Arnold, Tennyson, and a host of others—her very abstractedness was a recommendation. She only asked, she said, to be allowed to sit quiet in the sun and remember. That was all Mrs. Arbuthnot and Mrs. Wilkins asked of their sharers. It was their idea of a perfect sharer that she should sit quiet in the sun and remember, rousing herself on Saturday evenings sufficiently to pay her share. Mrs. Fisher was very fond, too, she said, of flowers, and once when she was spending a week-end with her father at Box Hill——

' Who lived at Box Hill ? ' interrupted Mrs. Wilkins, who hung on Mrs. Fisher's reminiscences, intensely excited by meeting somebody who had actually been familiar with all the really and truly and undoubtedly great,—actually seen them, heard them talking, touched them.

Mrs. Fisher looked at her over the top of her glasses in some surprise. Mrs. Wilkins, in her eagerness to tear the heart out quickly of Mrs. Fisher's reminiscences, afraid that at any moment Mrs. Arbuthnot would take her away and she wouldn't have heard half, had already interrupted several times with questions which appeared ignorant to Mrs. Fisher.

'Meredith of course,' said Mrs. Fisher rather shortly. 'I remember a particular week-end '—she continued. 'My father often took me, but I always remember this week-end particularly—— '

'Did you know Keats?' eagerly interrupted Mrs. Wilkins.

Mrs. Fisher, after a pause, said with sub-acid reserve that she had been unacquainted with both Keats and Shakespeare.

'Oh of course—how ridiculous of me!' cried Mrs. Wilkins, flushing scarlet. 'It's because '— she floundered—' it's because the immortals somehow still seem alive, don't they—as if they were here, going to walk into the room in another minute—and one forgets they are dead. In fact one knows perfectly well they're not dead—not nearly so dead as you and I even now,' she assured Mrs. Fisher, who observed her over the top of her glasses.

'I thought I *saw* Keats the other day,' Mrs. Wilkins incoherently proceeded, driven on by Mrs. Fisher's look over the top of her glasses. 'In Hampstead—crossing

the road in front of that house—you know—the house
where he lived——'

Mrs. Arbuthnot said they must be going.

Mrs. Fisher did nothing to prevent them.

' I *really* thought I saw him,' protested Mrs. Wilkins,
appealing for belief first to one and then to the other
while waves of colour passed over her face, and totally
unable to stop because of Mrs. Fisher's glasses and the
steady eyes looking at her over their tops.   ' I believe
I *did* see him—he was dressed in a——'

Even Mrs. Arbuthnot looked at her now, and in her
gentlest voice said they would be late for lunch.

It was at this point that Mrs. Fisher asked for references.   She had no wish to find herself shut up for four
weeks with somebody who saw things.   It is true that
there were three sitting-rooms, besides the garden and
the battlements at San Salvatore, so that there would
be opportunities of withdrawal from Mrs. Wilkins ; but
it would be disagreeable to Mrs. Fisher, for instance, if
Mrs. Wilkins were suddenly to assert that she saw Mr.
Fisher.   Mr. Fisher was dead ; let him remain so.   She
had no wish to be told he was walking about the garden.
The only reference she really wanted, for she was much
too old and firmly seated in her place in the world for
questionable associates to matter to her, was one with
regard to Mrs. Wilkins's health.   Was her health quite

normal ? Was she an ordinary, everyday, sensible woman ? Mrs. Fisher felt that if she were given even one address she would be able to find out what she needed. So she asked for references, and her visitors appeared to be so much taken aback—Mrs. Wilkins, indeed, was instantly sobered—that she added, ' It is usual.'

Mrs. Wilkins found her speech first. ' But,' she said, ' aren't we the ones who ought to ask for some from you ? '

And this seemed to Mrs. Arbuthnot too the right attitude. Surely it was they who were taking Mrs. Fisher into their party, and not Mrs. Fisher who was taking them into it ?

For answer Mrs. Fisher, leaning on her stick, went to the writing-table and in a firm hand wrote down three names and offered them to Mrs. Wilkins, and the names were so respectable, more, they were so momentous, they were so nearly august, that just to read them was enough. The President of the Royal Academy, the Archbishop of Canterbury, and the Governor of the Bank of England,—who would dare disturb such personages in their meditations with inquiries as to whether a female friend of theirs was all she should be ?

' They have known me since I was little,' said Mrs.

Fisher,—everybody seemed to have known Mrs. Fisher since or when she was little.

'I don't think references are nice things at all between —between ordinary decent women,' burst out Mrs. Wilkins, made courageous by being, as she felt, at bay; for she very well knew that the only reference she could give without getting into trouble was Shoolbred, and she had little confidence in that, as it would be entirely based on Mellersh's fish. 'We're not business people. We needn't distrust each other——'

And Mrs. Arbuthnot said, with a dignity that yet was sweet, 'I'm afraid references do bring an atmosphere into our holiday plan that isn't quite what we want, and I don't think we'll take yours up or give you any ourselves. So that I suppose you won't wish to join us.'

And she held out her hand in good-bye.

Then Mrs. Fisher, her gaze diverted to Mrs. Arbuthnot, who inspired trust and liking even in Tube officials, felt that she would be idiotic to lose the opportunity of being in Italy in the particular conditions offered, and that she and this calm-browed woman between them would certainly be able to curb the other one when she had her attacks. So she said, taking Mrs. Arbuthnot's offered hand, 'Very well. I waive references.'

She waived references.

The two as they walked to the station in Kensington

High Street could not help thinking that this way of putting it was lofty. Even Mrs. Arbuthnot, spendthrift of excuses for lapses, thought Mrs. Fisher might have used other words; and Mrs. Wilkins, by the time she got to the station, and the walk and the struggle on the crowded pavement with other people's umbrellas had warmed her blood, actually suggested waiving Mrs. Fisher.

'If there is any waiving to be done, do let us be the ones who waive,' she said eagerly.

But Mrs. Arbuthnot, as usual, held on to Mrs. Wilkins; and presently, having cooled down in the train, Mrs. Wilkins announced that at San Salvatore Mrs. Fisher would find her level. 'I *see* her finding her level there,' she said, her eyes very bright.

Whereupon Mrs. Arbuthnot, sitting with her quiet hands folded, turned over in her mind how best she could help Mrs. Wilkins not to see quite so much; or at least, if she must see, to see in silence.

IV

IT had been arranged that Mrs. Arbuthnot and Mrs. Wilkins, travelling together, should arrive at San Salvatore on the evening of March 31st—the owner, who told them how to get there, appreciated their disinclination to begin their time in it on April 1st— and Lady Caroline and Mrs. Fisher, as yet unacquainted and therefore under no obligations to bore each other on the journey, for only towards the end would they find out by a process of sifting who they were, were to arrive on the morning of April 2nd. In this way everything would be got nicely ready for the two who seemed, in spite of the equality of the sharing, yet to have something about them of guests.

There were disagreeable incidents towards the end of March, when Mrs. Wilkins, her heart in her mouth and her face a mixture of guilt, terror and determination, told her husband that she had been invited to Italy, and he declined to believe it. Of course he declined to believe it. Nobody had ever invited his wife to Italy

52

before. There was no precedent. He required proofs. The only proof was Mrs. Arbuthnot, and Mrs. Wilkins had produced her; but after what entreaties, what passionate persuading! For Mrs. Arbuthnot had not imagined she would have to face Mr. Wilkins and say things to him that were short of the truth, and it brought home to her what she had for some time suspected, that she was slipping more and more away from God.

Indeed, the whole of March was filled with unpleasant, anxious moments. It was an uneasy month. Mrs. Arbuthnot's conscience, made super-sensitive by years of pampering, could not reconcile what she was doing with its own high standard of what was right. It gave her little peace. It nudged her at her prayers. It punctuated her entreaties for divine guidance with disconcerting questions, such as, 'Are you not a hypocrite? Do you really mean that? Would you not, frankly, be disappointed if that prayer were granted?'

The prolonged wet, raw weather was on the side too of her conscience, producing far more sickness than usual among the poor. They had bronchitis; they had fevers; there was no end to the distress. And here she was going off, spending precious money on going off, simply and solely to be happy. One woman. One woman being happy, and these piteous multitudes. . . .

She was unable to look the vicar in the face. He did not know, nobody knew, what she was going to do, and from the very beginning she was unable to look anybody in the face. She excused herself from making speeches appealing for money. How could she stand up and ask people for money when she herself was spending so much on her own selfish pleasure ? Nor did it help her or quiet her that, having actually told Frederick, in her desire to make up for what she was squandering, that she would be grateful if he would let her have some money, he instantly gave her a cheque for £100. He asked no questions. She was scarlet. He looked at her a moment and then looked away. It was a relief to Frederick that she should take some money. She gave it all immediately to the organisation she worked with, and found herself more tangled in doubts than ever.

Mrs. Wilkins, on the contrary, had no doubts. She was quite certain that it was a most proper thing to have a holiday, and altogether right and beautiful to spend one's own hard-collected savings on being happy.

' Think how much nicer we shall be when we come back,' she said to Mrs. Arbuthnot, encouraging that pale lady.

No, Mrs. Wilkins had no doubts, but she had fears ; and March was for her too an anxious month, with the unconscious Mr. Wilkins coming back daily to his dinner and eating his fish in the silence of imagined security.

Also things happen so awkwardly. It really is astonishing, how awkwardly they happen. Mrs. Wilkins, who was very careful all this month to give Mellersh only the food he liked, buying it and hovering over its cooking with a zeal more than common, succeeded so well that Mellersh was pleased; definitely pleased; so much pleased that he began to think that he might, after all, have married the right wife instead of, as he had frequently suspected, the wrong one. The result was that on the third Sunday in the month—Mrs. Wilkins had made up her trembling mind that on the fourth Sunday, there being five in that March and it being on the fifth of them that she and Mrs. Arbuthnot were to start, she would tell Mellersh of her invitation—on the third Sunday, then, after a very well-cooked lunch in which the Yorkshire pudding had melted in his mouth and the apricot tart had been so perfect that he ate it all, Mellersh, smoking his cigar by the brightly burning fire the while hail gusts banged on the window, said: ' I am thinking of taking you to Italy for Easter.' And paused for her astounded and grateful ecstasy.

None came. The silence in the room, except for

the hail hitting the windows and the gay roar of the fire, was complete. Mrs. Wilkins could not speak. She was dumbfoundered. The next Sunday was the day she had meant to break her news to him, and she had not yet even prepared the form of words in which she would break it.

Mr. Wilkins, who had not been abroad since before the war, and was noticing with increasing disgust, as week followed week of wind and rain, the peculiar persistent vileness of the weather, had slowly conceived a desire to get away from England for Easter. He was doing very well in his business. He could afford a trip. Switzerland was useless in April. There was a familiar sound about Easter in Italy. To Italy he would go ; and as it would cause comment if he did not take his wife, take her he must,—besides, she would be useful ; a second person was always useful in a country whose language one did not speak for holding things, for waiting with the luggage.

He had expected an explosion of gratitude and excitement. The absence of it was incredible. She could not, he concluded, have heard. Probably she was absorbed in some foolish day-dream. It was regrettable how childish she remained.

He turned his head—their chairs were in front of the fire—and looked at her. She was staring straight into the fire, and it was no doubt the fire that made her face so red.

'I am thinking,' he repeated, raising his clear, cultivated voice and speaking with acerbity, for inattention at such a moment was deplorable, 'of taking you to Italy for Easter. Did you not hear me ? '

Yes, she had heard him, and she had been wondering at the extraordinary coincidence—really most extraordinary—she was just going to tell him how—how she had been invited—a friend had invited her—Easter, too—Easter was in April, wasn't it ?—her friend had a —had a house there.

In fact Mrs. Wilkins, driven by terror, guilt and surprise, had been more incoherent if possible than usual.

It was a dreadful afternoon. Mellersh, profoundly indignant, besides having his intended treat coming back on him like a blessing to roost, cross-examined her with the utmost severity. He demanded that she refuse the invitation. He demanded that, since she had so outrageously accepted it without consulting him, she should write and cancel her acceptance. Finding himself up against an unsuspected, shocking rock of obstinacy in her, he then declined to believe she had been invited to Italy at all. He declined to believe in this Mrs. Arbuthnot, of whom till that moment he had never heard ; and it was only when the gentle creature was brought round—with such difficulty, with such a desire on her part to throw the whole thing up rather than tell Mr. Wilkins less than the truth—and herself endorsed his wife's statements that he was able to give them credence. He could not but believe Mrs. Arbuthnot. She produced the precise effect on him that she did on Tube officials. She hardly needed to say anything. But that made no difference to her conscience, which knew and would not let her forget that she had given him an incomplete impression. 'Do you,' asked her conscience, 'see any real difference between an incomplete impression and a completely stated lie? God sees none.'

The remainder of March was a confused bad dream. Both Mrs. Arbuthnot and Mrs. Wilkins were shattered; try as they would not to, both felt extraordinarily guilty; and when on the morning of the 30th they did finally get off there was no exhilaration about the departure, no holiday feeling at all.

'We've been too good—*much* too good,' Mrs. Wilkins kept on murmuring as they walked up and down the platform at Victoria, having arrived there an hour before they need have, ' and that's why we feel as though we're doing wrong. We're brow-beaten—we're not any longer real human beings. Real human beings aren't ever as good as we've been. Oh '—she clenched her thin hands—' to *think* that we ought to be so happy now, here on the very station, actually starting, and we're not, and it's being spoilt for us just simply because we've spoilt *them*! What have we done—what have we done, I should like to know,' she inquired of Mrs. Arbuthnot indignantly, ' except for once want to go away by ourselves and have a little rest from *them* ? '

Mrs. Arbuthnot, patiently pacing, did not ask who she meant by *them*, because she knew. Mrs. Wilkins meant their husbands, persisting in her assumption that Frederick was as indignant as Mellersh over the departure of his wife, whereas Frederick did not even know his wife had gone.

Mrs. Arbuthnot, always silent about him, had said nothing of this to Mrs. Wilkins. Frederick went too deep into her heart for her to talk about him. He was having an extra bout of work finishing another of those dreadful books, and had been away practically continually the last few weeks, and was away when she left. Why should she tell him beforehand ? Sure as she so miserably was that he would have no objection to anything she did, she merely wrote him a note and put it on the hall-table ready for him if and when he should come home. She said she was going for a month's holiday as she needed a rest and she had not had one for so long, and that Gladys, the efficient parlourmaid,

had orders to see to his comforts. She did not say
where she was going; there was no reason why she
should; he would not be interested, he would not care.

The day was wretched, blustering and wet; the
crossing was atrocious, and they were very sick. But
after having been very sick, just to arrive at Calais
and not be sick was happiness, and it was there that
the real splendour of what they were doing first began
to warm their benumbed spirits. It got hold of Mrs.
Wilkins first, and spread from her like a rose-coloured
flame over her pale companion. Mellersh at Calais,
where they restored themselves with soles because of
Mrs. Wilkins's desire to eat a sole Mellersh wasn't having,
—Mellersh at Calais had already begun to dwindle and
seem less important. None of the French porters knew
him; not a single official at Calais cared a fig for Mellersh.
In Paris there was no time to think of him because their
train was late and they only just caught the Turin train
at the Gare de Lyons; and by the afternoon of the next
day when they got into Italy, England, Frederick,
Mellersh, the vicar, the poor, Hampstead, the club,
Shoolbred, everybody and everything, the whole in-
flamed sore dreariness, had faded to the dimness of a
dream.

It was cloudy in Italy, which surprised them. They had expected brilliant sunshine. But never mind : it was Italy, and the very clouds looked fat. Neither of them had ever been there before. Both gazed out of the windows with rapt faces. The hours flew as long as it was daylight, and after that there was the excitement of getting nearer, getting quite near, getting there. At Genoa it had begun to rain—Genoa ! imagine actually being at Genoa, seeing its name written up in the station just like any other name—at Nervi it was pouring, and when at last towards midnight, for again the train was late, they got to Mezzago, the rain was coming down in what seemed solid sheets. But it was Italy. Nothing it did could be bad. The very rain was different,— straight rain, falling properly on to one's umbrella ; not that violently blowing English stuff that got in everywhere. And it did leave off ; and when it did, behold the earth would be strewn with roses.

Mr. Briggs, San Salvatore's owner, had said, ' You

get out at Mezzago, and then you drive.' But he had forgotten what he amply knew, that trains in Italy are sometimes late, and he had imagined his tenants arriving at Mezzago at eight o'clock and finding a string of flys to choose from.

The train was four hours late, and when Mrs. Arbuthnot and Mrs. Wilkins scrambled down the ladder-like high steps of their carriage into the black downpour, their skirts sweeping off great pools of sooty wet because their hands were full of suit-cases, if it had not been for the vigilance of Domenico, the gardener at San Salvatore, they would have found nothing for them to drive in.   All ordinary flys had long since gone home. Domenico, foreseeing this, had sent his aunt's fly, driven by her son his cousin ; and his aunt and her fly lived in Castagneto, the village crouching at the feet of San Salvatore, and therefore, however late the train was, the fly would not dare come home without containing that which it had been sent to fetch.

Domenico's cousin's name was Beppo, and he presently emerged out of the dark where Mrs. Arbuthnot and Mrs. Wilkins stood, uncertain what to do next after the train had gone on, for they could see no porter and they thought from the feel of it that they were standing not so much on a platform as in the middle of the permanent way.

Beppo, who had been searching for them, emerged from the dark with a kind of pounce and talked Italian to them vociferously. Beppo was a most respectable young man, but he did not look as if he were, especially not in the dark, and he had a dripping hat slouched over one eye. They did not like the way he seized their suit-cases. He could not be, they thought, a porter. However, they presently from out of his streaming talk discerned the words San Salvatore, and after that they kept on saying them to him, for it was the only Italian they knew, as they hurried after him, unwilling to lose sight of their suit-cases, stumbling across rails and through puddles out to where in the road a small, high fly stood.

Its hood was up, and its horse was in an attitude of thought. They climbed in, and the minute they were in—Mrs. Wilkins, indeed, could hardly be called in—the horse awoke with a start from its reverie and immediately began going home rapidly ; without Beppo ; without the suit-cases.

Beppo darted after him, making the night ring with his shouts, and caught the hanging reins just in time. He explained proudly, and as it seemed to him with perfect clearness, that the horse always did that, being a fine animal full of corn and blood, and cared for by him, Beppo, as if he were his own son, and the ladies

must not be alarmed,—he had noticed they were clutching each other; but clear, and loud, and profuse of
words though he was, they only looked at him blankly.

He went on talking, however, while he piled the
suit-cases up round them, sure that sooner or later they
must understand him, especially as he was careful to
talk very loud and illustrate everything he said with
the simplest elucidatory gestures, but they both continued only to look at him. They both, he noticed
sympathetically, had white faces, fatigued faces, and
they both had big eyes, fatigued eyes. They were
beautiful ladies, he thought, and their eyes, looking
at him over the tops of the suit-cases watching his
every movement—there were no trunks, only numbers
of suit-cases—were like the eyes of the Mother of God.
The only thing the ladies said, and they repeated it
at regular intervals, even after they had started, gently
prodding him as he sat on his box to call his attention
to it, was, ' San Salvatore ? '

And each time he answered vociferously, encouragingly, ' Si, si—San Salvatore.'

' We don't *know* of course if he's taking us there,'
said Mrs. Arbuthnot at last in a low voice, after they
had been driving as it seemed to them a long while,
and had got off the paving-stones of the sleep-shrouded
town and were out on a winding road with what they

could just see was a low wall on their left beyond which was a great black emptiness and the sound of the sea. On their right was something close and steep and high and black,—rocks, they whispered to each other; huge rocks.

'No—we don't *know*,' agreed Mrs. Wilkins, a slight coldness passing down her spine.

They felt very uncomfortable. It was so late. It was so dark. The road was so lonely. Suppose a wheel came off. Suppose they met Fascisti, or the opposite of Fascisti. How sorry they were now that they had not slept at Genoa and come on the next morning in daylight.

'But that would have been the first of April,' said Mrs. Wilkins, in a low voice.

'It is that now,' said Mrs. Arbuthnot beneath her breath.

'So it is,' murmured Mrs. Wilkins.

They were silent.

Beppo turned round on his box,—a disquieting habit already noticed, for surely his horse ought to be carefully watched—and again addressed them with what he was convinced was lucidity,—no *patois*, and the clearest explanatory movements.

How much they wished their mothers had made them learn Italian when they were little. If only now

they could have said, 'Please sit round the right way
and look after the horse.' They did not even know
what horse was in Italian. It was contemptible to be
so ignorant.

In their anxiety, for the road twisted round great
jutting rocks, and on their left was only the low wall
to keep them out of the sea should anything happen,
they too began to gesticulate, waving their hands at
Beppo, pointing ahead. They wanted him to turn
round again and face his horse, that was all. He
thought they wanted him to drive faster; and there
followed a terrifying ten minutes during which, as he
supposed, he was gratifying them. He was proud of
his horse, and it could go very fast. He rose in his
seat, the whip cracked, the horse rushed forward, the
rocks leaped towards them, the little fly swayed, the
suit-cases heaved, Mrs. Arbuthnot and Mrs. Wilkins
clung. In this way they continued, swaying, heaving,
clattering, clinging, till at a point near Castagneto
there was a rise in the road, and on reaching the foot
of the rise the horse, who knew every inch of the way,
stopped suddenly, throwing everything in the fly into
a heap, and then proceeded up at the slowest of walks.

Beppo twisted himself round to receive their admiration, laughing with pride in his horse.

There was no answering laugh from the beautiful

ladies. Their eyes, fixed on him, seemed bigger than ever, and their faces against the black of the night showed milky.

But here at least, once they were up the slope, were houses. The rocks left off, and there were houses; the low wall left off, and there were houses; the sea shrunk away, and the sound of it ceased, and the loneliness of the road was finished. No lights anywhere, of course, nobody to see them pass; and yet Beppo, when the houses began, after looking over his shoulder and shouting 'Castagneto' at the ladies, once more stood up and cracked his whip and once more made his horse dash forward.

'We shall be there in a minute,' Mrs. Arbuthnot said to herself, holding on.

'We shall soon stop now,' Mrs. Wilkins said to herself, holding on. They said nothing aloud, because nothing would have been heard above the whip-cracking and the wheel-clattering and the boisterous inciting noises Beppo was making at his horse.

Anxiously they strained their eyes for any sight of the beginning of San Salvatore.

They had supposed and hoped that after a reasonable amount of village a mediaeval archway would loom upon them, and through it they would drive into a garden and draw up at an open, welcoming door, with light streaming from it and those servants standing in it who, according to the advertisement, remained.

Instead the fly suddenly stopped.

Peering out they could see they were still in the village street, with small dark houses each side; and Beppo, throwing the reins over the horse's back as if completely confident this time that he would not go any farther, got down off his box. At the same moment, springing as it seemed out of nothing, a man and several half-grown boys appeared on each side of the fly and began dragging out the suit-cases.

' No, no—San Salvatore, San Salvatore'—— exclaimed Mrs. Wilkins, trying to hold on to what suit-cases she could.

' *Si*, *si*—San Salvatore, San Salvatore,' they all shouted, pulling.

' This *can't* be San Salvatore,' said Mrs. Wilkins, turning to Mrs. Arbuthnot, who sat quite still watching her suit-cases being taken from her with the same patience she applied to lesser evils. She knew she could do nothing if these men were wicked men determined to have her suit-cases.

' I don't think it can be,' she admitted, and could not refrain from a moment's wonder at the ways of God. Had she really been brought here, she and poor Mrs. Wilkins, after so much trouble in arranging it, so much difficulty and worry, along such devious paths of prevarication and deceit, only to be——

She checked her thoughts, and gently said to Mrs. Wilkins, while the ragged youths disappeared with the suit-cases into the night and the man with the lantern helped Beppo pull the rug off her, that they were both in God's hands ; and for the first time, on hearing this, Mrs. Wilkins was afraid.

There was nothing for it but to get out. Useless to try to go on sitting in the fly repeating San Salvatore. Every time they said it, and their voices each time were fainter, Beppo and the other man merely echoed it in a series of loud shouts. If only they had learned Italian when they were little. If only they could have said, ' We wish to be driven to the door.' But they did not even know what door was in Italian. Such ignorance was not only contemptible, it was, they now saw, definitely dangerous. Useless, however, to lament it now. Useless to put off whatever it was that was going to happen to them by trying to go on sitting in the fly. They therefore got out.

The two men opened their umbrellas for them and handed them to them. From this they received a faint encouragement, because they could not believe that if these men were wicked they would pause to open umbrellas. The man with the lantern then made signs

to them to follow him, talking loud and quickly, and
Beppo, they noticed, remained behind. Ought they to
pay him ? Not, they thought, if they were going to
be robbed and perhaps murdered. Surely on such an
occasion one did not pay. Besides, he had not after
all brought them to San Salvatore. Where they had
got to was evidently somewhere else. Also, he did not
show the least wish to be paid ; he let them go away
into the night with no clamour at all. This, they
could not help thinking, was a bad sign. He asked for
nothing because presently he was to get so much.

They came to some steps. The road ended abruptly
in a church and some descending steps. The man held
the lantern low for them to see the steps.

' San Salvatore ? ' said Mrs. Wilkins once again, very
faintly, before committing herself to the steps. It was
useless to mention it now, of course, but she could not
go down steps in complete silence. No mediaeval castle,
she was sure, was ever built at the bottom of steps.

Again, however, came the echoing shout,—' Si, si—
San Salvatore.'

They descended gingerly, holding up their skirts just
as if they would be wanting them another time and
had not in all probability finished with skirts for
ever.

The steps ended in a steeply sloping path with flat

stone slabs down the middle. They slipped a good deal on these wet slabs, and the man with the lantern, talking loud and quickly, held them up. His way of holding them up was polite.

'Perhaps,' said Mrs. Wilkins in a low voice to Mrs. Arbuthnot, 'it is all right after all.'

'We're in God's hands,' said Mrs. Arbuthnot again; and again Mrs. Wilkins was afraid.

They reached the bottom of the sloping path, and the light of the lantern flickered over an open space with houses round three sides. The sea was the fourth side, lazily washing backwards and forwards on pebbles.

'San Salvatore,' said the man, pointing with his lantern to a black mass curved round the water like an arm flung about it.

They strained their eyes. They saw the black mass, and on the top of it a light.

'San Salvatore?' they both repeated incredulously, for where were the suit-cases, and why had they been forced to get out of the fly?

'Si, si—San Salvatore.'

They went along what seemed to be a quay, right on the edge of the water. There was not even a low wall here,—nothing to prevent the man with the lantern tipping them in if he wanted to. He did not, however, tip them in. Perhaps it was all right after all, Mrs.

Wilkins again suggested to Mrs. Arbuthnot on noticing this, who this time was herself beginning to think that it might be, and said no more about God's hands.

The flicker of the lantern danced along, reflected in the wet pavement of the quay. Out to the left, in the darkness and evidently at the end of a jetty, was a red light. They came to an archway with a heavy iron gate. The man with the lantern pushed the gate open. This time they went up steps instead of down, and at the top of them was a little path that wound upwards among flowers. They could not see the flowers, but the whole place was evidently full of them.

It here dawned on Mrs. Wilkins that perhaps the reason why the fly had not driven them up to the door was that there was no road, only a footpath. That also would explain the disappearance of the suit-cases. She began to feel confident that they would find their suit-cases waiting for them when they got up to the top. San Salvatore was, it seemed, on the top of a hill, as a mediaeval castle should be. At a turn of the path they saw above them, much nearer now and shining more brightly, the light they had seen from the quay. She told Mrs. Arbuthnot of her dawning belief, and Mrs. Arbuthnot agreed that it was very likely a true one.

Once more, but this time in a tone of real hopefulness, Mrs. Wilkins said, pointing upwards at the black outline against the only slightly less black sky, 'San Salvatore ? ' And once more, but this time comfortingly, encouragingly, came back the assurance, ' Si, si—San Salvatore.'

They crossed a little bridge, over what was apparently a ravine, and then came a flat bit with long grass at the sides and more flowers. They felt the grass, flicking wet against their stockings, and the invisible flowers were everywhere. Then up again through trees, along a zigzag path with the smell all the way of the flowers they could not see. The warm rain was bringing out all the sweetness. Higher and higher they went in this sweet darkness, and the red light on the jetty dropped farther and farther below them.

The path wound round to the other side of what appeared to be a little peninsula ; the jetty and the red light disappeared ; across the emptiness on their left were distant lights.

' Mezzago,' said the man, waving his lantern at the lights.

' Si, si,' they answered, for they had by now learned si, si. Upon which the man congratulated them in a great flow of polite words, not one of which they understood, on their magnificent Italian ; for this was Domenico, the vigilant and accomplished gardener of San Salvatore, the prop and stay of the establishment, the resourceful, the gifted, the eloquent, the courteous, the intelligent Domenico. Only they did not know that yet; and he did in the dark, and even sometimes in the light, look, with his knife-sharp swarthy features and swift, panther movements, very like somebody wicked.

They passed along another flat bit of path, with a black shape like a high wall towering above them on their right, and then the path went up again under trellises, and trailing sprays of scented things caught at them and shook raindrops on them, and the light of the lantern flickered over lilies, and then came a flight of ancient steps worn with centuries, and then another iron gate, and then they were inside, though still climbing a twisting flight of stone steps with old walls on either side like the walls of dungeons, and with a vaulted roof.

At the top was a wrought-iron door, and through it shone a flood of electric light.

'*Ecco*,' said Domenico, lithely running up the last few steps ahead and pushing the door open.

And there they were, arrived; and it was San Salvatore; and their suit-cases were waiting for them; and they had not been murdered.

They looked at each other's white faces and blinking eyes very solemnly.

It was a great, a wonderful moment. Here they

were, in their mediaeval castle at last. Their feet
touched its stones.

Mrs. Wilkins put her arm round Mrs. Arbuthnot's
neck and kissed her.

'The first thing to happen in this house,' she said
softly, solemnly, 'shall be a kiss.'

'Dear Lotty,' said Mrs. Arbuthnot.

'Dear Rose,' said Mrs. Wilkins, her eyes brimming
with gladness.

Domenico was delighted. He liked to see beautiful
ladies kiss. He made them a most appreciative speech
of welcome, and they stood arm in arm, holding each
other up, for they were very tired, blinking smilingly
at him, and not understanding a word.

VI

WHEN Mrs. Wilkins woke next morning she lay in bed a few minutes before getting up and opening the shutters. What would she see out of her window? A shining world, or a world of rain? But it would be beautiful; whatever it was would be beautiful.

She was in a little bedroom with bare white walls and a stone floor and sparse old furniture. The beds—there were two—were made of iron, enamelled black and painted with bunches of gay flowers. She lay putting off the great moment of going to the window as one puts off opening a precious letter, gloating over it. She had no idea what time it was; she had forgotten to wind up her watch ever since, centuries ago, she last went to bed in Hampstead. No sounds were to be heard in the house, so she supposed it was very early, yet she felt as if she had slept a long while,—so completely rested, so perfectly content. She lay with her arms clasped round her head thinking how happy she was, her lips curved upwards in a delighted smile.

76

In bed by herself : adorable condition. She had not been in bed without Mellersh once now for five whole years ; and the cool roominess of it, the freedom of one's movements, the sense of recklessness, of audacity, in giving the blankets a pull if one wanted to, or twitching the pillows more comfortable ! It was like the discovery of an entirely new joy.

Mrs. Wilkins longed to get up and open the shutters, but where she was was really so very delicious. She gave a sigh of contentment, and went on lying there looking round her, taking in everything in her room, her own little room, her very own to arrange just as she pleased for this one blessed month, her room bought with her own savings, the fruit of her careful denials, whose door she could bolt if she wanted to, and nobody had the right to come in. It was such a strange little room, so different from any she had known, and so sweet. It was like a cell. Except for the two beds, it suggested a happy austerity. ' And the name of the chamber,' she thought, quoting and smiling round at it, ' was Peace.'

Well, this was delicious, to lie there thinking how happy she was, but outside those shutters it was more delicious still. She jumped up, pulled on her slippers, for there was nothing on the stone floor but one small rug, ran to the window and threw open the shutters.

'*Oh!*' cried Mrs. Wilkins.

All the radiance of April in Italy lay gathered together at her feet. The sun poured in on her. The sea lay asleep in it, hardly stirring. Across the bay the lovely mountains, exquisitely different in colour, were asleep too in the light; and underneath her window, at the bottom of the flower-starred grass slope from which the wall of the castle rose up, was a great cypress, cutting through the delicate blues and violets and rose-colours of the mountains and the sea like a great black sword.

She stared. Such beauty; and she there to see it. Such beauty; and she alive to feel it. Her face was bathed in light. Lovely scents came up to the window and caressed her. A tiny breeze gently lifted her hair. Far out in the bay a cluster of almost motionless fishing boats hovered like a flock of white birds on the tranquil sea. How beautiful, how beautiful. Not to have died before this . . . to have been allowed to see, breathe, feel this. . . . She stared, her lips parted. Happy? Poor, ordinary, everyday word. But what could one say, how could one describe it? It was as though she could hardly stay inside herself, it was as though she were too small to hold so much of joy, it was as though she were washed through with light. And how astonishing to feel this sheer bliss, for here she was, not doing and not going to do a single unselfish thing, not

going to do a thing she didn't want to do. According
to everybody she had ever come across she ought at
least to have twinges. She had not one twinge. Something was wrong somewhere. Wonderful that at home
she should have been so good, so terribly good, and
merely felt tormented. Twinges of every sort had
there been her portion; aches, hurts, discouragements,
and she the whole time being steadily unselfish. Now
she had taken off all her goodness and left it behind
her like a heap of rain-sodden clothes, and she only felt
joy. She was naked of goodness, and was rejoicing in
being naked. She was stripped, and exulting. And
there, away in the dim mugginess of Hampstead, was
Mellersh being angry.

She tried to visualise Mellersh, she tried to see him
having breakfast and thinking bitter things about her;
and lo, Mellersh himself began to shimmer, became rose-
colour, became delicate violet, became an enchanting
blue, became formless, became iridescent. Actually
Mellersh, after quivering a minute, was lost in light.

' *Well*,' thought Mrs. Wilkins, staring, as it were,
after him. How extraordinary not to be able to visualise Mellersh; and she who used to know every feature,
every expression of his by heart. She simply could not
see him as he was. She could only see him resolved
into beauty, melted into harmony with everything

else. The familiar words of the General Thanksgiving
came quite naturally into her mind, and she found herself
blessing God for her creation, preservation, and all the
blessings of this life, but above all for His inestimable
Love ; out loud ; in a burst of acknowledgment.
While Mellersh, at that moment angrily pulling on his
boots before going out into the dripping streets, was
indeed thinking bitter things about her.

She began to dress, choosing clean white clothes in
honour of the summer's day, unpacking her suit-cases,
tidying her adorable little room. She moved about
with quick, purposeful steps, her long thin body held
up straight, her small face, so much puckered at home
with effort and fear, smoothed out. All she had been
and done before this morning, all she had felt and
worried about, was gone. Each of her worries behaved
as the image of Mellersh had behaved, and dissolved
into colour and light. And she noticed things she had
not noticed for years,—when she was doing her hair
in front of the glass she noticed it, and thought, ' Why,
what pretty stuff.' For years she had forgotten she
had such a thing as hair, plaiting it in the evening and
unplaiting it in the morning with the same hurry and
indifference with which she laced and unlaced her shoes.
Now she suddenly saw it, and she twisted it round her
fingers before the glass, and was glad it was so pretty.

Mellersh couldn't have seen it either, for he had never said a word about it. Well, when she got home she would draw his attention to it. 'Mellersh,' she would say, 'look at my hair. Aren't you pleased you've got a wife with hair like curly honey?'

She laughed. She had never said anything like that to Mellersh yet, and the idea of it amused her. But why had she not? Oh yes—she used to be afraid of him. Funny to be afraid of anybody; and especially of one's husband, whom one saw in his more simplified moments, such as asleep, and not breathing properly through his nose.

When she was ready she opened her door to go across to see if Rose, who had been put the night before by a sleepy maidservant into a cell opposite, were awake. She would say good-morning to her, and then she would run down and stay with that cypress tree till breakfast was ready, and after breakfast she wouldn't so much as look out of a window till she had helped Rose get everything ready for Lady Caroline and Mrs. Fisher. There was much to be done that day, settling in, arranging the rooms; she mustn't leave Rose to do it alone. They would make it all so lovely for the two to come, have such an entrancing vision ready for them of little cells bright with flowers. She remembered she had wanted Lady Caroline not to come; fancy wanting to shut some one out of heaven because she thought she

would be shy of her! And as though it mattered if
she were, and as though she would be anything so self-
conscious as shy. Besides, what a reason. She could
not accuse herself of goodness over that. And she
remembered she had wanted not to have Mrs. Fisher
either, because she had seemed lofty. How funny of
her. So funny to worry about such little things, making
them important.

The bedrooms and two of the sitting-rooms at San
Salvatore were on the top floor, and opened into a roomy
hall with a wide glass window at the north end. San
Salvatore was rich in small gardens in different parts
and on different levels. The garden this window looked
down on was made on the highest part of the walls,
and could only be reached through the corresponding
spacious hall on the floor below. When Mrs. Wilkins
came out of her room this window stood wide open,
and beyond it in the sun was a Judas tree in full flower.
There was no sign of anybody, no sound of voices or
feet. Tubs of arum lilies stood about on the stone
floor, and on a table flamed a huge bunch of fierce
nasturtiums. Spacious, flowery, silent, with the wide
window at the end opening into the garden, and the
Judas tree absurdly beautiful in the sunshine, it seemed
to Mrs. Wilkins, arrested on her way across to Mrs.
Arbuthnot, too good to be true. Was she really going

to live in this for a whole month ?   Up to now she had
had to take what beauty she could as she went along,
snatching at little bits of it when she came across it,—
a patch of daisies on a fine day in a Hampstead field,
a flash of sunset between two chimney pots. She had
never been in definitely, completely beautiful places.
She had never been even in a venerable house ; and
such a thing as a profusion of flowers in her rooms was
unattainable to her. Sometimes in the spring she had
bought six tulips at Shoolbred's, unable to resist them,
conscious that Mellersh if he knew what they had cost
would think it inexcusable ; but they had soon died,
and then there were no more. As for the Judas tree,
she hadn't an idea what it was, and gazed at it out
there against the sky with the rapt expression of one
who sees a heavenly vision.

Mrs. Arbuthnot, coming out of her room, found her
there like that, standing in the middle of the hall staring.

' Now what does she think she sees now ? ' thought
Mrs. Arbuthnot.

' We *are* in God's hands,' said Mrs. Wilkins, turning
to her, speaking with extreme conviction.

' Oh ! ' said Mrs. Arbuthnot quickly, her face, which
had been covered with smiles when she came out of
her room, falling. ' Why, what has happened ? '

For Mrs. Arbuthnot had woken up with such a de-

lightful feeling of security, of relief, and she did not
want to find she had not after all escaped from the need
of refuge. She had not even dreamed of Frederick.
For the first time for years she had been spared the
nightly dream that he was with her, that they were
heart to heart, and its miserable awakening. She had
slept like a baby, and had woken up confident; she
had found there was nothing she wished to say in her
morning prayer except Thank you. It was disconcerting to be told she was after all in God's hands.

'I hope nothing has happened?' she asked
anxiously.

Mrs. Wilkins looked at her a moment, and laughed.
'How funny,' she said, kissing her.

'What is funny?' asked Mrs. Arbuthnot, her face
clearing because Mrs. Wilkins laughed.

'We are. This is. Everything. It's all so wonderful. It's so funny and so adorable that we should be
in it. I daresay when we finally reach heaven—the
one they talk about so much—we shan't find it a bit
more beautiful.'

Mrs. Arbuthnot relaxed to smiling security again.
'Isn't it divine?' she said.

'Were you ever, ever in your life so happy?' asked
Mrs. Wilkins, catching her by the arm.

'No,' said Mrs. Arbuthnot. Nor had she been; not

ever; not even in her first love-days with Frederick. Because always pain had been close at hand in that other happiness, ready to torture with doubts, to torture even with the very excess of her love; while this was the simple happiness of complete harmony with her surroundings, the happiness that asks for nothing, that just accepts, just breathes, just is.

'Let's go and look at that tree close,' said Mrs. Wilkins. 'I don't believe it can only be a tree.'

And arm in arm they went along the hall, and their husbands would not have known them their faces were so young with eagerness, and together they stood at the open window, and when their eyes, having feasted on the marvellous pink thing, wandered farther among the beauties of the garden, they saw sitting on the low wall at the east edge of it, gazing out over the bay, her feet in lilies, Lady Caroline.

They were astonished. They said nothing in their astonishment, but stood quite still, arm in arm, staring down at her.

She too had on a white frock, and her head was bare. They had had no idea that day in London, when her hat was down to her nose and her furs were up to her ears, that she was so pretty. They had merely thought her different from the other women in the club, and so had the other women themselves, and so had all the waitresses, eyeing her sideways and eyeing her again as they passed the corner where she sat talking; but they had had no idea she was so pretty. She was exceedingly pretty. Everything about her was very much that which it was. Her fair hair was very fair, her lovely grey eyes were very lovely and grey, her dark eyelashes were very dark, her white skin was very white, her red mouth was very red. She was extravagantly slender,—the merest thread of a girl, though not without little curves beneath her thin frock where little curves should be. She was looking out across the bay, and was sharply defined against the background of empty blue. She was full in the sun. Her feet dangled among the leaves and flowers of the lilies just as if it did not matter that they should be bent or bruised.

' She ought to have a headache,' whispered Mrs. Arbuthnot at last, ' sitting there in the sun like that.'

' She ought to have a hat,' whispered Mrs. Wilkins.

' She's treading on lilies.'

' But they're hers as much as ours.'

' Only one-fourth of them.'

Lady Caroline turned her head. She looked up at them a moment, surprised to see them so much younger than they had seemed that day at the club, and so much less unattractive. Indeed, they were really almost quite attractive, if any one could ever be really quite attractive in the wrong clothes. Her eyes, swiftly glancing over them, took in every inch of each of them in the half second before she smiled and waved her hand and called out Good-morning. There was nothing, she saw at once, to be hoped for in the way of interest from their clothes. She did not consciously think this, for she was having a violent reaction against beautiful clothes and the slavery they impose on one, her experience being that the instant one had got them they took one in hand and gave one no peace till they had been everywhere and been seen by everybody. You didn't take your clothes to parties ; they took you. It was quite a mistake to think that a woman, a really well-dressed woman, wore out her clothes ; it was the clothes that wore out the woman,—dragging her about at all hours of the day and night. No wonder men stayed young longer. Just new trousers couldn't excite them. She couldn't suppose that even the newest trousers ever behaved like that, taking the bit between their teeth. Her images were disorderly, but she thought as she chose, she used what images she liked. As she got off the wall and came towards the window, it seemed a restful thing to know she was going to spend an entire month with people in dresses made as she dimly remembered dresses used to be made five summers ago.

' I got here yesterday morning,' she said, looking up

at them and smiling. She really was bewitching. She
had everything, even a dimple.

'It's a great pity,' said Mrs. Arbuthnot, smiling back,
'because we were going to choose the nicest room for
you.'

'Oh, but I've done that,' said Lady Caroline. 'At
least, I think it's the nicest. It looks two ways—I adore
a room that looks two ways, don't you? Over the sea
to the west, and over this Judas tree to the north.'

'And we had meant to make it pretty for you with
flowers,' said Mrs. Wilkins.

'Oh, Domenico did that. I told him to directly I
got here. He's the gardener. He's wonderful.'

'It's a good thing, of course,' said Mrs. Arbuthnot
a little hesitatingly, 'to be independent, and to know
exactly what one wants.'

'Yes, it saves trouble,' agreed Lady Caroline.

'But one shouldn't be so independent,' said Mrs.
Wilkins, 'as to leave no opportunity for other people
to exercise their benevolences on one.'

Lady Caroline, who had been looking at Mrs.
Arbuthnot, now looked at Mrs. Wilkins. That day at
that queer club she had had merely a blurred impression
of Mrs. Wilkins, for it was the other one who did all the
talking, and her impression had been of somebody so
shy, so awkward that it was best to take no notice of

her. She had not even been able to say good-bye
properly, doing it in an agony, turning red, turning
damp. Therefore she now looked at her in some surprise;
and she was still more surprised when Mrs. Wilkins added,
gazing at her with the most obvious sincere admiration,
speaking indeed with a conviction that refused to remain
unuttered, ' I didn't realise you were *so* pretty.'

She stared at Mrs. Wilkins. She was not usually
told this quite so immediately and roundly. Abundantly
as she was used to it—impossible not to be after twenty-
eight solid years—it surprised her to be told it with such
bluntness, and by a woman.

' It's very kind of you to think so,' she said.

' Why, you're lovely,' said Mrs. Wilkins. ' Quite,
quite lovely.'

' I hope,' said Mrs. Arbuthnot pleasantly, ' you make
the most of it.'

Lady Caroline then stared at Mrs. Arbuthnot. ' Oh
yes,' she said. ' I make the most of it. I've been doing
that ever since I can remember.'

' Because,' said Mrs. Arbuthnot, smiling and raising
a warning forefinger, ' it won't last.'

Then Lady Caroline began to be afraid these two
were originals. If so, she would be bored. Nothing
bored her so much as people who insisted on being
original, who came and buttonholed her and kept her

waiting while they were being original. And the one who admired her—it would be tiresome if she dogged her about in order to look at her. What she wanted of this holiday was complete escape from all she had had before, she wanted the rest of complete contrast. Being admired, being dogged, wasn't contrast, it was repetition; and as for originals, to find herself shut up with two on the top of a precipitous hill in a mediaeval castle built for the express purpose of preventing easy goings out and in, would not, she was afraid, be especially restful. Perhaps she had better be a little less encouraging. They had seemed such timid creatures, even the dark one—she couldn't remember their names—that day at the club, that she had felt it quite safe to be very friendly. Here they had come out of their shells; already; indeed, at once. There was no sign of timidity about either of them here. If they had got out of their shells so immediately, at the very first contact, unless she checked them they would soon begin to press upon her, and then good-bye to her dream of thirty restful, silent days, lying unmolested in the sun, getting her feathers smooth again, not being spoken to, not waited on, not grabbed at and monopolised, but just recovering from the fatigue, the deep and melancholy fatigue, of the too much.

Besides, there was Mrs. Fisher. She too must be

checked. Lady Caroline had started two days earlier
than had been arranged for two reasons : first, because
she wished to arrive before the others in order to pick
out the room or rooms she preferred, and second, because
she judged it likely that otherwise she would have to
travel with Mrs. Fisher. She did not want to travel
with Mrs. Fisher. She did not want to arrive with
Mrs. Fisher. She saw no reason whatever why for a
single moment she should have to have anything at all
to do with Mrs. Fisher.

But unfortunately Mrs. Fisher also was filled with a
desire to get to San Salvatore first and pick out the room
or rooms she preferred, and she and Lady Caroline had
after all travelled together. As early as Calais they
began to suspect it ; in Paris they feared it ; at Modane
they knew it ; at Mezzago they concealed it, driving out
to Castagneto in two separate flys, the nose of the one
almost touching the back of the other the whole way.
But when the road suddenly left off at the church and
the steps, further evasion was impossible ; and faced by
this abrupt and difficult finish to their journey there was
nothing for it but to amalgamate.

Because of Mrs. Fisher's stick Lady Caroline had to
see about everything. Mrs. Fisher's intentions, she
explained from her fly when the situation had become
plain to her, were active, but her stick prevented their

being carried out. The two drivers told Lady Caroline boys would have to carry the luggage up to the castle, and she went in search of some, while Mrs. Fisher waited in the fly because of her stick. Mrs. Fisher could speak Italian, but only, she explained, the Italian of Dante, which Matthew Arnold used to read with her when she was a girl, and she thought this might be above the heads of boys. Therefore Lady Caroline, who spoke ordinary Italian very well, was obviously the one to go and do things.

' I am in your hands,' said Mrs. Fisher, sitting firmly in her fly. ' You must please regard me as merely an old woman with a stick.'

And presently, down the steps and cobbles to the piazza, and along the quay, and up the zigzag path, Lady Caroline found herself as much obliged to walk slowly with Mrs. Fisher as if she were her own grandmother.

' It's my stick,' Mrs. Fisher complacently remarked at intervals.

And when they rested at those bends of the zigzag path where seats were, and Lady Caroline, who would have liked to run on and get to the top quickly, was forced in common humanity to remain with Mrs. Fisher because of her stick, Mrs. Fisher told her how she had been on a zigzag path once with Tennyson.

'Isn't his cricket wonderful?' said Lady Caroline absently.

'*The* Tennyson,' said Mrs. Fisher, turning her head and observing her a moment over her spectacles.

'Isn't he?' said Lady Caroline.

'I am speaking,' said Mrs. Fisher, 'of Alfred.'

'Oh,' said Lady Caroline.

'And it was a path, too,' Mrs. Fisher went on severely, 'curiously like this. No eucalyptus tree, of course, but otherwise curiously like this. And at one of the bends he turned and said to me—I see him now turning and saying to me——'

Yes, Mrs. Fisher would have to be checked. And so would these two up at the window. She had better begin at once. She was sorry she had got off the wall. All she need have done was to have waved her hand, and waited till they came down and out into the garden to her.

So she ignored Mrs. Arbuthnot's remark and raised forefinger, and said with marked coldness—at least, she tried to make it sound marked—that she supposed they would be going to breakfast, and that she had had hers; but it was her fate that however coldly she sent forth her words they came out sounding quite warm and agreeable. That was because she had a sympathetic and delightful voice, due entirely to some special formation of her throat and the roof of her mouth, and having nothing whatever to do with what she was feeling. Nobody in consequence ever believed they were being snubbed. It was most tiresome. And if she stared icily it did not look icy at all, because her eyes, lovely to begin with, had the added loveliness of very long, soft, dark eyelashes. No icy stare could come out of eyes like that; it got caught and lost in the soft eyelashes, and the persons stared at merely thought they were being regarded with a flattering and exquisite attentiveness. And if ever she was out of humour or definitely cross,—and who would not be sometimes in such a world ?—she only looked so pathetic that people all rushed to comfort her, if possible by means of kissing. It was more than tiresome, it was maddening. Nature was determined that she should look and sound angelic. She could never be disagreeable or rude without being completely misunderstood.

'I had my breakfast in my room,' she said, trying her utmost to sound curt. 'Perhaps I'll see you later.'

And she nodded, and went back to where she had been sitting on the wall, with the lilies being nice and cool round her feet.

THEIR eyes followed her admiringly. They had no idea they had been snubbed. It was a disappointment, of course, to find she had forestalled them and that they were not to have the happiness of preparing for her, of watching her face when she arrived and first saw everything, but there was still Mrs. Fisher. They would concentrate on Mrs. Fisher, and would watch her face instead; only, like everybody else, they would have preferred to watch Lady Caroline's.

Perhaps, then, as Lady Caroline had talked of breakfast, they had better begin by going and having it, for there was too much to be done that day to spend any more time gazing at the scenery,—servants to be interviewed, the house to be gone through and examined, and finally Mrs. Fisher's room to be got ready and adorned.

They waved their hands gaily at Lady Caroline, who seemed absorbed in what she saw and took no notice, and turning away found the maidservant of the night before had come up silently behind them in cloth slippers with string soles.

She was Francesca, the elderly parlour-maid, who had been with the owner, he had said, for years, and whose presence made inventories unnecessary ; and after wishing them good-morning and hoping they had slept well, she told them breakfast was ready in the dining-room on the floor below, and if they would follow her she would lead.

They did not understand a single word of the very many in which Francesca succeeded in clothing this simple information, but they followed her, for it at least was clear that they were to follow, and going down the stairs, and along the broad hall like the one above except for glass doors at the end instead of a window opening into the garden, they were shown into the dining-room ; where, sitting at the head of the table having her breakfast, was Mrs. Fisher.

This time they exclaimed. Even Mrs. Arbuthnot exclaimed, though her exclamation was only ' Oh.'

Mrs. Wilkins exclaimed at greater length. ' Why, but it's like having the bread taken out of one's mouth ! ' exclaimed Mrs. Wilkins.

' How do you do,' said Mrs. Fisher. ' I can't get up because of my stick.' And she stretched out her hand across the table.

They advanced and shook it.

'We had no idea you were here,' said Mrs. Arbuthnot.

'Yes,' said Mrs. Fisher, resuming her breakfast. 'Yes. I am here.' And with composure she removed the top of her egg.

'It's a great disappointment,' said Mrs. Wilkins. 'We had meant to give you *such* a welcome.'

This was the one, Mrs. Fisher remembered, briefly glancing at her, who when she came to Prince of Wales Terrace said she had seen Keats. She must be careful with this one,—curb her from the beginning.

She therefore ignored Mrs. Wilkins and said gravely, with a downward face of impenetrable calm bent on her egg, 'Yes. I arrived yesterday with Lady Caroline.'

'It's really dreadful,' said Mrs. Wilkins, exactly as if she had not been ignored. 'There's nobody left to get anything ready for now. I feel thwarted. I feel as if the bread had been taken out of my mouth just when I was going to be happy swallowing it.'

'Where will you sit?' asked Mrs. Fisher of Mrs. Arbuthnot,—markedly of Mrs. Arbuthnot; the comparison with the bread seemed to her most unpleasant.

'Oh, thank you——' said Mrs. Arbuthnot, sitting down rather suddenly next to her.

There were only two places she could sit down in, the places laid on either side of Mrs. Fisher. She there-

fore sat down in one, and Mrs. Wilkins sat down opposite
her in the other.

Mrs. Fisher was at the head of the table. Round
her was grouped the coffee and the tea. Of course
they were all sharing San Salvatore equally, but it
was she herself and Lotty, Mrs. Arbuthnot mildly
reflected, who had found it, who had had the work of
getting it, who had chosen to admit Mrs. Fisher into
it. Without them, she could not help thinking, Mrs.
Fisher would not have been there. Morally Mrs. Fisher
was a guest. There was no hostess in this party, but
supposing there had been a hostess it would not have
been Mrs. Fisher, nor Lady Caroline, it would have
been either herself or Lotty. Mrs. Arbuthnot could not
help feeling this as she sat down, and Mrs. Fisher, the
hand which Ruskin had wrung suspended over the pots
before her, inquired, ' Tea or coffee ? ' She could not
help feeling it even more definitely when Mrs. Fisher
touched a small gong on the table beside her as though
she had been used to that gong and that table ever
since she was little, and, on Francesca's appearing, bade
her in the language of Dante bring more milk. There
was a curious air about Mrs. Fisher, thought Mrs.
Arbuthnot, of being in possession ; and if she herself
had not been so happy she would have perhaps minded.

Mrs. Wilkins noticed it too, but it only made her

discursive brain think of cuckoos. She would no doubt immediately have begun to talk of cuckoos, incoherently, unrestrainably and deplorably, if she had been in the condition of nerves and shyness she was in last time she saw Mrs. Fisher. But happiness had done away with shyness,—she was very serene ; she could control her conversation ; she did not have, horrified, to listen to herself saying things she had no idea of saying when she began ; she was quite at her ease, and completely natural. The disappointment of not going to be able to prepare a welcome for Mrs. Fisher had evaporated at once, for it was impossible to go on being disappointed in heaven. Nor did she mind her behaving as hostess. What did it matter ? You did not mind things in heaven. She and Mrs. Arbuthnot, therefore, sat down more willingly than they otherwise would have done, one on either side of Mrs. Fisher, and the sun, pouring through the two windows facing east across the bay, flooded the room, and there was an open door leading into the garden, and the garden was full of many lovely things, especially freesias.

The delicate and delicious fragrance of the freesias came in through the door and floated round Mrs. Wilkins's enraptured nostrils. Freesias in London were quite beyond her. Occasionally she went into a shop and asked what they cost, so as just to have an excuse for

lifting up a bunch and smelling them, well knowing
that it was something awful like a shilling for about
three flowers. Here they were everywhere,—bursting
out of every corner and carpeting the rose-beds. Imagine
it—having freesias to pick in armsful if you wanted to,
and with glorious sunshine flooding the room, and in
your summer frock, and its being only the first of April!

' I suppose you realise, don't you, that we've got
to heaven ? ' she said, beaming at Mrs. Fisher with all
the familiarity of a fellow-angel.

' They are considerably younger than I had supposed,'
thought Mrs. Fisher, ' and not nearly so plain.' And
she mused a moment, while she took no notice of Mrs.
Wilkins's exuberance, on their instant and agitated
refusal that day at Prince of Wales Terrace to have
anything to do with the giving or the taking of references.

Nothing could affect her, of course ; nothing that
anybody did. She was far too solidly seated in respectability. At her back stood massively in a tremendous
row those three great names she had offered, and they
were not the only ones she could turn to for support
and countenance. Even if these young women—she
had no grounds for believing the one out in the garden
to be really Lady Caroline Dester, she had merely
been told she was—even if these young women should
all turn out to be what Browning used to call—how

well she remembered his amusing and delightful way of putting things—Fly-by-Nights, what could it possibly, or in any way matter to her? Let them fly by night if they wished. One was not sixty-five for nothing. In any case there would only be four weeks of it, at the end of which she would see no more of them. And in the meanwhile there were plenty of places where she could sit quietly away from them and remember. Also there was her own sitting-room, a charming room, all honey-coloured furniture and pictures, with windows to the sea towards Genoa, and a door opening on to the battlements. The house possessed two sitting-rooms, and she had explained to that pretty creature Lady Caroline—certainly a pretty creature, whatever else she was; Tennyson would have enjoyed taking her for blows on the downs—who had seemed inclined to appropriate the honey-coloured one, that she needed some little refuge entirely to herself because of her stick.

' Nobody wants to see an old woman hobbling about everywhere,' she had said. ' I shall be quite content to spend much of my time by myself in here or sitting out on these convenient battlements.'

And she had a very nice bedroom, too; it looked two ways, across the bay to the morning sun—she liked the morning sun—and on to the garden. There were only two of these bedrooms with cross-views in the house, she and Lady Caroline had discovered, and they were by far the airiest. They each had two beds in them, and she and Lady Caroline had had the extra beds taken out at once and put into two of the other rooms. In this way there was much more space and comfort. Lady Caroline, indeed, had turned hers into a bed-sitting-room, with the sofa out of the bigger drawing-room and the writing-table and the most comfortable chair, but she herself had not had to do that because she had her own sitting-room, equipped with what was necessary. Lady Caroline had thought at first of taking the bigger sitting-room entirely for her own, because the dining-room on the floor below could quite well be used between meals to sit in by the two others, and was a very pleasant room with nice chairs, but she had not liked the bigger sitting-room's shape,—it was a round room in the tower, with deep slit windows pierced through the massive walls, and a domed and ribbed ceiling arranged to look like an open umbrella, and it seemed a little dark. Undoubtedly Lady Caroline had cast covetous glances at the honey-coloured room, and if she, Mrs. Fisher, had been less firm would have installed herself in it. Which would have been absurd.

'I hope,' said Mrs. Arbuthnot, smilingly making an attempt to convey to Mrs. Fisher that though she, Mrs. Fisher, might not be exactly a guest she certainly was not in the very least a hostess, 'your room is comfortable.'

'Quite,' said Mrs. Fisher. 'Will you have some more coffee ? '

'No, thank you. Will you ? '

'No, thank you. There were two beds in my bedroom, filling it up unnecessarily, and I had one taken out. It has made it much more convenient.'

'Oh *that's* why I've got two beds in my room ! ' exclaimed Mrs. Wilkins, illuminated ; the second bed in her little cell had seemed an unnatural and inappropriate object from the moment she saw it.

'I gave no directions,' said Mrs. Fisher, addressing Mrs. Arbuthnot. 'I merely asked Francesca to remove it.'

'I have two in my room as well,' said Mrs. Arbuthnot.

'Your second one must be Lady Caroline's. She had hers removed too,' said Mrs. Fisher. 'It seems foolish to have more beds in a room than there are occupiers.'

'But *we* haven't got any husbands here either,' said Mrs. Wilkins, 'and I don't see any use in extra beds in one's room if one hasn't got husbands to put in them. Can't we have them taken away too ? '

'Beds,' said Mrs. Fisher coldly, 'cannot be removed from one room after another. They must remain somewhere.'

Mrs. Wilkins's remarks seemed to Mrs. Fisher persistently unfortunate. Each time she opened her mouth she said something best left unsaid. Loose talk about husbands had never in Mrs. Fisher's circle been encouraged. In the 'eighties, when she chiefly flourished, husbands were taken seriously, as the only real obstacles to sin. Beds too, if they had to be mentioned, were approached with caution; and a decent reserve prevented them and husbands ever being spoken of in the same breath.

She turned more markedly than ever to Mrs. Arbuthnot. ' Do let me give you a little more coffee,' she said.

' No, thank you. But won't you have some more ? '

' No indeed. I never have more than two cups at breakfast. Would you like an orange ? '

' No, thank you. Would you ? '

' No, I don't eat fruit at breakfast. It is an American fashion which I am too old now to adopt. Have you had all you want ? '

' Quite. Have you ? '

Mrs. Fisher paused before replying. Was this a habit, this trick of answering a simple question with the same question ? If so it must be curbed, for no one could live four weeks in any real comfort with somebody who had a habit.

She glanced at Mrs. Arbuthnot, and her parted hair and gentle brow reassured her. No ; it was accident, not habit, that had produced those echoes. She could as soon imagine a dove having tiresome habits as Mrs. Arbuthnot. Considering her, she thought what a splendid wife she would have been for poor Carlyle. So much better than that horrid clever Jane. She would have soothed him.

' Then shall we go ? ' she suggested.

' Let me help you up,' said Mrs. Arbuthnot, all consideration.

' Oh, thank you—I can manage perfectly. It's only sometimes that my stick prevents me——'

Mrs. Fisher got up quite easily ; Mrs. Arbuthnot had hovered over her for nothing.

' *I'm* going to have one of these gorgeous oranges,' said Mrs. Wilkins, staying where she was and reaching across to a black bowl piled with them. ' Rose, how can you resist them. Look—have this one. Do have this beauty——' And she held out a big one.

' No, I'm going to see to my duties,' said Mrs. Arbuthnot, moving towards the door. ' You'll forgive me for leaving you, won't you,' she added politely to Mrs. Fisher.

Mrs. Fisher moved towards the door too ; quite easily ; almost quickly ; her stick did not hinder her at all. She had no intention of being left with Mrs. Wilkins.

'What time would you like to have lunch?' Mrs. Arbuthnot asked her, trying to keep her head as at least a non-guest, if not precisely a hostess, above water.

'Lunch,' said Mrs. Fisher, 'is at half-past twelve.'

'You shall have it at half-past twelve then,' said Mrs. Arbuthnot. 'I'll tell the cook. It will be a great struggle,' she continued, smiling, 'but I've brought a little dictionary——'

'The cook,' said Mrs. Fisher, 'knows.'

'Oh?' said Mrs. Arbuthnot.

'Lady Caroline has already told her,' said Mrs. Fisher.

'Oh?' said Mrs. Arbuthnot again.

'Yes. Lady Caroline speaks the kind of Italian cooks understand. I am prevented going into the kitchen because of my stick. And even if I were able to go, I fear I shouldn't be understood.'

'But——' began Mrs. Arbuthnot.

'But it's *too* wonderful,' Mrs. Wilkins finished for her from the table, delighted with these unexpected simplifications in her and Rose's lives. 'Why, we've got positively nothing to do here, either of us, except just be happy. You wouldn't believe,' she said, turning her head and speaking straight to Mrs. Fisher, portions of orange in either hand, 'how terribly good Rose and I have been for years without stopping, and how much now we need a perfect rest.'

And Mrs. Fisher, going without answering her out of the room, said to herself, ' She must, she shall be curbed.'

of maize in either hand, 'how terribly good Rose and I have been for years about shopping, and how much now we need a perfect rest.'

And Mrs. Fisher, going without answering her out the room, said to herself, 'She must, she shall be curbed.'

VIII

PRESENTLY, when Mrs. Wilkins and Mrs. Arbuthnot, unhampered by any duties, wandered out and down the worn stone steps and under the pergola into the lower garden, Mrs. Wilkins said to Mrs. Arbuthnot, who seemed pensive, ' Don't you see that if somebody else does the ordering it frees us ? '

Mrs. Arbuthnot said she did see, but nevertheless she thought it rather silly to have everything taken out of their hands.

' I love things to be taken out of my hands,' said Mrs. Wilkins.

' But we found San Salvatore,' said Mrs. Arbuthnot, ' and it *is* rather silly that Mrs. Fisher should behave as if it belonged only to her.'

' What is rather silly,' said Mrs. Wilkins with much serenity, ' is to mind. I can't see the least point in being in authority at the price of one's liberty.'

Mrs. Arbuthnot said nothing to that for two reasons, —first, because she was struck by the remarkable and

growing calm of the hitherto incoherent and excited
Lotty, and secondly because what she was looking at
was so very beautiful.

All down the stone steps on either side were periwinkles in full flower, and she could now see what it
was that had caught at her the night before and brushed,
wet and scented, across her face. It was wistaria.
Wistaria and sunshine . . . she remembered the
advertisement. Here indeed were both in profusion.
The wistaria was tumbling over itself in its excess of
life, its prodigality of flowering; and where the pergola
ended the sun blazed on scarlet geraniums, bushes of
them, and nasturtiums in great heaps, and marigolds
so brilliant that they seemed to be burning, and red
and pink snapdragons, all outdoing each other in bright,
fierce colour. The ground behind these flaming things
dropped away in terraces to the sea, each terrace a
little orchard, where among the olives grew vines on
trellises, and fig-trees, and peach-trees, and cherry-trees.
The cherry-trees and peach-trees were in blossom,—
lovely showers of white and deep rose-colour among the
trembling delicacy of the olives; the fig-leaves were
just big enough to smell of figs, the vine-buds were
only beginning to show. And beneath these trees were
groups of blue and purple irises, and bushes of lavender,
and grey, sharp cactuses, and the grass was thick with

dandelions and daisies, and right down at the bottom
was the sea. Colour seemed flung down anyhow, anywhere ; every sort of colour, piled up in heaps, pouring
along in rivers—the periwinkles looked exactly as if
they were being poured down each side of the steps
—and flowers that grow only in borders in England,
proud flowers keeping themselves to themselves over
there, such as the great blue irises and the lavender,
were being jostled by small, shining common things
like dandelions and daisies and the white bells of the
wild onion, and only seemed the better and the more
exuberant for it.

They stood looking at this crowd of loveliness, this
happy jumble, in silence. No, it didn't matter what
Mrs. Fisher did ; not here ; not in such beauty. Mrs.
Arbuthnot's discomposure melted out of her. In the
warmth and light of what she was looking at, of what
to her was a manifestation, an entirely new side, of
God, how could one be discomposed ? If only Frederick
were with her, seeing it too, seeing as he would have
seen it when first they were lovers, in the days
when he saw what she saw and loved what she
loved. . . .

She sighed.

'You mustn't sigh in heaven,' said Mrs. Wilkins.
'One doesn't.'

'I was thinking how one longs to share this with those one loves,' said Mrs. Arbuthnot.

'You mustn't long in heaven,' said Mrs. Wilkins. 'You're supposed to be quite complete there. And it *is* heaven, isn't it, Rose? See how everything has been let in together,—the dandelions and the irises, the vulgar and the superior, me and Mrs. Fisher—all welcome, all mixed up anyhow, and all so visibly happy and enjoying ourselves.'

'Mrs. Fisher doesn't seem happy—not visibly, anyhow,' said Mrs. Arbuthnot, smiling.

'She'll begin soon, you'll see.'

Mrs. Arbuthnot said she didn't believe that after a certain age people began anything.

Mrs. Wilkins said she was sure no one, however old and tough, could resist the effects of perfect beauty. Before many days, perhaps only hours, they would see Mrs. Fisher bursting out into every kind of exuberance. 'I'm quite sure,' said Mrs. Wilkins, 'that we've got to heaven, and once Mrs. Fisher realises that that's where she is, she's bound to be different. You'll see. She'll leave off being ossified, and go all soft and able to stretch, and we shall get quite—why, I shouldn't be surprised if we get quite fond of her.'

The idea of Mrs. Fisher bursting out into anything, she who seemed so particularly firmly fixed inside her buttons, made Mrs. Arbuthnot laugh. She condoned Lotty's loose way of talking of heaven, because in such a place, on such a morning, condonation was in the very air. Besides, what an excuse there was.

And Lady Caroline, sitting where they had left her before breakfast on the wall, peeped over when she heard laughter, and saw them standing on the path below, and thought what a mercy it was they were laughing down there and had not come up and done it round her. She disliked jokes at all times, but in the morning she hated them; especially close up; especially crowding in her ears. She hoped the originals were on their way out for a walk, and not on their way back from one. They were laughing more and more. What could they possibly find to laugh at?

She looked down on the tops of their heads with a very serious face, for the thought of spending a month with laughers was a grave one, and they, as though they felt her eyes, turned suddenly and looked up.

The dreadful geniality of those women. . . .

She shrank away from their smiles and wavings, but she could not shrink out of sight without falling into the lilies. She neither smiled nor waved back, and turning her eyes to the more distant mountains surveyed them carefully till the two, tired of waving, moved away along the path and turned the corner and disappeared.

This time they both did notice that they had been met with, at least, unresponsiveness.

'If we weren't in heaven,' said Mrs. Wilkins serenely, 'I should say we had been snubbed, but as nobody snubs anybody there of course we can't have been.'

'Perhaps she is unhappy,' said Mrs. Arbuthnot.

'Whatever it is she is she'll get over it here,' said Mrs. Wilkins with conviction.

'We must try and help her,' said Mrs. Arbuthnot.

'Oh, but nobody helps anybody in heaven. That's finished with. You don't try to be, or do. You simply *are*.'

Well, Mrs. Arbuthnot wouldn't go into that,—not here, not to-day. The vicar, she knew, would have called Lotty's talk levity, if not profanity. How old he seemed from here ; an old, old vicar.

They left the path, and clambered down the olive terraces, down and down, to where at the bottom the warm, sleepy sea heaved gently among the rocks. There a pine-tree grew close to the water, and they sat under it, and a few yards away was a fishing-boat lying motionless and green-bellied on the water. The ripples of the sea made little gurgling noises at their feet. They screwed up their eyes to be able to look into the blaze of light beyond the shade of their tree. The hot smell from the pine-needles and from the cushions of wild thyme that padded the spaces between the rocks, and sometimes a smell of pure honey from a clump of warm irises up behind them in the sun, puffed across their faces. Very soon Mrs. Wilkins took her shoes and stockings off, and let her feet hang in the water. After watching her a minute Mrs. Arbuthnot did the same. Their happiness was then complete. Their husbands would not have known them. They left off talking. They ceased to mention heaven. They were just cups of acceptance.

Meanwhile Lady Caroline, on her wall, was considering her position. The garden on the top of the wall was a delicious garden, but its situation made it insecure and exposed to interruptions. At any moment the others might come and want to use it, because both the hall and the dining-room had doors opening straight into it. Perhaps, thought Lady Caroline, she could arrange that it should be solely hers. Mrs. Fisher had the battlements, delightful with flowers, and a watch-tower all to herself, besides having snatched the one really nice room in the house. There were plenty of places the originals could go to,—she had herself seen at least two other little gardens, while the hill the castle

stood on was itself a garden, with walks and seats.
Why should not this one spot be kept exclusively for
her ? She liked it ; she liked it best of all. It had
the Judas tree and an umbrella pine, it had the freesias
and the lilies, it had a tamarisk beginning to flush
pink, it had the convenient low wall to sit on, it had
from each of its three sides the most amazing views,—
to the east the bay and mountains, to the north the
village across the tranquil clear green water of the little
harbour and the hills dotted with white houses and
orange groves, and to the west was the thin thread of
land by which San Salvatore was tied to the mainland,
and then the open sea and the coast line beyond Genoa
reaching away into the blue dimness of France. Yes,
she would say she wanted to have this entirely to
herself. How obviously sensible if each of them had
their own special place to sit in apart. It was essential
to her comfort that she should be able to be apart,
left alone, not talked to. The others ought to like
it best too. Why herd ? One had enough of that in
England, with one's relations and friends—oh, the
numbers of them !—pressing on one continually. Having
successfully escaped them for four weeks why continue,
and with persons having no earthly claim on one, to
herd ?

She lit a cigarette. She began to feel secure. Those

two had gone for a walk. There was no sign of Mrs. Fisher. How very pleasant this was.

Somebody came out through the glass doors, just as she was drawing a deep breath of security. Surely it couldn't be Mrs. Fisher, wanting to sit with her ? Mrs. Fisher had her battlements. She ought to stay on them, having snatched them. It would be too tiresome if she wouldn't, and wanted not only to have them and her sitting-room but to establish herself in this garden as well.

No ; it wasn't Mrs. Fisher ; it was the cook.

She frowned. Was she going to have to go on ordering the food ? Surely one or other of those two waving women would do that now.

The cook, who had been waiting in increasing agitation in the kitchen, watching the clock getting nearer to lunch-time while she still was without knowledge of what lunch was to consist of, had gone at last to Mrs. Fisher, who had immediately waved her away. She then wandered about the house seeking a mistress, any mistress, who would tell her what to cook, and finding none ; and at last, directed by Francesca, who always knew where everybody was, came out to Lady Caroline.

Domenica had provided this cook. She was Costanza, the sister of that one of his cousins who kept a restaurant down on the piazza. She helped her brother in his cooking when she had no other job, and knew every sort of fat, mysterious Italian dish such as the workmen of Castagneto, who crowded the restaurant at midday, and the inhabitants of Mezzago when they came over on Sundays, loved to eat. She was a fleshless spinster of fifty, grey-haired, nimble, rich of speech, and thought Lady Caroline more beautiful than any one she had ever seen; and so did Domenico; and so did the boy Giuseppe who helped Domenico and was, besides, his nephew; and so did the girl Angela who helped Francesca and was, besides, Domenico's niece; and so did Francesca herself. Domenico and Francesca, the only two who had seen them, thought the two ladies who arrived last very beautiful, but compared to the fair young lady who arrived first they were as candles to the electric light that had lately been installed, and as the tin tubs in the bedrooms to the wonderful new bathroom their master had had arranged on his last visit.

Lady Caroline scowled at the cook. The scowl, as usual, was transformed on the way into what appeared to be an intent and beautiful gravity, and Costanza threw up her hands and took the saints aloud to witness that here was the very picture of the Mother of God.

Lady Caroline asked her crossly what she wanted, and Costanza's head went on one side with delight at the sheer music of her voice. She said, after waiting a moment in case the music was going to continue, for she didn't wish to miss any of it, that she wanted orders ; she had been to the Signorina's mother, but in vain.

'She is not my mother,' repudiated Lady Caroline angrily ; and her anger sounded like the regretful wail of a melodious orphan.

Costanza poured forth pity. She too, she explained, had no mother——

Lady Caroline interrupted with the curt information that her mother was alive and in London.

Costanza praised God and the saints that the young lady did not yet know what it was like to be without a mother. Quickly enough did misfortunes overtake one ; no doubt the young lady already had a husband.

'No,' said Lady Caroline icily. Worse than jokes in the morning did she hate the idea of husbands. And everybody was always trying to press them on her,— all her relations, all her friends, all the evening papers. After all, she could only marry one, anyhow ; but you would think from the way everybody talked, and especially those persons who wanted to be husbands, that she could marry at least a dozen.

Her soft, pathetic ' No ' made Costanza, who was standing close to her, well with sympathy.

' Poor little one,' said Costanza, moved actually to pat her encouragingly on the shoulder, ' take hope. There is still time.'

' For lunch,' said Lady Caroline freezingly, marvelling as she spoke that she should be patted, she who had taken so much trouble to come to a place, remote and hidden, where she could be sure that among other things of a like oppressive nature pattings also were not, ' we will have——'

Costanza became business-like. She interrupted with suggestions, and her suggestions were all admirable and all expensive.

Lady Caroline did not know they were expensive, and fell in with them at once. They sounded very nice. Every sort of young vegetables and fruits came into them, and much butter and a great deal of cream and incredible numbers of eggs. Costanza said enthusiastically at the end, as a tribute to this acquiescence, that of the many ladies and gentlemen she had worked for on temporary jobs such as this she preferred the English ladies and gentlemen. She more than preferred them,—they roused devotion in her. For they knew what to order ; they did not skimp ; they refrained from grinding down the faces of the poor.

From this Lady Caroline concluded that she had been extravagant, and promptly countermanded the cream.

Costanza's face fell, for she had a cousin who had a cow, and the cream was to have come from them both.

' And perhaps we had better not have chickens,' said Lady Caroline.

Costanza's face fell more, for her brother at the restaurant kept chickens in his back-yard, and many of them were ready for killing.

' Also do not order strawberries till I have consulted with the other ladies,' said Lady Caroline, remembering that it was only the first of April, and that perhaps people who lived in Hampstead might be poor; indeed, must be poor, or why live in Hampstead ? ' It is not I who am mistress here.'

' Is it the old one ? ' asked Costanza, her face very long.

' No,' said Lady Caroline.

' Which of the other two ladies is it ? '

' Neither,' said Lady Caroline.

Then Costanza's smiles returned, for the young lady was having fun with her and making jokes. She told her so, in her friendly Italian way, and was genuinely delighted.

'I never make jokes,' said Lady Caroline briefly. 'You had better go, or lunch will certainly not be ready by half-past twelve.'

And these curt words came out sounding so sweet that Costanza felt as if kind compliments were being paid her, and forgot her disappointment about the cream and the chickens, and went away all gratitude and smiles.

'This,' thought Lady Caroline, 'will never do. I haven't come here to housekeep, and I won't.'

She called Costanza back. Costanza came running. The sound of her name in that voice enchanted her.

'I have ordered the lunch for to-day,' said Lady Caroline, with the serious angel face that was hers when she was annoyed, 'and I have also ordered the dinner, but from now on you will go to one of the other ladies for orders. I give no more.'

The idea that she would go on giving orders was too absurd. She never gave orders at home. Nobody there dreamed of asking her to do anything. That such a very tiresome activity should be thrust upon her here, simply because she happened to be able to talk Italian, was ridiculous. Let the originals give orders if Mrs. Fisher refused to. Mrs. Fisher, of course, was the one Nature intended for such a purpose. She had the very air of a competent housekeeper. Her clothes were the clothes of a housekeeper, and so was the way she did her hair.

Having delivered herself of her ultimatum with an acerbity that turned sweet on the way, and accompanied it by a peremptory gesture of dismissal that had the grace and loving-kindness of a benediction, it was annoying that Costanza should only stand still with her head on one side gazing at her in obvious delight.

' Oh, *go* away ! ' exclaimed Lady Caroline in English, suddenly exasperated.

There had been a fly in her bedroom that morning which had stuck just as Costanza was sticking; only one, but it might have been a myriad it was so tiresome from daylight on. It was determined to settle on her face, and she was determined it should not. Its persistence was uncanny. It woke her, and would not let her go to sleep again. She hit at it, and it eluded her without fuss or effort and with an almost visible blandness, and she had only hit herself. It came back again instantly, and with a loud buzz alighted on her cheek. She hit at it again and hurt herself, while it skimmed gracefully away. She lost her temper, and sat up in bed and waited, watching to hit at it and kill it. She kept on hitting at it at last with fury and with all her strength, as if it were a real enemy deliberately trying

to madden her; and it elegantly skimmed in and out
of her blows, not even angry, to be back again the next
instant. It succeeded every time in getting on to
her face, and was quite indifferent how often it was
driven away. That was why she had dressed and come
out so early. Francesca had already been told to put
a net over her bed, for she was not going to allow herself
to be annoyed twice like that. People were exactly like
flies. She wished there were nets for keeping them off
too. She hit at them with words and frowns, and like
the fly they slipped between her blows and were untouched. Worse than the fly, they seemed unaware
that she had even tried to hit them. The fly at least
did for a moment go away. With human beings the
only way to get rid of them was to go away herself.
That was what, so tired, she had done this April; and
having got here, having got close up to the details of
life at San Salvatore, it appeared that here, too, she
was not to be let alone.

Viewed from London there had seemed to be no
details. San Salvatore from there seemed to be an
empty, a delicious blank. Yet, after only twenty-four
hours of it, she was discovering that it was not a blank
at all, and that she was having to ward off as actively as
ever. Already she had been much stuok to. Mrs.
Fisher had stuck nearly the whole of the day before, and

this morning there had been no peace, not ten minutes uninterruptedly alone.

Costanza of course had finally to go because she had to cook, but hardly had she gone before Domenico came. He came to water and tie up. That was natural, since he was the gardener, but he watered and tied up all the things that were nearest to her; he hovered closer and closer; he watered to excess; he tied plants that were as straight and steady as arrows. Well, at least he was a man, and therefore not quite so annoying, and his smiling good-morning was received with an answering smile; upon which Domenico forgot his family, his wife, his mother, his grown-up children and all his duties, and only wanted to kiss the young lady's feet.

He could not do that, unfortunately, but he could talk while he worked, and talk he did; voluminously; pouring out every kind of information, illustrating what he said with gestures so lively that he had to put down the watering-pot, and thus delay the end of the watering.

Lady Caroline bore it for a time but presently was unable to bear it, and as he would not go, and she could not tell him to, seeing that he was engaged in his proper work, once again it was she who had to.

She got off the wall and moved to the other side of the garden, where in a wooden shed were some comfortable low cane chairs. All she wanted was to turn one of these round with its back to Domenico and its front to the sea towards Genoa. Such a little thing to want. One would have thought she might have been allowed to do that unmolested. But he, who watched her every movement, when he saw her approaching the chairs darted after her and seized one and asked to be told where to put it.

Would she never get away from being waited on, being made comfortable, being asked where she wanted things put, having to say thank you? She was short with Domenico, who instantly concluded the sun had given her a headache, and ran in and fetched her a sunshade and a cushion and a footstool, and was skilful, and was wonderful, and was one of Nature's gentlemen.

She shut her eyes in a heavy resignation. She could not be unkind to Domenico. She could not get up and walk indoors as she would have done if it had been one of the others. Domenico was intelligent and very competent. She had at once discovered that it was he who really ran the house, who really did everything. And his manners were definitely delightful, and he undoubtedly was a charming person. It was only that she did so much long to be let alone. If only, only she could be left quite quiet for this one month, she felt that she might perhaps make something of herself after all.

She kept her eyes shut, because then he would think she wanted to sleep and would go away.

Domenico's romantic Italian soul melted within him at the sight, for having her eyes shut was extraordinarily becoming to her. He stood entranced, quite still, and she thought he had stolen away, so she opened them again.

No ; there he was, staring at her. Even he. There was no getting away from being stared at.

' I have a headache,' she said, shutting them again.

' It is the sun,' said Domenico, ' and sitting on the wall without a hat.'

' I wish to sleep.'

' *Si signorina,*' he said sympathetically ; and went softly away.

She opened her eyes with a sigh of relief. The gentle closing of the glass doors showed her that he had not only gone quite away but had shut her out in the garden so that she should be undisturbed. Now perhaps she would be alone till lunch-time.

It was very curious, and no one in the world could have been more surprised than she herself, but she wanted to think. She had never wanted to do that before. Everything else that it is possible to do without too much inconvenience she had either wanted to do or had done at one period or another of her life, but not before had she wanted to think. She had come to San Salvatore with the single intention of lying comatose for four weeks in the sun, somewhere where her parents and friends were not, lapped in forgetfulness, stirring herself only to be fed, and she had not been there more than a few hours when this strange new desire took hold of her.

There had been wonderful stars the evening before, and she had gone out into the top garden after dinner, leaving Mrs. Fisher alone over her nuts and wine, and, sitting on the wall at the place where the lilies crowded their ghost heads, she had looked out into the gulf of the night, and it had suddenly seemed as if her life had been a noise all about nothing.

She had been intensely surprised. She knew stars and darkness did produce unusual emotions because, in others, she had seen them being produced, but they had not before done it in herself. A noise all about nothing. Could she be quite well ? she had wondered. For a long while past she had been aware that her life was a noise, but it had seemed to be very much about something ; a noise, indeed, about so much that she felt she must get out of earshot for a little or she would be completely, and perhaps permanently, deafened. But suppose it was only a noise about nothing ?

She had not had a question like that in her mind

before. It had made her feel lonely. She wanted to be alone, but not lonely. That was very different; that was something that ached and hurt dreadfully right inside one. It was what one dreaded most. It was what made one go to so many parties; and lately even the parties had seemed once or twice not to be a perfectly certain protection. Was it possible that loneliness had nothing to do with circumstances, but only with the way one met them? Perhaps, she had thought, she had better go to bed. She couldn't be very well.

She went to bed; and in the morning, after she had escaped the fly and had her breakfast and got out again into the garden, there was this same feeling again, and in broad daylight. Once more she had that really rather disgusting suspicion that her life till now had not only been loud but empty. Well, if that were so, and if her first twenty-eight years—the best ones—had gone just in meaningless noise, she had better stop a moment and look round her; pause, as they said in tiresome novels, and consider. She hadn't got many sets of twenty-eight years. One more would see her growing very like Mrs. Fisher. Two more—— She averted her eyes.

Her mother would have been concerned if she had known. Her mother doted. Her father would have been concerned too, for he also doted. Everybody doted. And when, melodiously obstinate, she had insisted on going off to entomb herself in Italy for a whole month with queer people she had got out of an advertisement, refusing even to take her maid, the only explanation her friends could imagine was that poor Scrap—such was her name among them—had overdone it and was feeling a little nervy.

Her mother had been distressed at her departure. It was such an odd thing to do, such a sign of disappointment. She encouraged the general idea of the verge of a nervous breakdown. If she could have seen her adored Scrap, more delightful to look upon than any other mother's daughter had ever yet been, the object of her utmost pride, the source of all her fondest hopes, sitting staring at the empty noonday Mediterranean considering her three possible sets of twenty-eight years, she would have been miserable. To go away alone was bad ; to think was worse. No good could come out of the thinking of a beautiful young woman. Complications could come out of it in profusion, but no good. The thinking of the beautiful was bound to result in hesitations, in reluctances, in unhappiness all round. And here, if she could have seen her, sat her Scrap thinking quite hard. And such things. Such old things. Things nobody ever began to think till they were at least forty.

IX

THAT one of the two sitting-rooms which Mrs. Fisher had taken for her own was a room of charm and character. She surveyed it with satisfaction on going into it after breakfast, and was glad it was hers. It had a tiled floor, and walls the colour of pale honey, and inlaid furniture the colour of amber, and mellow books, many in ivory or lemon-coloured covers. There was a big window overlooking the sea towards Genoa, and a glass door through which she could proceed out on to the battlements and walk along past the quaint and attractive watch-tower, in itself a room with chairs and a writing table, to where on the other side of the tower the battlements ended in a marble seat, and one could see the western bay and the point round which began the Gulf of Spezia. Her south view, between these two stretches of sea, was another hill, higher than San Salvatore, the last of the little peninsula, with the bland turrets of a smaller and uninhabited castle on the top, on

which the setting sun still shone when everything else
was sunk in shadow. Yes, she was very comfortably
established here ; and receptacles—Mrs. Fisher did not
examine their nature closely, but they seemed to be
small stone troughs, or perhaps little sarcophagi—ringed
round the battlements with flowers.

These battlements, she thought, considering them,
would have been a perfect place for her to pace up and
down gently in moments when she least felt the need
of her stick, or to sit in on the marble seat, having first
put a cushion on it, if there had not unfortunately been
a second glass door opening on to them, destroying
their complete privacy, spoiling her feeling that the
place was only for her. The second door belonged to
the round drawing-room, which both she and Lady
Caroline had rejected as too dark. That room would
probably be sat in by the women from Hampstead,
and she was afraid they would not confine themselves
to sitting in it, but would come out through the glass
door and invade her battlements. This would ruin
the battlements. It would ruin them as far as she was
concerned if they were to be overrun ; or even if, not
actually overrun, they were liable to be raked by the
eyes of persons inside the room. No one could be
perfectly at ease if they were being watched and knew
it. What she wanted, what she surely had a right to,

was privacy. She had no wish to intrude on the others; why then should they intrude on her? And she could always relax her privacy if, when she became better acquainted with her companions, she should think it worth while, but she doubted whether any of the three would so develop as to make her think it worth while.

Hardly anything was really worth while, reflected Mrs. Fisher, except the past. It was astonishing, it was simply amazing, the superiority of the past to the present. Those friends of hers in London, solid persons of her own age, knew the same past that she knew, could talk about it with her, could compare it as she did with the tinkling present, and in remembering great men forget for a moment the trivial and barren young people who still, in spite of the war, seemed to litter the world in such numbers. She had not come away from these friends, these conversable ripe friends, in order to spend her time in Italy chatting with three persons of another generation and defective experience; she had come away merely to avoid the treacheries of a London April. It was true what she had told the two who came to Prince of Wales Terrace, that all she wished to do at San Salvatore was to sit by herself in the sun and remember. They knew this, for she had told them. It had been plainly expressed and clearly

understood.   Therefore she had a right to expect them
to stay inside the round drawing-room and not to emerge
interruptingly on to her battlements.

But would they ?   The doubt spoilt her morning.
It was only towards lunch-time that she saw a way to
be quite safe, and ringing for Francesca, bade her, in
slow and majestic Italian, shut the shutters of the glass
door of the round drawing-room, and then, going with
her into the room, which had become darker than ever
in consequence, but also, Mrs. Fisher observed to Francesca, who was being voluble, would because of this
very darkness remain agreeably cool, and after all there
were the numerous slit-windows in the walls to let in
light and it was nothing to do with her if they did not
let it in, she directed the placing of a cabinet of curios
across the door on its inside.

This would discourage egress.

Then she rang for Domenico, and caused him to
move one of the flower-filled sarcophagi across the door
on its outside.

This would discourage ingress.

' No one,' said Domenico, hesitating, ' will be able to
use the door.'

' No one,' said Mrs. Fisher firmly, ' will wish to.'

She then retired to her sitting-room, and from a
chair placed where she could look straight on to them,

gazed at her battlements, secured to her now completely, with calm pleasure.

Being here, she reflected placidly, was much cheaper than being in an hotel and, if she could keep off the others, immeasurably more agreeable. She was paying for her rooms—extremely pleasant rooms, now that she was arranged in them—£3 a week, which came to about eight shillings a day, battlements, watch-tower and all. Where else abroad could she live as well for so little, and have as many baths as she liked, for eight shillings a day? Of course she did not yet know what her food would cost, but she would insist on carefulness over that, though she would also insist on its being carefulness combined with excellence. The two were perfectly compatible if the caterer took pains. The servants' wages, she had ascertained, were negligible, owing to the advantageous exchange, so that there was only the food to cause her anxiety. If she saw signs of extravagance she would propose that they each hand over a reasonable sum every week to Lady Caroline which should cover the bills, any of it that was not used to be returned, and if it were exceeded the loss to be borne by the caterer.

Mrs. Fisher was well off and had the desire for comforts proper to her age, but she disliked expenses. So well off was she that, had she so chosen, she could have

lived in an opulent part of London and driven from it
and to it in a Rolls-Royce. She had no such wish. It
needed more vitality than went with true comfort to
deal with a house in an opulent spot and a Rolls-Royce.
Worries attended such possessions, worries of every
kind, crowned by bills. In the sober gloom of Prince
of Wales Terrace she could obscurely enjoy inexpensive
yet real comfort, without being snatched at by predatory
men-servants or collectors for charities, and a taxi stand
was at the end of the road. Her annual outlay was
small. The house was inherited. Death had furnished
it for her. She trod in the dining-room on the Turkey
carpet of her fathers; she regulated her day by the
excellent black marble clock on the mantelpiece which
she remembered from childhood; her walls were entirely
covered by the photographs her illustrious deceased
friends had given either herself or her father, with their
own handwriting across the lower parts of their bodies,
and the windows, shrouded by the maroon curtains of
all her life, were decorated besides with the selfsame
aquariums to which she owed her first lessons in sea-
lore, and in which still swam slowly the goldfishes of
her youth.

Were they the same goldfish? She did not know.
Perhaps, like carp, they outlived everybody. Perhaps,
on the other hand, behind the deep-sea vegetation

provided for them at the bottom, they had from time
to time as the years went by withdrawn and replaced
themselves. Were they or were they not, she sometimes
wondered, contemplating them between the courses of
her solitary meals, the same goldfish that had that day
been there when Carlyle—how well she remembered it—
angrily strode up to them in the middle of some argu-
ment with her father that had grown heated, and striking
the glass smartly with his fist had put them to flight,
shouting as they fled, ' Och, ye deaf deevils ! Och, ye
lucky deaf deevils ! Ye can't hear anything of the
blasted, blethering, doddering, glaikit fool-stuff yer
maister talks, can ye ? ' Or words to that effect.

Dear, great-souled Carlyle. Such natural gushings
forth ; such true freshness ; such real grandeur. Rugged,
if you will—yes, undoubtedly sometimes rugged, and
startling in a drawing-room, but magnificent. Who
was there now to put beside him ? Who was there to
mention in the same breath ? Her father, than whom
no one had had more *flair*, said : ' Thomas is immortal.'
And here was this generation, this generation of puni-
ness, raising its little voice in doubts, or, still worse,
not giving itself the trouble to raise it at all, not—it
was incredible, but it had been thus reported to her—
even reading him. Mrs. Fisher did not read him either,
but that was different. She had read him ; she had

certainly read him. Of course she had read him.
There was Teufelsdröck—she quite well remembered a
tailor called Teufelsdröck. So like Carlyle to call him
that. Yes, she must have read him, though naturally
details escaped her.

The gong sounded. Lost in reminiscence Mrs.
Fisher had forgotten time, and hastened to her bedroom
to wash her hands and smoothe her hair. She did not
wish to be late and set a bad example, and perhaps find
her seat at the head of the table taken. One could put
no trust in the manners of the younger generation;
especially not in those of that Mrs. Wilkins.

She was, however, the first to arrive in the dining-
room. Francesca in a white apron stood ready with
an enormous dish of smoking hot, glistening maccaroni,
but nobody was there to eat it.

Mrs. Fisher sat down, looking stern. Lax, lax.

' Serve me,' she said to Francesca, who showed a
disposition to wait for the others.

Francesca served her. Of the party she liked Mrs.
Fisher least, in fact she did not like her at all. She
was the only one of the four ladies who had not yet
smiled. True she was old, true she was unbeautiful,
true she therefore had no reason to smile, but kind
ladies smiled, reason or no. They smiled, not because
they were happy but because they wished to make

happy. This one of the four ladies could not then, Francesca decided, be kind ; so she handed her the maccaroni, being unable to hide any of her feelings, morosely.

It was very well cooked, but Mrs. Fisher had never cared for maccaroni, especially not this long, worm-shaped variety. She found it difficult to eat,—slippery, wriggling off her fork, making her look, she felt, un-dignified when, having got it as she supposed into her mouth, ends of it yet hung out. Always, too, when she ate it she was reminded of Mr. Fisher. He had during their married life behaved very much like maccaroni. He had slipped, he had wriggled, he had made her feel undignified, and when at last she had got him safe, as she thought, there had invariably been little bits of him that still, as it were, hung out.

Francesca from the sideboard watched Mrs. Fisher's way with maccaroni gloomily, and her gloom deepened when she saw her at last take her knife to it and chop it small.

Mrs. Fisher really did not know how else to get hold of the stuff. She was aware that knives in this con-nection were improper, but one did finally lose patience. Maccaroni was never allowed to appear on her table in London. Apart from its tiresomeness she did not even like it, and she would tell Lady Caroline not to order it

again. Years of practice, reflected Mrs. Fisher, chop-
ping it up, years of actual living in Italy, would be
necessary to learn the exact trick. Browning managed
maccaroni wonderfully. She remembered watching him
one day when he came to lunch with her father, and a
dish of it had been ordered as a compliment to his con-
nection with Italy. Fascinating, the way it went in.
No chasing round the plate, no slidings off the fork, no
subsequent protrusions of loose ends—just one dig, one
whisk, one thrust, one gulp, and lo, yet another poet
had been nourished.

'Shall I go and seek the young lady?' asked Francesca, unable any longer to look on at good maccaroni
being cut with a knife.

Mrs. Fisher came out of her reminiscent reflections
with difficulty. 'She knows lunch is at half-past
twelve,' she said. 'They all know.'

'She may be asleep,' said Francesca. 'The other
ladies are further away, but this one is not far
away.'

'Beat the gong again then,' said Mrs. Fisher.

What manners, she thought; what, what manners.
It was not an hotel, and considerations were due. She
must say she was surprised at Mrs. Arbuthnot, who had
not looked like somebody unpunctual. Lady Caroline,
too—she had seemed amiable and courteous, whatever

else she might be. From the other one, of course, she expected nothing.

Francesca fetched the gong, and took it out into the garden and advanced, beating it as she advanced, close up to Lady Caroline, who, still stretched in her low chair, waited till she had done, and then turned her head and in the sweetest tones poured forth what appeared to be music but was really invective.

Francesca did not recognise the liquid flow as invective; how was she to, when it came out sounding like that? And with her face all smiles, for she could not but smile when she looked at this young lady, she told her the maccaroni was getting cold.

'When I do not come to meals it is because I do not wish to come to meals,' said the irritated Scrap, 'and you will not in future disturb me.'

'Is She ill?' asked Francesca, sympathetic but unable to stop smiling. Never, never had she seen hair so beautiful. Like pure flax; like the hair of northern babes. On such a little head only blessing could rest, on such a little head the nimbus of the holiest saints could fitly be placed.

Scrap shut her eyes and refused to answer. In this she was injudicious, for its effect was to convince Francesca, who hurried away full of concern to tell Mrs.

Fisher, that she was indisposed. And Mrs. Fisher, being prevented, she explained, from going out to Lady Caroline herself because of her stick, sent the two others instead, who had come in at that moment heated and breathless and full of excuses, while she herself proceeded to the next course, which was a very well-made omelette, bursting most agreeably at both its ends with young green peas.

'Serve me,' she directed Francesca, who again showed a disposition to wait for the others.

'*Oh*, why won't they leave me alone—oh, why *won't* they leave me alone ? ' Scrap asked herself when she heard more scrunchings on the little pebbles which took the place of grass, and therefore knew some one else was approaching.

She kept her eyes tight shut this time. Why should she go in to lunch if she didn't want to ? This wasn't a private house ; she was in no way tangled up in duties towards a tiresome hostess. For all practical purposes San Salvatore was an hotel, and she ought to be let alone to eat or not to eat exactly as if she really had been in an hotel.

But the unfortunate Scrap could not just sit still and close her eyes without rousing that desire to stroke and pet in her beholders with which she was only too familiar. Even the cook had patted her. And now a gentle hand

—how well she knew and how much she dreaded gentle hands—was placed on her forehead.

'I'm afraid you're not well,' said a voice that was not Mrs. Fisher's, and therefore must belong to one of the originals.

'I have a headache,' murmured Scrap. Perhaps it was best to say that; perhaps it was the shortest cut to peace.

'I'm *so* sorry,' said Mrs. Arbuthnot softly, for it was her hand being gentle.

'And I,' said Scrap to herself, 'who thought if I came here I would escape mothers.'

'Don't you think some tea would do you good?' asked Mrs. Arbuthnot tenderly.

Tea? The idea was abhorrent to Scrap. In this heat to be drinking tea in the middle of the day. . . .

'No,' she murmured.

'I expect what would really be best for her,' said another voice, 'is to be left quiet.'

How sensible, thought Scrap; and raised the eye-lashes of one eye just enough to peep through and see who was speaking.

It was the freckled original. The dark one, then, was the one with the hand. The freckled one rose in her esteem.

'But I can't bear to think of you with a headache

and nothing being done for it,' said Mrs. Arbuthnot.
' Would a cup of strong black coffee——? '

Scrap said no more. She waited, motionless and
dumb, till Mrs. Arbuthnot should remove her hand.
After all, she couldn't stand there all day, and when
she went away she would have to take her hand with
her.

' I do think,' said the freckled one, ' that she wants
nothing except quiet.'

And perhaps the freckled one pulled the one with
the hand by the sleeve, for the hold on Scrap's forehead
relaxed, and after a minute's silence, during which no
doubt she was being contemplated—she was always
being contemplated—the footsteps began to scrunch the
pebbles again, and grew fainter, and were gone.

' Lady Caroline has a headache,' said Mrs. Arbuthnot,
re-entering the dining-room and sitting down in her place
next to Mrs. Fisher.   ' I can't persuade her to have even
a little tea, or some black coffee.   Do you know what
aspirin is in Italian ? '

' The proper remedy for headaches,' said Mrs. Fisher
firmly, ' is castor oil.'

' But she hasn't got a headache,' said Mrs. Wilkins.

' Carlyle,' said Mrs. Fisher, who had finished her
omelette and had leisure, while she waited for the
next course, to talk, ' suffered at one period terribly

from headaches, and he constantly took castor oil as a
remedy.   He took it, I should say, almost to excess, and
called it, I remember, in his interesting way the oil of
sorrow.   My father said it coloured for a time his whole
attitude to life, his whole philosophy.   But that was
because he took too much.   What Lady Caroline wants
is one dose, and one only.   It is a mistake to keep on
taking castor oil.'

'Do you know the Italian for it?' asked Mrs.
Arbuthnot.

'Ah, that I'm afraid I don't.   However, she would
know.   You can ask her.'

'But she hasn't got a headache,' repeated Mrs.
Wilkins, who was struggling with the maccaroni.   'She
only wants to be let alone.'

They both looked at her.   The word shovel crossed
Mrs. Fisher's mind in connection with Mrs. Wilkins's
actions at that moment.

'Then why should she say she has?' asked Mrs.
Arbuthnot.

'Because she is still trying to be polite.   Soon she
won't try, when the place has got more into her—she'll
really be it.   Without trying.   Naturally.'

'Lotty, you see,' explained Mrs. Arbuthnot, smiling
to Mrs. Fisher, who sat waiting with a stony patience
for her next course, delayed because Mrs. Wilkins would

go on trying to eat the maccaroni, which must be less worth eating than ever now that it was cold ; ' Lotty, you see, has a theory about this place——'

But Mrs. Fisher had no wish to hear any theory of Mrs. Wilkins's.

' I am sure I don't know,' she interrupted, looking severely at Mrs. Wilkins, ' why you should assume Lady Caroline is not telling the truth.'

' I don't assume—I know,' said Mrs. Wilkins.

' And pray how do you know ? ' asked Mrs. Fisher icily, for Mrs. Wilkins was actually helping herself to more maccaroni, offered her officiously and unnecessarily a second time by Francesca.

' When I was out there just now I saw inside her.'

Well, Mrs. Fisher wasn't going to say anything to that ; she wasn't going to trouble to reply to downright idiocy. Instead she sharply rapped the little table-gong by her side, though there was Francesca standing at the sideboard, and said, for she would wait no longer for her next course, ' Serve me.'

And Francesca—it must have been wilful—offered her the maccaroni again.

THERE was no way of getting into or out of the top garden at San Salvatore except through the two glass doors, unfortunately side by side, of the dining-room and the hall. A person in the garden who wished to escape unseen could not, for the person to be escaped from would be met on the way. It was a small, oblong garden, and concealment was impossible. What trees there were—the Judas tree, the tamarisk, the umbrella-pine—grew close to the low parapets. Rose-bushes gave no real cover; one step to right or left of them, and the person wishing to be private was discovered. Only in the north-west corner was a little place jutting out from the great wall, a kind of excrescence or loop, no doubt used in the old distrustful days for observation, where it was possible to sit really unseen, because between it and the house was a thick clump of daphne.

Scrap, after glancing round to see that no one was looking, got up and carried her chair into this place, stealing away as carefully on tiptoe as those steal whose

purpose is sin. There was another excrescence on the
walls just like it at the north-east corner, but this,
though the view from it was almost more beautiful, for
from it you could see the bay and the lovely mountains
behind Mezzago, was exposed. No bushes grew near
it, nor had it any shade. The north-west loop then was
where she would sit, and she settled into it, and nestling
her head in her cushion and putting her feet comfortably
on the parapet, from whence they appeared to the
villagers on the piazza below as two white doves, thought
that now indeed she would be safe.

Mrs. Fisher found her there, guided by the smell of
her cigarette. The incautious Scrap had not thought
of that. Mrs. Fisher did not smoke herself, and all the
more distinctly could she smell the smoke of others.
The virile smell met her directly she went out into the
garden from the dining-room after lunch in order to
have her coffee. She had bidden Francesca set the
coffee in the shade of the house just outside the glass
door, and when Mrs. Wilkins, seeing a table being carried
there, reminded her, very officiously and tactlessly
Mrs. Fisher considered, that Lady Caroline wanted to
be alone, she retorted—and with what propriety—that
the garden was for everybody.

Into it accordingly she went, and was immediately
aware that Lady Caroline was smoking. She said to

herself, ' These modern young women,' and proceeded
to find her ; her stick, now that lunch was over, being
no longer the hindrance to action that it was before her
meal had been securely, as Browning once said—surely
it was Browning ? yes, she remembered how much
diverted she had been—roped in.

Nobody diverted her now, reflected Mrs. Fisher,
making straight for the clump of daphne ; the world
had grown very dull, and had entirely lost its sense of
humour.   Probably they still had their jokes, these
people,—in fact she knew they did, for *Punch* still went
on ; but how differently it went on, and what jokes.
Thackeray, in his inimitable way, would have made
mincemeat of this generation.   Of how much it needed
the tonic properties of that astringent pen it was of
course unaware.   It no longer even held him—at least,
so she had been informed—in any particular esteem.
Well, she could not give it eyes to see and ears to hear
and a heart to understand, but she could and would
give it, represented and united in the form of Lady
Caroline, a good dose of honest medicine.

' I hear you are not well,' she said, standing in the
narrow entrance of the loop and looking down with
the inflexible face of one who is determined to do good
at the motionless and apparently sleeping Scrap.

Mrs. Fisher had a deep voice, very like a man's, for

she had been overtaken by that strange masculinity that sometimes pursues a woman during the last laps of her life.

Scrap tried to pretend that she was asleep, but if she had been her cigarette would not have been held in her fingers but would have been lying on the ground.

She forgot this. Mrs. Fisher did not, and coming inside the loop, sat down on a narrow stone seat built out of the wall. For a little she could sit on it; for a little, till the chill began to penetrate.

She contemplated the figure before her. Undoubtedly a pretty creature, and one that would have had a success at Farringford. Strange how easily even the greatest men were moved by exteriors. She had seen with her own eyes Tennyson turn away from everybody—turn, positively, his back on a crowd of eminent people assembled to do him honour, and withdraw to the window with a young person nobody had ever heard of, who had been brought there by accident and whose one and only merit—if it be a merit, that which is conferred by chance—was beauty. Beauty! All over before you can turn round. An affair, one might almost say, of minutes. Well, while it lasted it did seem able to do what it liked with men. Even husbands were not immune. There had been passages in the life of Mr. Fisher . . .

'I expect the journey has upset you,' she said in her deep voice. 'What you want is a good dose of some simple medicine. I shall ask Domenico if there is such a thing in the village as castor oil.'

Scrap opened her eyes and looked straight at Mrs. Fisher.

'Ah,' said Mrs. Fisher, 'I knew you were not asleep. If you had been you would have let your cigarette fall to the ground.'

Scrap threw the cigarette over the parapet.

'Waste,' said Mrs. Fisher. 'I don't like smoking for women, but I still less like waste.'

'What *does* one do with people like this?' Scrap asked herself, her eyes fixed on Mrs. Fisher in what felt to her an indignant stare but appeared to Mrs. Fisher as really charming docility.

'Now you'll take my advice,' said Mrs. Fisher, touched, 'and not neglect what may very well turn into an illness. We are in Italy, you know, and one has to be careful. You ought, to begin with, to go to bed.'

'I never go to bed,' snapped Scrap; and it sounded as moving, as forlorn, as that line spoken years and years ago by an actress playing the part of Poor Jo in a dramatised version of Bleak House,—'I'm always moving on,' said Poor Jo in this play, urged to do so by a policeman; and Mrs. Fisher, then a girl, had laid her head on the red velvet parapet of the front row of the dress circle and wept aloud.

It was wonderful, Scrap's voice. It had given her, in the ten years since she came out, all the triumphs that intelligence and wit can have, because it made whatever she said seem memorable. She ought, with a throat formation like that, to have been a singer, but in every kind of music Scrap was dumb except this one music of the speaking voice; and what a fascination, what a spell lay in that. Such was the loveliness of her face and the beauty of her colouring that there was not a man into whose eyes at the sight of her there did not leap a flame of intensest interest; but, when he heard her voice, the flame in that man's eyes was caught and fixed. It was the same with every man, educated and uneducated, old, young, desirable themselves or un-desirable, men of her own world and bus-conductors, generals and Tommies,—during the war she had had a perplexing time—bishops equally with vergers,—round about her confirmation startling occurrences had taken place—wholesome and unwholesome, rich and penniless, brilliant or idiotic; and it made no difference at all what they were, or how long and securely married: into the eyes of every one of them, when they saw her, leapt this flame, and when they heard her it stayed there.

Scrap had had enough of this look. It only led to difficulties. At first it had delighted her. She had been excited, triumphant. To be apparently incapable of doing or saying the wrong thing, to be applauded, listened to, petted, adored wherever she went, and when she came home to find nothing there either but the most indulgent proud fondness,—why, how extremely pleasant. And so easy, too. No preparation necessary for this achievement, no hard work, nothing to learn. She need take no trouble. She had only to appear, and presently say something.

But gradually experiences gathered round her. After all, she had to take trouble, she had to make efforts, because, she discovered with astonishment and rage, she had to defend herself. That look, that leaping look, meant that she was going to be grabbed at. Some of those who had it were more humble than others, especially if they were young, but they all, according to their several ability, grabbed ; and she who had entered the world so jauntily, with her head in the air and the completest confidence in anybody whose hair was grey, began to distrust, and then to dislike, and soon to shrink away from, and presently to be indignant. Sometimes it was just as if she didn't belong to herself, wasn't her own at all, but was regarded as a universal thing, a sort of beauty-of-all-work. Really men . . . And she found herself involved in queer, vague quarrels, being curiously hated. Really women . . . And when the war came, and she flung herself into it along with everybody else, it finished her. Really generals . . .

The war finished Scrap. It killed the one man she felt safe with, whom she would have married, and it finally disgusted her with love. Since then she had been embittered. She was struggling as angrily in the sweet stuff of life as a wasp got caught in honey. Just as desperately did she try to unstick her wings. It gave her no pleasure to outdo other women ; she didn't want their tiresome men. What could one do with men when one had got them ? None of them would talk to her of anything but the things of love, and how foolish and fatiguing that became after a bit. It was as though a healthy person with a normal hunger was given nothing whatever to eat but sugar. Love, love . . . the very word made her want to slap somebody. ' *Why* should I love you ? *Why* should I ? ' she would ask amazed sometimes when somebody was trying— somebody was always trying—to propose to her. But she never got a real answer, only further incoherence.

A deep cynicism took hold of the unhappy Scrap. Her inside grew hoary with disillusionment, while her gracious and charming outside continued to make the world more beautiful. What had the future in it for her ? She would not be able, after such a preparation, to take hold of it. She was fit for nothing; she had wasted all this time being beautiful. Presently she wouldn't be beautiful, and what then ? Scrap didn't know what then, it appalled her to wonder even. Tired as she was of being conspicuous she was at least used to that, she had never known anything else ; and to become inconspicuous, to fade, to grow shabby and dim, would probably be most painful. And once she began, what years and years of it there would be ! Imagine, thought Scrap, having most of one's life at the wrong end. Imagine being old for two or three times as long as being young. Stupid, stupid. Everything was stupid. There wasn't a thing she wanted to do. There were thousands of things she didn't want to do. Avoidance, silence, invisibility, if possible unconsciousness—these negations were all she asked for at the moment ; and here, even here, she was not allowed a minute's peace, and this absurd woman must come pretending, merely because she wanted to exercise power and make her go to bed and make her—hideous —drink castor oil, that she thought she was ill.

'I'm sure,' said Mrs. Fisher, who felt the cold of the stone beginning to come through and knew she could not sit much longer, ' you'll do what is reasonable. Your mother would wish—have you a mother ? '

A faint wonder came into Scrap's eyes. Have you a mother ? If ever anybody had a mother it was Scrap. It had not occurred to her that there could be people who had never heard of her mother. She was one of the major marchionesses—there being, as no one knew better than Scrap, marchionesses and marchionesses—and had held high positions at Court. Her father, too, in his day had been most prominent. His day was a little over, poor dear, because in the war he had made some important mistakes, and besides he was now grown old ; still, there he was, an excessively well-known person. How restful, how extraordinarily restful to have found some one who had never heard of any of her lot, or at least had not yet connected her with them.

She began to like Mrs. Fisher. Perhaps the originals didn't know anything about her either. When she first wrote to them and signed her name, that great name of Dester which twisted in and out of English history like a bloody thread, for its bearers constantly killed, she had taken it for granted that they would know who she was ; and at the interview in Shaftesbury Avenue she was sure they did know, because they hadn't asked, as they otherwise would have, for references.

Scrap began to cheer up. If nobody at San Salvatore had ever heard of her, if for a whole month she could shed herself, get right away from everything connected

with herself, be allowed really to forget the clinging
and the clogging and all the noise, why, perhaps she
might make something of herself after all. She might
really think; really clear up her mind; really come
to some conclusion.

'What I want to do here,' she said, leaning forward
in her chair and clasping her hands round her knees
and looking up at Mrs. Fisher, whose seat was higher
than hers, almost with animation, so much pleased was
she that Mrs. Fisher knew nothing about her, 'is to
come to a conclusion. That's all. It isn't much to
want, is it ? Just that.'

She gazed at Mrs. Fisher, and thought that almost
any conclusion would do ; the great thing was to get
hold of something, catch something tight, cease to drift.

Mrs. Fisher's little eyes surveyed her. 'I should
say,' she said, 'that what a young woman like you wants
is a husband and children.'

'Well, that's one of the things I'm going to consider,' said Scrap amiably. 'But I don't think it would
be a conclusion.'

'And meanwhile,' said Mrs. Fisher, getting up, for
the cold of the stone was now through, 'I shouldn't
trouble my head if I were you with considerings and
conclusions. Women's heads weren't made for thinking,
I assure you. I should go to bed and get well.'

' I am well,' said Scrap.

' Then why did you send a message that you were ill ? '

' I didn't.'

' Then I've had all the trouble of coming out here for nothing.'

' But wouldn't you prefer coming out and finding me well than coming out and finding me ill ? ' asked Scrap, smiling.

Even Mrs. Fisher was caught by the smile.

' Well, you're a pretty creature,' she said forgivingly. ' It's a pity you weren't born fifty years ago. My friends would have liked looking at you.'

' I'm very glad I wasn't,' said Scrap. ' I dislike being looked at.'

' Absurd,' said Mrs. Fisher, growing stern again. ' That's what you are made for, young women like you. For what else, pray ? And I assure you that if my friends had looked at you, you would have been looked at by some very great people.'

' I dislike very great people,' said Scrap, frowning. There had been an incident quite recently — really potentates. . . .

' What *I* dislike,' said Mrs. Fisher, now as cold as the stone she had got up from, ' is the pose of the modern young woman.   It seems to me pitiful, positively pitiful, in its silliness.'

And, her stick crunching the pebbles, she walked away.

'That's all right,' Scrap said to herself, dropping back into her comfortable position with her head in the cushion and her feet on the parapet; if only people would go away she didn't in the least mind why they went.

'Don't you think darling Scrap is growing a little, just a little, peculiar?' her mother had asked her father a short time before that latest peculiarity of the flight to San Salvatore, uncomfortably struck by the very odd things Scrap said and the way she had taken to slinking out of reach whenever she could and avoiding everybody except—such a sign of age—quite young men, almost boys.

'Eh? What? Peculiar? Well, let her be peculiar if she likes. A woman with her looks can be any damned thing she pleases,' was the infatuated answer.

'I do let her,' said her mother meekly; and indeed if she did not, what difference would it make?

Mrs. Fisher was sorry she had bothered about Lady Caroline. She went along the hall towards her private sitting-room, and her stick as she went struck the stone floor with a vigour in harmony with her feelings. Sheer silliness, these poses. She had no patience with them. Unable to be or do anything of themselves, the

young of the present generation tried to achieve a
reputation for cleverness by decrying all that was
obviously great and obviously good and by praising
everything, however obviously bad, that was different.
Apes, thought Mrs. Fisher, roused. Apes. Apes. And
in her sitting-room she found more apes, or what seemed
to her in her present mood more, for there was Mrs.
Arbuthnot placidly drinking coffee, while at the writing-
table, the writing-table she already looked upon as
sacred, using her pen, her own pen brought for her
hand alone from Prince of Wales Terrace, sat Mrs.
Wilkins writing; at the table; in her room; with
her pen.

'Isn't this a delightful place ? ' said Mrs. Arbuthnot
cordially.   ' We have just discovered it.'

' I'm writing to Mellersh,' said Mrs. Wilkins, turning
her head and also cordially,—as though, Mrs. Fisher
thought, she cared a straw who she was writing to and
anyhow knew who the person she called Mellersh was.
' He'll want to know,' said Mrs. Wilkins, optimism
induced by her surroundings, ' that I've got here safely.'

XI

THE sweet smells that were everywhere in San Salvatore were alone enough to produce concord. They came into the sitting-room from the flowers on the battlements, and met the ones from the flowers inside the room, and almost, thought Mrs. Wilkins, could be seen greeting each other with a holy kiss. Who could be angry in the middle of such gentlenesses ? Who could be acquisitive, selfish, in the old rasped London way, in the presence of this bounteous beauty ?

Yet Mrs. Fisher seemed to be all three of these things.

There was so much beauty, so much more than enough for every one, that it did appear to be a vain activity to try and make a corner in it.

Yet Mrs. Fisher was trying to make a corner in it, and had railed off a portion for her exclusive use.

Well, she would get over that presently ; she would get over it inevitably, Mrs. Wilkins was sure, after a day or two in the extraordinary atmosphere of peace in that place.

Meanwhile she obviously hadn't even begun to get over it. She stood looking at her and Rose with an expression that appeared to be one of anger. Anger. Fancy. Silly old nerve-racked London feelings, thought Mrs. Wilkins, whose eyes saw the room full of kisses, and everybody in it being kissed, Mrs. Fisher as copiously as she herself and Rose.

'You don't like us being in here,' said Mrs. Wilkins, getting up and at once, after her manner, fixing on the truth. 'Why?'

'I should have thought,' said Mrs. Fisher leaning on her stick, ' you could have seen that it is my room.'

'You mean because of the photographs,' said Mrs. Wilkins.

Mrs. Arbuthnot, who was a little red and surprised, got up too.

'And the notepaper,' said Mrs. Fisher. 'Notepaper with my London address on it. That pen——'

She pointed. It was still in Mrs. Wilkins's hand.

'Is yours. I'm very sorry,' said Mrs. Wilkins, laying it on the table. And she added, smiling, that it had just been writing some very amiable things.

'But why,' asked Mrs. Arbuthnot, who found herself unable to acquiesce in Mrs. Fisher's arrangements without at least a gentle struggle, ' ought we not to be here? It's a sitting-room.'

'There is another one,' said Mrs. Fisher. 'You and your friend cannot sit in two rooms at once, and if I have no wish to disturb you in yours I am unable to see why you should wish to disturb me in mine.'

'But why——' began Mrs. Arbuthnot again.

'It's quite natural,' Mrs. Wilkins interrupted, for Rose was looking stubborn ; and turning to Mrs. Fisher she said that although sharing things with friends was pleasant she could understand that Mrs. Fisher, still steeped in the Prince of Wales Terrace attitude to life, did not yet want to, but that she would get rid of that after a bit and feel quite different. 'Soon you'll *want* us to share,' said Mrs. Wilkins reassuringly. 'Why, you may even get so far as *asking* me to use your pen if you knew I hadn't got one.'

Mrs. Fisher was moved almost beyond control by this speech. To have a ramshackle young woman from Hampstead patting her on the back as it were, in breezy certitude that quite soon she would improve, stirred her more deeply than anything had stirred her since her first discovery that Mr. Fisher was not what he seemed. Mrs. Wilkins must certainly be curbed. But how ? There was a curious imperviousness about her. At that moment, for instance, she was smiling as pleasantly and with as unclouded a face as if she were saying nothing in the least impertinent. Would she know she was being curbed ? If she didn't know, if she were too tough to feel it, then what ? Nothing, except avoidance ; except, precisely, one's own private sitting-room.

'I'm an old woman,' said Mrs. Fisher, ' and I need a room to myself. I cannot get about, because of my stick. As I cannot get about I have to sit. Why should I not sit quietly and undisturbed, as I told you in London I intended to ? If people are to come in and out all day long, chattering and leaving doors open, you will have broken the agreement, which was that I was to be quiet.'

'But we haven't the least wish——' began Mrs. Arbuthnot, who was again cut short by Mrs. Wilkins.

'We're only too glad,' said Mrs. Wilkins, 'for you to have this room if it makes you happy. We didn't know about it, that's all. We wouldn't have come in if we had,—not till you invited us, anyhow. I expect,' she finished looking down cheerfully at Mrs. Fisher, 'you soon will.' And picking up her letter she took Mrs. Arbuthnot's hand and drew her towards the door.

Mrs. Arbuthnot did not want to go. She, the mildest of women, was filled with a curious and surely unchristian desire to stay and fight. Not, of course, really, nor even with any definitely aggressive words. No ;

she only wanted to reason with Mrs. Fisher, and to reason patiently. But she did feel that something ought to be said, and that she ought not to allow herself to be rated and turned out as if she were a schoolgirl caught in ill behaviour by Authority.

Mrs. Wilkins, however, drew her firmly to and through the door, and once again Rose wondered at Lotty, at her balance, her sweet and equable temper,— she who in England had been such a thing of gusts. From the moment they got into Italy it was Lotty who seemed the elder. She certainly was very happy ; blissful, in fact. Did happiness so completely protect one ? Did it make one so untouchable, so wise ? Rose was happy herself, but not anything like *so* happy. Evidently not, for not only did she want to fight Mrs. Fisher but she wanted something else, something more than this lovely place, something to complete it ; she wanted Frederick. For the first time in her life she was surrounded by perfect beauty, and her one thought was to show it to him, to share it with him. She wanted Frederick. She yearned for Frederick. Ah, if only, only Frederick . . .

'Poor old thing,' said Mrs. Wilkins, shutting the door gently on Mrs. Fisher and her triumph. 'Fancy on a day like this.'

'She's a very rude old thing,' said Mrs. Arbuthnot.

'She'll get over that. I'm sorry we chose just her room to go and sit in.'

'It's much the nicest,' said Mrs. Arbuthnot. 'And it isn't hers.'

'Oh but there are lots of other places, and she's such a poor old thing. Let her have the room. Whatever does it matter?'

And Mrs. Wilkins said she was going down to the village to find out where the post-office was and post her letter to Mellersh, and would Rose go too.

'I've been thinking about Mellersh,' said Mrs. Wilkins as they walked, one behind the other, down the narrow zigzag path up which they had climbed in the rain the night before.

She went first. Mrs. Arbuthnot, quite naturally now, followed. In England it had been the other way about,—Lotty, timid, hesitating, except when she burst out so awkwardly, getting behind the calm and reasonable Rose whenever she could.

'I've been thinking about Mellersh,' repeated Mrs. Wilkins over her shoulder, as Rose seemed not to have heard.

'Have you?' said Rose, a faint distaste in her voice, for her experiences with Mellersh had not been of a kind to make her enjoy remembering him. She had deceived Mellersh; therefore she didn't like him. She was unconscious that this was the reason of her dislike, and thought it was that there didn't seem to be much, if any, of the grace of God about him. And yet how wrong to feel that, she rebuked herself, and how presumptuous. No doubt Lotty's husband was far, far nearer to God than she herself was ever likely to be. Still, she didn't like him.

' I've been a mean dog,' said Mrs. Wilkins.

' A what ? ' asked Mrs. Arbuthnot, incredulous of her hearing.

' All this coming away and leaving him in that dreary place while I rollick in heaven. He had planned to take me to Italy for Easter himself. Did I tell you ? '

' No,' said Mrs. Arbuthnot ; and indeed she had discouraged talk about husbands. Whenever Lotty had begun to blurt out things she had swiftly changed the conversation. One husband led to another, in conversation as well as in life, she felt, and she could not, she would not, talk of Frederick. Beyond the bare fact that he was there, he had not been mentioned. Mellersh had had to be mentioned, because of his obstructiveness, but she had carefully kept him from overflowing outside the limits of necessity.

' Well, he did,' said Mrs. Wilkins. ' He had never done such a thing in his life before, and I was horrified. Fancy—just as I had planned to come to it myself.'

She paused on the path and looked up at Rose.

' Yes,' said Rose, trying to think of something else to talk about.

' Now you see why I say I've been a mean dog. *He* had planned a holiday in Italy with me, and *I* had planned a holiday in Italy leaving him at home. I think,' she went on, her eyes fixed on Rose's face, ' Mellersh has every reason to be both angry and hurt.'

Mrs. Arbuthnot was astonished. The extraordinary quickness with which, hour by hour, under her very eyes, Lotty became more selfless, disconcerted her. She was turning into something surprisingly like a saint. Here she was now being affectionate about Mellersh,— Mellersh, who only that morning, while they hung their feet into the sea, had seemed a mere iridescence, Lotty had told her, a thing of gauze. That was only that morning; and by the time they had had lunch Lotty had developed so far as to have got him solid enough again to write to, and to write to at length. And now, a few minutes later, she was announcing that he had every reason to be angry with her and hurt, and that she herself had been—the language was unusual, but it did express real penitence—a mean dog.

Rose stared at her astonished. If she went on like this, soon a nimbus might be expected round her head, was there already, if one didn't know it was the sun through the tree-trunks catching her sandy hair.

A great desire to love and be friends, to love everybody, to be friends with everybody, seemed to be invading Lotty,—a desire for sheer goodness. Rose's own experience was that goodness, the state of being good, was only reached with difficulty and pain. It took a long time to get to it; in fact one never did get to it, or, if for a flashing instant one did, it was only for a flashing instant. Desperate perseverance was needed to struggle along its path, and all the way was dotted with doubts. Lotty simply flew along. She had certainly, thought Rose, not got rid of her impetuousness. It had merely taken another direction. She was now impetuously becoming a saint. Could one really attain goodness so violently? Wouldn't there be an equally violent reaction?

' I shouldn't,' said Rose with caution, looking down into Lotty's bright eyes—the path was steep, so that Lotty was well below her—' I shouldn't be sure of that too quickly.'

' But I am sure of it, and I've written and told him so.'

Rose stared. ' Why, but only this morning——' she began.

' It's all in this,' interrupted Lotty, tapping the envelope and looking pleased.

' What—everything ? '

' You mean about the advertisement and my savings being spent ? Oh no—not yet. But I'll tell him all that when he comes.'

' When he comes ? ' repeated Rose.

' I've invited him to come and stay with us.'

Rose could only go on staring.

' It's the least I could do. Besides—look at this.' Lotty waved her hand. ' Disgusting not to share it. I was a mean dog to go off and leave him, but no dog I've ever heard of was ever as mean as I'd be if I didn't try and persuade Mellersh to come out and enjoy this too. It's barest decency that he should have some of the fun out of my nest-egg. After all, he has housed me and fed me for years. One shouldn't be churlish.'

' But—do you think he'll come ? '

' Oh, I *hope* so,' said Lotty with the utmost earnestness ; and added, ' Poor lamb.'

At that Rose felt she would like to sit down. Mellersh a poor lamb ? That same Mellersh who a few hours before was mere shimmer ? There was a seat at the bend of the path, and Rose went to it and sat down. She wished to get her breath, gain time. If she had time she might perhaps be able to catch up the leaping Lotty, and perhaps be able to stop her before she committed herself to what she probably presently would be

sorry for.   Mellersh at San Salvatore ?   Mellersh, from
whom Lotty had taken such pains so recently to escape ?

'I *see* him here,' said Lotty, as if in answer to her
thoughts.

Rose looked at her with real concern : for every time
Lotty said in that convinced voice, ' I *see*,' what she
saw came true.   Then it was to be supposed that
Mr. Wilkins too would presently come true.

' I wish,' said Rose anxiously, ' I understood you.'

' Don't try,' said Lotty, smiling.

' But I must, because I love you.'

' Dear Rose,' said Lotty, swiftly bending down and
kissing her.

' You're so quick,' said Rose.   ' I can't follow your
developments.   I can't keep touch.   It was what
happened with Freder——'

She broke off and looked frightened.

' The whole idea of our coming here,' she went on
again, as Lotty didn't seem to have noticed, ' was to get
away, wasn't it ?   Well, we've got away.   And now,
after only a single day of it, you want to write to the very
people——'

She stopped.

' The very people we were getting away from,'
finished Lotty.   ' It's quite true.   It seems idiotically
illogical.   But I'm so happy, I'm so well, I feel so fear-

fully wholesome. This place—why, it makes me feel *flooded* with love.'

And she stared down at Rose in a kind of radiant surprise.

Rose was silent a moment. Then she said, ' And do you think it will have the same effect on Mr. Wilkins ? '

Lotty laughed. ' I don't know,' she said. ' But even if it doesn't, there's enough love about to flood fifty Mr. Wilkinses, as you call him. The great thing is to have lots of love *about*. I don't see,' she went on, ' at least I don't see here, though I did at home, that it matters who loves as long as somebody does. I was a stingy beast at home, and used to measure and count. I had a queer obsession about justice. As though justice mattered. As though justice can really be distinguished from vengeance. It's only love that's any good. At home I wouldn't love Mellersh unless he loved me back, exactly as much, absolute fairness. Did you ever. And as he didn't, neither did I, and the *aridity* of that house ! The *aridity* . . .'

Rose said nothing. She was bewildered by Lotty. One odd effect of San Salvatore on her rapidly developing friend was her sudden free use of robust words. She had not used them in Hampstead. Beast and dog were more robust than Hampstead cared about. In words, too, Lotty had come unchained.

But how she wished, oh how Rose wished, that she too could write to her husband and say ' Come.' The Wilkins *ménage*, however pompous Mellersh might be, and he had seemed to Rose pompous, was on a healthier, more natural footing than hers. Lotty could write to Mellersh and would get an answer. She couldn't write to Frederick, for only too well did she know he wouldn't answer. At least, he might answer,— a hurried scribble, showing how much bored he was at doing it, with perfunctory thanks for her letter. But that would be worse than no answer at all ; for his handwriting, her name on an envelope addressed by him, stabbed her heart. Too acutely did it bring back the letters of their beginnings together, the letters from him so desolate with separation, so aching with love and longing. To see apparently one of these very same letters arrive, and open it and find :

DEAR ROSE—Thanks for letter. Glad you're having a good time. Don't hurry back. Say if you want any money. Everything going splendidly here.—Yours,

FREDERICK.

—no, it couldn't be borne.

' I don't think I'll come down to the village with you to-day,' she said, looking up at Lotty with eyes suddenly gone dim. ' I think I want to think.'

'All right,' said Lotty, at once starting off briskly down the path. 'But don't think too long,' she called back over her shoulder. 'Write and invite him at once.'

'Invite whom?' asked Rose, startled.

'Your husband.'

XII

At the evening meal, which was the first time the whole four sat round the dining-room table together, Scrap appeared.

She appeared quite punctually, and in one of those wrappers or tea-gowns which are sometimes described as ravishing. This one really was ravishing. It certainly ravished Mrs. Wilkins, who could not take her eyes off the enchanting figure opposite. It was a shell-pink garment, and clung to the adorable Scrap as though it, too, loved her.

'What a beautiful dress!' exclaimed Mrs. Wilkins eagerly.

'What—this old rag?' said Scrap, glancing down at it as if to see which one she had got on. 'I've had it a hundred years.' And she concentrated on her soup.

'You must be very cold in it,' said Mrs. Fisher, thin-lipped; for it showed a great deal of Scrap,—the whole of her arms, for instance, and even where it covered her up it was so thin that you still saw her.

174

'Who—me ? ' said Scrap, looking up a moment. ' Oh no.'

And she continued her soup.

'You mustn't catch a chill, you know,' said Mrs. Arbuthnot, feeling that such loveliness must at all costs be preserved unharmed. ' There's a great difference here when the sun goes down.'

' I'm quite warm,' said Scrap, industriously eating her soup.

' You look as if you had nothing at all on underneath,' said Mrs. Fisher.

' I haven't. At least, hardly anything,' said Scrap, finishing her soup.

' How very imprudent,' said Mrs. Fisher, ' and how highly improper.'

Whereupon Scrap stared at her.

Mrs. Fisher had arrived at dinner feeling friendly towards Lady Caroline. She at least had not intruded into her room and sat at her table and written with her pen. She did, Mrs. Fisher had supposed, know how to behave. Now it appeared that she did not know, for was this behaving, to come dressed—no, undressed— like that to a meal ? Such behaviour was not only exceedingly improper but also most inconsiderate, for the indelicate creature would certainly catch a chill, and then infect the entire party. Mrs. Fisher had a great

objection to other people's chills. They were always
the fruit of folly ; and then they were handed on to her,
who had done nothing at all to deserve them.

'Bird-brained,' thought Mrs. Fisher, sternly contemplating Lady Caroline. 'Not an idea in her head
except vanity.'

'But there are no men here,' said Mrs. Wilkins, 'so
how can it be improper ? Have you noticed,' she inquired of Mrs. Fisher, who endeavoured to pretend she
did not hear, 'how difficult it is to be improper without
men ? '

Mrs. Fisher neither answered her nor looked at her ;
but Scrap looked at her, and did that with her mouth
which in any other mouth would have been a faint grin.
Seen from without, across the bowl of nasturtiums, it
was the most beautiful of brief and dimpled smiles.

She had a very alive sort of face, that one, thought
Scrap, observing Mrs. Wilkins with a dawn of interest,
It was rather like a field of corn swept by lights and
shadows. Both she and the dark one, Scrap noticed,
had changed their clothes, but only in order to put on
silk jumpers. The same amount of trouble would have
been enough to dress them properly, reflected Scrap.
Naturally they looked like nothing on earth in the
jumpers. It didn't matter what Mrs. Fisher wore ;
indeed, the only thing for her, short of plumes and ermine,

was what she did wear. But these others were quite young still, and quite attractive. They really definitely had faces. How different life would be for them if they made the most of themselves instead of the least. And yet,—Scrap was suddenly bored, and turned away her thoughts and absently ate toast. What did it matter? If you did make the best of yourself, you only collected people round you who ended by wanting to grab.

'I've had the most wonderful day,' began Mrs. Wilkins, her eyes shining.

Scrap lowered hers. 'Oh,' she thought, 'she's going to gush.'

'As though anybody were interested in her day,' thought Mrs. Fisher, lowering hers also.

In fact, whenever Mrs. Wilkins spoke Mrs. Fisher deliberately cast down her eyes. Thus would she mark her disapproval. Besides, it seemed the only safe thing to do with her eyes, for no one could tell what the uncurbed creature would say next. That which she had just said, for instance, about men—addressed, too, to her—what could she mean? Better not conjecture, thought Mrs. Fisher; and her eyes, though cast down, yet saw Lady Caroline stretch out her hand to the Chianti flask and fill her glass again.

Again. She had done it once already, and the fish was only just going out of the room. Mrs. Fisher could

see that the other respectable member of the party,
Mrs. Arbuthnot, was noticing it too. Mrs. Arbuthnot
was, she hoped and believed, respectable and well-
meaning. It is true she also had invaded her sitting-
room, but no doubt she had been dragged there by the
other one, and Mrs. Fisher had little if anything against
Mrs. Arbuthnot, and observed with approval that
she only drank water. That was as it should be. So,
indeed, to give her her dues, did the freckled one ; and
very right at their age. She herself drank wine, but
with what moderation : one meal, one glass. And she
was sixty-five, and might properly, and even bene-
ficially, have had at least two.

'That,' she said to Lady Caroline, cutting right
across what Mrs. Wilkins was telling them about her
wonderful day and indicating the wine-glass, ' is very
bad for you.'

Lady Caroline, however, could not have heard, for
she continued to sip, her elbow on the table, and listen
to what Mrs. Wilkins was saying.

And what was it she was saying ? She had invited
somebody to come and stay ? A man ?

Mrs. Fisher could not credit her ears. Yet it evidently
was a man, for she spoke of the person as he.

Suddenly and for the first time—but then this was
most important—Mrs. Fisher addressed Mrs. Wilkins

directly. She was sixty-five, and cared very little what
sorts of women she happened to be with for a month,
but if the women were to be mixed with men it was a
different proposition altogether. She was not going to
be made a cat's-paw of. She had not come out there
to sanction by her presence what used in her day to be
called fast behaviour. Nothing had been said at the
interview in London about men; if there had been
she would have declined, of course, to come.

'What is his name?' asked Mrs. Fisher, abruptly
interposing.

Mrs. Wilkins turned to her with a slight surprise.
'Wilkins,' she said.

'Wilkins?'

'Yes.'

'Your name?'

'And his.'

'A relation?'

'Not blood.'

'A connection?'

'A husband.'

Mrs. Fisher once more cast down her eyes. She could
not talk to Mrs. Wilkins. There was something about
the things she said. . . . 'A husband.' Suggesting
one of many. Always that unseemly twist to everything.
Why could she not say 'My husband'? Besides, Mrs.

Fisher had, she herself knew not for what reason, taken both the Hampstead young women for widows. War ones. There had been an absence of mention of husbands at the interview which would not, she considered, be natural if such persons did after all exist. And if a husband was not a relation, who was ? ' Not blood.' What a way to talk. Why, a husband was the first of all relations. How well she remembered Ruskin— no, it was not Ruskin, it was the Bible that said a man should leave his father and mother and cleave only to his wife ; showing that she became by marriage an even more than blood relation. And if the husband's father and mother were to be nothing to him compared to his wife, how much less than nothing ought the wife's father and mother be to her compared to her husband. She herself had been unable to leave her father and mother in order to cleave to Mr. Fisher because they were no longer, when she married, alive, but she certainly would have left them if they had been there to leave. Not blood, indeed. Silly talk.

The dinner was very good. Succulence succeeded succulence. Costanza had determined to do as she chose in the matter of cream and eggs the first week, and see what happened at the end of it when the bills had to be paid. Her experience of the English was that they were quiet about bills. They were shy of words. They believed readily. Besides, who was the mistress here ? In the absence of a definite one, it occurred to Costanza that she might as well be the mistress herself. So she did as she chose about the dinner, and it was very good.

The four, however, were so much preoccupied by their own conversation that they ate it without noticing how good it was. Even Mrs. Fisher, she who in such matters was manly, did not notice. The entire excellent cooking was to her as though it were not ; which shows how much she must have been stirred.

She was stirred. It was that Mrs. Wilkins. She was enough to stir anybody. And she was undoubtedly encouraged by Lady Caroline, who, in her turn, was no doubt influenced by the Chianti.

Mrs. Fisher was very glad there were no men present, for they certainly would have been foolish about Lady Caroline. She was precisely the sort of young woman to unbalance them ; especially, Mrs. Fisher recognised, at that moment. Perhaps it was the Chianti momentarily intensifying her personality, but she was undeniably most attractive ; and there were few things Mrs. Fisher disliked more than having to look on while sensible, intelligent men, who the moment before were talking seriously and interestingly about real matters, became merely foolish and simpering—she had seen them actually simpering—just because in walked a bit of bird-brained beauty. Even Mr. Gladstone, that great wise statesman, whose hand had once rested for an unforgettable moment solemnly on her head, would have, she felt, on perceiving Lady Caroline left off talking sense and horribly embarked on badinage.

'You see,' Mrs. Wilkins said—a silly trick that, with which she mostly began her sentences; Mrs. Fisher each time wished to say, 'Pardon me—I do not see, I hear'—but why trouble?—'You see,' said Mrs. Wilkins, leaning across towards Lady Caroline, 'we arranged, didn't we, in London that if any of us wanted to we could each invite one guest. So now I'm doing it.'

'I don't remember that,' said Mrs. Fisher, her eyes on her plate.

'Oh yes, we did—didn't we, Rose?'

'Yes—I remember,' said Lady Caroline. 'Only it seemed so incredible that one could ever want to. One's whole idea was to get away from one's friends.'

'And one's husbands.'

Again that unseemly plural. But how altogether unseemly, thought Mrs. Fisher. Such implications. Mrs. Arbuthnot clearly thought so too, for she had turned red.

'And family affection,' said Lady Caroline—or was it the Chianti speaking? Surely it was the Chianti.

'And the want of family affection,' said Mrs. Wilkins,

—what a light she was throwing on her home life and real character.

' That wouldn't be so bad,' said Lady Caroline. ' I'd stay with that. It would give one room.'

' Oh no, no—it's dreadful,' cried Mrs. Wilkins. ' It's as if one had no clothes on.'

' But I like that,' said Lady Caroline.

' Really——' said Mrs. Fisher.

' It's a divine feeling, getting rid of things,' said Lady Caroline, who was talking altogether to Mrs. Wilkins and paid no attention to the other two.

' Oh, but in a bitter wind to have nothing on and know there never will be anything on and you going to get colder and colder till at last you die of it—that's what it was like, living with somebody who didn't love one.'

These confidences, thought Mrs. Fisher . . . and no excuse whatever for Mrs. Wilkins, who was making them entirely on plain water. Mrs. Arbuthnot, judging from her face, quite shared Mrs. Fisher's disapproval; she was fidgeting.

' But didn't he ? ' asked Lady Caroline,—every bit as shamelessly unreticent as Mrs. Wilkins.

' Mellersh ? He showed no signs of it.'

' Delicious,' murmured Lady Caroline.

' Really——' said Mrs. Fisher.

'I didn't think it was at all delicious. I was miserable. And now, since I've been here, I simply stare at myself being miserable. As miserable as that. And about Mellersh.'

'You mean he wasn't worth it.'

'Really——' said Mrs. Fisher.

'No, I don't. I mean I've suddenly got well.'

Lady Caroline, slowly twisting the stem of her glass in her fingers, scrutinised the lit-up face opposite.

'And now I'm well I find I can't sit here and gloat all to myself. I can't be happy, shutting him out. I must share. I understand exactly what the Blessed Damozel felt like.'

'What was the Blessed Damozel?' asked Scrap.

'Really——' said Mrs. Fisher; and with such emphasis this time that Lady Caroline turned to her.

'Ought I to know?' she asked. 'I don't know any natural history. It sounds like a bird.'

'It is a poem,' said Mrs. Fisher with extraordinary frost.

'Oh,' said Scrap.

'I'll lend it to you,' said Mrs. Wilkins, over whose face laughter rippled.

'No,' said Scrap.

'And its author,' said Mrs. Fisher icily, 'though not

perhaps quite what one would have wished him to be, was frequently at my father's table.'

'What a bore for you,' said Scrap. 'That's what mother's always doing—inviting authors. I hate authors. I wouldn't mind them so much if they didn't write books. Go on about Mellersh,' she said, turning to Mrs. Wilkins.

'Really——' said Mrs. Fisher.

'All those empty beds,' said Mrs. Wilkins.

'What empty beds?' asked Scrap.

'The ones in this house. Why, of course they each ought to have somebody happy inside them. Eight beds, and only four people. It's dreadful, dreadful to be so greedy and keep everything just for oneself. I want Rose to ask her husband out too. You and Mrs. Fisher haven't got husbands, but why not give some friend a glorious time?'

Rose bit her lip. She turned red, she turned pale. If only Lotty would keep quiet, she thought. It was all very well to have suddenly become a saint and want to love everybody, but need she be so tactless? Rose felt that all her poor sore places were being danced on. If only Lotty would keep quiet . . .

And Mrs. Fisher, with even greater frostiness than that with which she had received Lady Caroline's ignorance of the Blessed Damozel, said, 'There is only one unoccupied bedroom in this house.'

' Only one ? ' echoed Mrs. Wilkins, astonished. ' Then who are in all the others ? '

' We are,' said Mrs. Fisher.

' But we're not in all the bedrooms. There must be at least six. That leaves two over, and the owner told us there were eight beds—didn't he, Rose ? '

' There are six bedrooms,' said Mrs. Fisher ; for both she and Lady Caroline had thoroughly searched the house on arriving, in order to see which part of it they would be most comfortable in, and they both knew that there were six bedrooms, two of which were very small, and in one of these small ones Francesca slept in the company of a chair and a chest of drawers, and the other, similarly furnished, was empty.

Mrs. Wilkins and Mrs. Arbuthnot had hardly looked at the house, having spent most of their time out-of-doors gaping at the scenery, and had, in the agitated inattentiveness of their minds when first they began negotiating for San Salvatore, got into their heads that the eight beds of which the owner spoke were the same as eight bedrooms ; which they were not. There were indeed eight beds, but four of them were in Mrs. Wilkins's and Mrs. Arbuthnot's rooms.

' There are six bedrooms,' repeated Mrs. Fisher. ' We have four, Francesca has the fifth, and the sixth is empty.'

'So that,' said Scrap, 'however kind we feel we would be if we could, we can't. Isn't it fortunate ? '

'But then there's only room for one ? ' said Mrs. Wilkins, looking round at the three faces.

'Yes—and you've got him,' said Scrap.

Mrs. Wilkins was taken aback. This question of the beds was unexpected. In inviting Mellersh she had intended to put him in one of the four spare-rooms that she imagined were there. When there were plenty of rooms and enough servants there was no reason why they should, as they did in their small, two-servanted house at home, share the same one. Love, even universal love, the kind of love with which she felt herself flooded, should not be tried. Much patience and self-effacement were needed for successful married sleep. Placidity ; a steady faith ; these too were needed. She was sure she would be much fonder of Mellersh, and he not mind her nearly so much, if they were not shut up together at night, if in the morning they could meet with the cheery affection of friends between whom lies no shadow of differences about the window or the washing arrangements, or of absurd little choked-down resentments at something that had seemed to one of them unfair. Her happiness, she felt, and her ability to be friends with everybody, was the result of her sudden new freedom and its peace. Would there be that

sense of freedom, that peace, after a night shut up with
Mellersh ?   Would she be able in the morning to be full
towards him, as she was at that moment full, of nothing
at all but loving-kindness ?   After all, she hadn't been
very long in heaven. Suppose she hadn't been in it
long enough for her to have become fixed in blandness ?
And only that morning what an extraordinary joy it
had been to find herself alone when she woke, and
able to pull the bed-clothes any way she liked !

Francesca had to nudge her. She was so much
absorbed that she did not notice the pudding.

'If,' thought Mrs. Wilkins, distractedly helping herself, 'I share my room with Mellersh I risk losing all I
now feel about him. If on the other hand I put him
in the one spare-room, I prevent Mrs. Fisher and Lady
Caroline from giving somebody a treat. True they
don't seem to want to at present, but at any moment
in this place one or the other of them may be seized
with a desire to make somebody happy, and then they
wouldn't be able to because of Mellersh.'

'What a problem,' she said aloud, her eyebrows
puckered.

'What is ? ' asked Scrap.

'Where to put Mellersh.'

Scrap stared. 'Why, isn't one room enough for
him ? ' she asked.

'Oh yes, quite. But then there won't be any room left at all—any room for somebody *you* may want to invite.'

'I shan't want to,' said Scrap.

'Or *you*,' said Mrs. Wilkins to Mrs. Fisher. 'Rose, of course, doesn't count. I'm sure she would like sharing her room with her husband. It's written all over her.'

'Really——' said Mrs. Fisher.

'Really what?' asked Mrs. Wilkins, turning hopefully to her, for she thought the word this time was the preliminary to a helpful suggestion.

It was not. It stood by itself. It was, as before, mere frost.

Challenged, however, Mrs. Fisher did fasten it on to a sentence. 'Really am I to understand,' she asked, 'that you propose to reserve the one spare-room for the exclusive use of your own family?'

'He isn't my own family,' said Mrs. Wilkins. 'He's my husband. You see——'

'I see nothing,' Mrs. Fisher could not this time refrain from interrupting—for what an intolerable trick. 'At the most I hear, and that reluctantly.'

But Mrs. Wilkins, as impervious to rebuke as Mrs. Fisher had feared, immediately repeated the tiresome formula and launched out into a long and excessively indelicate speech about the best place for the person she called Mellersh to sleep in.

Mellersh—Mrs. Fisher, remembering the Thomases and Johns and Alfreds and Roberts of her day, plain names that yet had all become glorious, thought it sheer affectation to be christened Mellersh—was, it seemed, Mrs. Wilkins's husband, and therefore his place was clearly indicated. Why this talk ? She herself, as if foreseeing his arrival, had had a second bed put in Mrs. Wilkins's room. There were certain things in life which were never talked about but only done. Most things connected with husbands were not talked about ; and to have a whole dinner-table taken up with a discussion as to where one of them should sleep was an affront to the decencies. How and where husbands slept should be known only to their wives. Sometimes it was not known to them, and then the marriage had less happy moments ; but these moments were not talked about either ; the decencies continued to be preserved. At least, it was so in her day. To have to hear whether Mr. Wilkins should or should not sleep with Mrs. Wilkins, and the reasons why he should and the reasons why he shouldn't, was both uninteresting and indelicate.

She might have succeeded in imposing propriety and changing the conversation if it had not been for Lady

Caroline. Lady Caroline encouraged Mrs. Wilkins, and
threw herself into the discussion with every bit as much
unreserve as Mrs. Wilkins herself. No doubt she was
impelled on this occasion by Chianti, but whatever the
reason there it was. And, characteristically, Lady
Caroline was all for Mr. Wilkins being given the solitary
spare-room. She took that for granted. Any other
arrangement would be impossible, she said; her expression was, Barbarous. Had she never read her Bible,
Mrs. Fisher was tempted to inquire,—*And they two shall
be one flesh*? Clearly also, then, one room. But Mrs.
Fisher did not inquire. She did not care even to allude
to such texts to some one unmarried.

However, there was one way she could force Mr.
Wilkins into his proper place and save the situation:
she could say she herself intended to invite a friend.
It was her right. They had all said so. Apart from
propriety, it was monstrous that Mrs. Wilkins should
want to monopolise the one spare-room, when in her
own room was everything necessary for her husband.
Perhaps she really would invite somebody,—not invite,
but suggest coming. There was Kate Lumley, for instance. Kate could perfectly afford to come and pay
her share; and she was of her own period and knew,
and had known, most of the people she herself knew
and had known. Kate, of course, had only been on

the fringe ; she used to be asked only to the big parties, not to the small ones, and she still was only on the fringe. There were some people who never got off the fringe, and Kate was one. Often, however, such people were more permanently agreeable to be with than the others, in that they remained grateful.

Yes ; she might really consider Kate. The poor soul had never married, but then everybody could not expect to marry, and she was quite comfortably off,— not too comfortably, but just comfortably enough to pay her own expenses if she came and yet be grateful. Yes ; Kate was the solution. If she came, at one stroke, Mrs. Fisher saw, would the Wilkinses be regularised and Mrs. Wilkins be prevented from having more than her share of the rooms. Also, Mrs. Fisher would save herself from isolation ; spiritual isolation. She desired physical isolation between meals, but she disliked that isolation which is of the spirit. Such isolation would, she feared, certainly be hers with these three alien-minded young women. Even Mrs. Arbuthnot was, owing to her friendship with Mrs. Wilkins, necessarily alien-minded. In Kate she would have a support. Kate, without intruding on her sitting-room, for Kate was tractable, would be there at meals to support her.

Mrs. Fisher said nothing at the moment ; but presently in the drawing-room, when they were gathered

round the wood fire—she had discovered there was
no fireplace in her own sitting-room, and therefore she
would after all be forced, so long as the evenings remained cool, to spend them in the other room—presently,
while Francesca was handing coffee round and Lady
Caroline was poisoning the air with smoke, Mrs. Wilkins,
looking relieved and pleased, said : ' Well, if nobody
really wants that room, and wouldn't use it anyhow,
I shall be very glad if Mellersh may have it.'

' Of course he must have it,' said Lady Caroline.

Then Mrs. Fisher spoke.

' I have a friend,' she said in her deep voice ; and
sudden silence fell upon the others.

' Kate Lumley,' said Mrs. Fisher.

Nobody spoke.

' Perhaps,' continued Mrs. Fisher, addressing Lady
Caroline, ' you know her ? '

No, Lady Caroline did not know Kate Lumley ;
and Mrs. Fisher, without asking the others if they did,
for she was sure they knew no one, proceeded. ' I
wish to invite her to join me,' said Mrs. Fisher.

Complete silence.

Then Scrap said, turning to Mrs. Wilkins, ' That
settles Mellersh, then.'

' It settles the question of Mr. Wilkins,' said Mrs.
Fisher, ' although I am unable to understand that there

should ever have been a question, in the only way that is right.'

'I'm afraid you're in for it, then,' said Lady Caroline, again to Mrs. Wilkins. 'Unless,' she added, 'he can't come.'

But Mrs. Wilkins, her brow perturbed—for suppose after all she were not yet quite stable in heaven?—could only say, a little uneasily, 'I *see* him here.'

THE uneventful days—only outwardly uneventful—
slipped by in floods of sunshine, and the servants,
watching the four ladies, came to the conclusion there
was very little life in them.

To the servants San Salvatore seemed asleep. No
one came to tea, nor did the ladies go anywhere to tea.
Other tenants in other springs had been far more active.
There had been stir and enterprise; the boat had been
used; excursions had been made; Beppo's fly was
ordered; people from Mezzago came over and spent
the day; the house rang with voices; even sometimes champagne had been drunk. Life was varied,
life was interesting. But this? What was this? The
servants were not even scolded. They were left completely to themselves. They yawned.

Perplexing, too, was the entire absence of gentlemen. How could gentlemen keep away from so much
beauty? For, added up, and even after the sub-
traction of the old one, the three younger ladies

produced a formidable total of that which gentlemen usually sought.

Also the evident desire of each lady to spend long hours separated from the other ladies puzzled the servants. The result was a deathly stillness in the house, except at meal-times. It might have been as empty as it had been all the winter, for any sounds of life there were. The old lady sat in her room, alone ; the dark-eyed lady wandered off alone, loitering, so Domenico told them, who sometimes came across her in the course of his duties, incomprehensibly among the rocks ; the very beautiful fair lady lay in her low chair in the top garden, alone ; the less, but still beautiful fair lady went up the hills and stayed up them for hours, alone ; and every day the sun blazed slowly round the house, and disappeared at evening into the sea, and nothing at all had happened.

The servants yawned.

Yet the four visitors, while their bodies sat—that was Mrs. Fisher's—or lay—that was Lady Caroline's—or loitered—that was Mrs. Arbuthnot's—or went in solitude up into the hills—that was Mrs. Wilkins's—were anything but torpid really. Their minds were unusually busy. Even at night their minds were busy, and the dreams they had were clear, thin, quick things, entirely different from the heavy dreams of home. There was that in the atmosphere of San Salvatore which produced active-mindedness in all except the natives. They, as before, whatever the beauty around them, whatever the prodigal seasons did, remained immune from thoughts other than those they were accustomed to. All their lives they had seen, year by year, the amazing recurrent spectacle of April in the gardens, and custom had made it invisible to them. They were as blind to it, as unconscious of it, as Domenico's dog asleep in the sun.

The visitors could not be blind to it,—it was too arresting after London in a particularly wet and gloomy March. Suddenly to be transported to that place where the air was so still that it held its breath, where the light was so golden that the most ordinary things were transfigured,—to be transported into that delicate warmth, that caressing fragrance, and to have the old grey castle as the setting, and, in the distance, the serene clear hills of Perugini's backgrounds, was an astonishing contrast. Even Lady Caroline, used all her life to beauty, who had been everywhere and seen everything, felt the surprise of it. It was, that year, a particularly wonderful spring, and of all the months at San Salvatore April, if the weather was fine, was best. May scorched and withered; March was restless, and could be hard and cold in its brightness; but April came along softly like a blessing, and if it were a fine April it was so beautiful that it was impossible not to feel different, not to feel stirred and touched.

Mrs. Wilkins, we have seen, responded to it instantly. She, so to speak, at once flung off all her garments and dived straight into glory, unhesitatingly, with a cry of rapture.

Mrs. Arbuthnot was stirred and touched, but differently. She had odd sensations,—presently to be described.

Mrs. Fisher, being old, was of a closer, more impermeable texture, and offered more resistance; but she too had odd sensations, also in their place to be described.

Lady Caroline, already amply acquainted with beautiful houses and climates, to whom they could not come quite with the same surprise, yet was very nearly as quick to react as Mrs. Wilkins. The place had an almost instantaneous influence on her as well, and of one part of this influence she was aware : it had made her, beginning on the very first evening, want to think, and acted on her curiously like a conscience. What this conscience seemed to press upon her notice with an insistence that startled her—Lady Caroline hesitated to accept the word, but it would keep on coming into her head—was that she was tawdry.

Tawdry. She. Fancy.

She must think that out.

The morning after the first dinner together, she woke up in a condition of regret that she should have been so talkative to Mrs. Wilkins the night before. What had made her be, she wondered. Now, of course, Mrs. Wilkins would want to grab, she would want to be inseparable; and the thought of a grabbing and an inseparableness that should last four weeks made Scrap's spirit swoon within her. No doubt the encouraged Mrs. Wilkins would be lurking in the top garden waiting to waylay her when she went out, and would hail her with morning cheerfulness. How much she hated being hailed with morning cheerfulness,—or indeed hailed at all. She oughtn't to have encouraged Mrs. Wilkins the night before. Fatal to encourage. It was bad enough not to encourage, for just sitting there and saying nothing seemed usually to involve her, but actively to encourage was suicidal. What on earth had made her? Now she would have to waste all the precious time, the precious, lovely time for thinking in, for getting square with herself, in shaking Mrs. Wilkins off.

With great caution and on the tips of her toes, balancing herself carefully lest the pebbles should scrunch, she stole out when she was dressed to her corner; but the garden was empty. No shaking off was necessary. Neither Mrs. Wilkins nor anybody else was to be seen. She had it entirely to herself. Except for Domenico, who presently came and hovered, watering his plants, again especially all the plants that were nearest her, no one came out at all; and when, after a long while of following up thoughts which seemed to escape her just as she had got them, and dropping off exhausted to sleep in the intervals of this chase, she felt hungry and looked at her watch and saw that it was past three, she realised that nobody had even bothered to call her in to lunch. So that, Scrap could not but remark, if any one was shaken off it was she herself.

Well, but how delightful, and how very new. Now she would really be able to think, uninterruptedly. Delicious to be forgotten.

Still, she was hungry; and Mrs. Wilkins, after that excessive friendliness the night before, might at least have told her lunch was ready. And she had really been excessively friendly, — so nice about Mellersh's sleeping arrangements, wanting him to have the spare-room and all. She wasn't usually interested in arrange-ments, in fact she wasn't ever interested in them; so that Scrap considered she might be said almost to have gone out of her way to be agreeable to Mrs. Wilkins. And, in return, Mrs. Wilkins didn't even bother whether or not she had any lunch.

Fortunately, though she was hungry, she didn't mind missing a meal. Life was full of meals. They took up an enormous proportion of one's time ; and Mrs. Fisher was, she was afraid, one of those persons who at meals linger. Twice now had she dined with Mrs. Fisher, and each time she had been difficult at the end to dislodge, lingering on slowly cracking innumerable nuts and slowly drinking a glass of wine that seemed as if it would never be finished. Probably it would be a good thing to make a habit of missing lunch, and as it was quite easy to have tea brought out to her, and as she breakfasted in her room, only once a day would she have to sit at the dining-room table and endure the nuts.

Scrap burrowed her head comfortably in the cushions, and with her feet crossed on the low parapet gave herself up to more thought. She said to herself, as she had said at intervals throughout the morning : Now I'm going to think. But, never having thought out anything in her life, it was difficult. Extraordinary how one's attention wouldn't stay fixed ; extraordinary how one's mind slipped sideways. Settling herself down to a review of her past as a preliminary to the consideration of her future, and hunting in it to begin with for any justification of that distressing word tawdry, the next thing she knew was that she wasn't thinking about this at all, but had somehow switched on to Mr. Wilkins.

Well, Mr. Wilkins was quite easy to think about, though not pleasant. She viewed his approach with misgivings. For not only was it a profound and unexpected bore to have a man added to the party, and a man, too, of the kind she was sure Mr. Wilkins must be, but she was afraid—and her fear was the result of a drearily unvarying experience—that he might wish to hang about her.

This possibility had evidently not yet occurred to Mrs. Wilkins, and it was not one to which she could very well draw her attention; not, that is, without being too fatuous to live. She tried to hope that Mr. Wilkins would be a wonderful exception to the dreadful rule. If only he were, she would be so much obliged to him that she believed she might really quite like him.

But—she had misgivings. Suppose he hung about her so that she was driven from her lovely top garden; suppose the light in Mrs. Wilkins's funny, flickering face was blown out. Scrap felt she would particularly dislike this to happen to Mrs. Wilkins's face, yet she had never in her life met any wives, not any at all, who had been able to understand that she didn't in the least want their husbands. Often she had met wives who didn't want their husbands either, but that made them none the less indignant if they thought somebody else did, and none the less sure, when they saw them hanging round Scrap, that she was trying to get them. Trying to get them! The bare thought, the bare recollection of these situations, filled her with a boredom so extreme that it instantly sent her to sleep again.

When she woke up she went on with Mr. Wilkins.

Now if, thought Scrap, Mr. Wilkins were not an exception and behaved in the usual way, would Mrs. Wilkins understand, or would it just simply spoil her holiday? She seemed quick, but would she be quick about just this? She seemed to understand and see inside one, but would she understand and see inside one when it came to Mr. Wilkins?

The experienced Scrap was full of doubts. She shifted her feet on the parapet; she jerked a cushion straight. Perhaps she had better try and explain to Mrs. Wilkins, during the days still remaining before the arrival,—explain in a general way, rather vague and talking at large,—her attitude towards such things. She might also expound to her her peculiar dislike of people's husbands, and her profound craving to be, at least for this one month, let alone.

But Scrap had her doubts about this too. Such talk meant a certain familiarity, meant embarking on a friendship with Mrs. Wilkins; and if, after having embarked on it and faced the peril it contained of too

much Mrs. Wilkins, Mr. Wilkins should turn out to be
artful—and people did get very artful when they were
set on anything—and manage after all to slip through
into the top garden, Mrs. Wilkins might easily believe
she had been taken in, and that she, Scrap, was deceitful.
Deceitful! And about Mr. Wilkins. Wives were really
pathetic.

At half-past four she heard sounds of saucers on the
other side of the daphne bushes. Was tea being sent
out to her?

No; the sounds came no closer, they stopped near
the house. Tea was to be in the garden, in her garden.
Scrap considered she might at least have been asked if she
minded being disturbed. They all knew she sat there.

Perhaps some one would bring hers to her in her corner.

No; nobody brought anything.

Well, she was too hungry not to go and have it with
the others to-day, but she would give Francesca strict
orders for the future.

She got up, and walked with that slow grace which
was another of her outrageous number of attractions
towards the sounds of tea. She was conscious not only
of being very hungry but of wanting to talk to Mrs.
Wilkins again. Mrs. Wilkins had not grabbed, she had
left her quite free all day in spite of the *rapprochement*
the night before. Of course she was an original, and

put on a silk jumper for dinner, but she hadn't grabbed.
This was a great thing. Scrap went towards the tea-
table quite looking forward to Mrs. Wilkins ; and when
she came in sight of it she saw only Mrs. Fisher and
Mrs. Arbuthnot.

Mrs. Fisher was pouring out the tea, and Mrs.
Arbuthnot was offering Mrs. Fisher macaroons. Every
time Mrs. Fisher offered Mrs. Arbuthnot anything—her
cup, or milk, or sugar—Mrs. Arbuthnot offered her
macaroons,—pressed them on her with an odd assiduous-
ness, almost with obstinacy. Was it a game ? Scrap
wondered, sitting down and seizing a macaroon.

' Where is Mrs. Wilkins ? ' asked Scrap.

They did not know. At least, Mrs. Arbuthnot, on
Scrap's inquiry, did not know ; Mrs. Fisher's face, at
the name, became elaborately uninterested.

It appeared that Mrs. Wilkins had not been seen
since breakfast. Mrs. Arbuthnot thought she had
probably gone for a picnic. Scrap missed her. She
ate the enormous macaroons, the best and biggest she
had ever come across, in silence. Tea without Mrs.
Wilkins was dull ; and Mrs. Arbuthnot had that fatal
flavour of motherliness about her, of wanting to pet one,
to make one very comfortable, coaxing one to eat,—
coaxing her, who was already so frankly, so even excessively, eating,—that seemed to have dogged Scrap's

steps through life. Couldn't people leave one alone ?
She was perfectly able to eat what she wanted un-
incited. She tried to quench Mrs. Arbuthnot's zeal by
being short with her. Useless. The shortness was not
apparent. It remained, as all Scrap's evil feelings remained, covered up by the impenetrable veil of her
loveliness.

Mrs. Fisher sat monumentally, and took no notice of
either of them. She had had a curious day, and was a
little worried. She had been quite alone, for none of
the three had come to lunch, and none of them had
taken the trouble to let her know they were not coming ;
and Mrs. Arbuthnot, drifting casually into tea, had
behaved oddly till Lady Caroline joined them and
distracted her attention.

Mrs. Fisher was prepared not to dislike Mrs.
Arbuthnot, whose parted hair and mild expression
seemed very decent and womanly, but she certainly had
habits that were difficult to like. Her habit of instantly
echoing any offer made her of food or drink, of throwing
the offer back on one, as it were, was not somehow what
one expected of her. ' Will you have some more tea ? '
was surely a question to which the answer was simply
yes or no ; but Mrs. Arbuthnot persisted in the trick
she had exhibited the day before at breakfast, of adding
to her yes or no the words, ' Will *you* ? ' She had done

it again that morning at breakfast, and here she was doing it at tea,—the two meals at which Mrs. Fisher presided and poured out. Why did she do it? Mrs. Fisher failed to understand.

But this was not what was worrying her; this was merely by the way. What was worrying her was that she had been quite unable that day to settle to anything, and had done nothing but wander restlessly from her sitting-room to her battlements and back again. It had been a wasted day, and how much she disliked waste. She had tried to read, and she had tried to write to Kate Lumley; but no,—a few words read, a few lines written, and up she got again and went out on to the battlements and stared at the sea.

It did not matter that the letter to Kate Lumley should not be written. There was time enough for that. Let the others suppose her coming was definitely fixed. All the better. So would Mr. Wilkins be kept out of the spare-room and put where he belonged. Kate would keep. She could be held in reserve. Kate in reserve was just as potent as Kate in actuality, and there were points about Kate in reserve which might be missing from Kate in actuality. For instance, if Mrs. Fisher were going to be restless, she would rather Kate were not there to see. There was a want of dignity about restlessness, about trotting backwards and forwards. But it did matter that she could not read a sentence of any of her great dead friends' writings ; no, not even of Browning's, who had been so much in Italy, nor of Ruskin's, whose *Stones of Venice* she had brought with her to re-read so nearly on the very spot ; nor even a sentence of a really interesting book like the one she had found in her sitting-room about the home life of the German Emperor, poor man—written in the nineties, when he had not yet begun to be more sinned against than sinning, which was, she was firmly convinced, what was the matter with him now, and full of exciting things about his birth and his right arm and *accoucheurs*—without having to put it down and go and stare at the sea.

Reading was very important ; the proper exercise and development of one's mind was a paramount duty. How could one read if one were constantly trotting in and out ? Curious, this restlessness. Was she going to be ill ? No, she felt well ; indeed, unusually well, and she went in and out quite quickly—trotted, in fact— and without her stick. Very odd that she shouldn't be able to sit still, she thought, frowning across the tops of some purple hyacinths at the Gulf of Spezia glittering beyond a headland ; very odd that she, who walked so slowly, with such dependence on her stick, should suddenly trot.

It would be interesting to talk to some one about it, she felt. Not to Kate,—to a stranger. Kate would only look at her and suggest a cup of tea. Kate always suggested cups of tea. Besides, Kate had a flat face. That Mrs. Wilkins, now,—annoying as she was, loose-tongued as she was, impertinent, objectionable, would probably understand, and perhaps know what was making her be like this. But she could say nothing to Mrs. Wilkins. She was the last person to whom one would admit sensations. Dignity alone forbade it. Confide in Mrs. Wilkins ? Never.

And Mrs. Arbuthnot, while she wistfully mothered the obstructive Scrap at tea, felt too that she had had a curious day. Like Mrs. Fisher's, it had been active, but, unlike Mrs. Fisher's, only active in mind. Her body had been quite still ; her mind had not been still at all, it had been excessively active. For years she had taken care to have no time to think. Her scheduled life in the parish had prevented memories and desires from intruding on her. That day they had crowded. She went back to tea feeling dejected, and that she should feel dejected in such a place with everything about her to make her rejoice, only dejected her the more. But how could she rejoice alone ? How could anybody rejoice and enjoy and appreciate, really appreciate, alone ? Except Lotty. Lotty seemed able to. She had

gone off down the hill directly after breakfast, alone
yet obviously rejoicing, for she had not suggested that
Rose should go too, and she was singing as she went.

Rose had spent the day by herself, sitting with her
hands clasping her knees, staring straight in front of
her. What she was staring at were the grey swords
of the agaves, and, on their tall stalks, the pale irises
that grew in the remote place she had found, while
beyond them, between the grey leaves and the blue
flowers, she saw the sea. The place she had found was
a hidden corner where the sun-baked stones were padded
with thyme, and nobody was likely to come. It was
out of sight and sound of the house; it was off any
path; it was near the end of the promontory. She
sat so quiet that presently lizards darted over her feet,
and some tiny birds like finches, frightened away at
first, came back again and flitted among the bushes
round her just as if she hadn't been there. How beautiful it was. And what was the good of it with no one
there, no one who loved being with one, who belonged
to one, to whom one could say, ' Look.' And wouldn't
one say, ' Look—*dearest* ? ' Yes, one would say *dearest*;
and the sweet word, just to say it to somebody who
loved one, would make one happy.

She sat quite still, staring straight in front of her.
Strange that in this place she did not want to pray.

She who had prayed so constantly at home didn't seem able to do it here at all. The first morning she had merely thrown up a brief thank you to heaven on getting out of bed, and had gone straight to the window to see what everything looked like,—thrown up the thank you as carelessly as a ball, and thought no more about it. That morning, remembering this and ashamed, she had knelt down with determination ; but perhaps determination was bad for prayers, for she had been unable to think of a thing to say. And as for her bed-time prayers, on neither of the nights had she said a single one. She had forgotten them. She had been so much absorbed in other thoughts that she had forgotten them ; and, once in bed, she was asleep and whirling along among bright, thin swift dreams before she had so much time as to stretch herself out.

What had come over her ? Why had she let go the anchor of prayer ? And she had difficulty, too, in remembering her poor, in remembering even that there were such things as poor. Holidays, of course, were good, and were recognised by everybody as good, but ought they so completely to blot out, to make such havoc of, the realities ? Perhaps it was healthy to forget her poor ; with all the greater gusto would she go back to them. But it couldn't be healthy to forget her prayers, and still less could it be healthy not to mind.

Rose did not mind. She knew she did not mind. And, even worse, she knew she did not mind not minding. In this place she was indifferent to both the things that had filled her life and made it seem as if it were happy for years. Well, if only she could rejoice in her wonderful new surroundings, have that much at least to set against the indifference, the letting go,—but she could not. She had no work ; she did not pray ; she was left empty.

Lotty had spoilt her day that day, as she had spoilt her day the day before,—Lotty, with her invitation to her husband, with her suggestion that she too should invite hers. Having flung Frederick into her mind again the day before, Lotty had left her ; for the whole afternoon she had left her alone with her thoughts. Since then they had been all of Frederick. Where at Hampstead he came to her only in her dreams, here he left her dreams free and was with her during the day instead. And again that morning, as she was struggling not to think of him, Lotty had asked her, just before disappearing singing down the path, if she had written yet and invited him, and again he was flung into her mind and she wasn't able to get him out.

How could she invite him ? It had gone on so long, their estrangement, such years ; she would hardly know what words to use ; and besides, he would not come. Why should he come ? He didn't care about being with her. What could they talk about ? Between them was the barrier of his work and her religion. She could not—how could she, believing as she did in purity, in responsibility for the effect of one's actions on others —bear his work, bear living by it ; and he, she knew, had at first resented and then been merely bored by her religion. He had let her slip away ; he had given her up ; he no longer minded ; he accepted her religion indifferently, as a settled fact. Both it and she—Rose's mind, becoming more luminous in the clear light of April at San Salvatore, suddenly saw the truth—bored him.

Naturally when she saw this, when that morning it flashed upon her for the first time, she did not like it ; she liked it so little that for a space the whole beauty of Italy was blotted out. What was to be done about it ? She could not give up believing in good and not liking evil, and it must be evil to live entirely on the proceeds of adulteries, however dead and distinguished they were. Besides, if she did, if she sacrificed her whole past, her bringing up, her work for the last ten years, would she bore him less ? Rose felt right down at her very roots that if you have once thoroughly bored somebody it is next to impossible to unbore him. Once a bore always a bore,—certainly, she thought, to the person originally bored.

Then, thought she, looking out to sea through eyes grown misty, better cling to her religion. It was better —she hardly noticed the reprehensibleness of her thought —than nothing. But oh, she wanted to cling to something tangible, to love something living, something that one could hold against one's heart, that one could see and touch and do things for. If her poor baby hadn't died . . . babies didn't get bored with one, it took them a long while to grow up and find one out. And perhaps one's baby never did find one out ; perhaps one would always be to it, however old and bearded it grew, somebody special, somebody different from every one else, and, if for no other reason, precious in that one could never be repeated.

Sitting with dim eyes looking out to sea she felt an extraordinary yearning to hold something of her very own tight to her bosom. Rose was slender, and as reserved in figure as in character, yet she felt a queer sensation of—how could she describe it ?—bosom. There was something about San Salvatore that made her feel all bosom. She wanted to gather to her bosom, to comfort and protect, soothing the dear head that should lie on it with softest strokings and murmurs of love. Frederick, Frederick's child,—come to her, pillowed on her, because they were unhappy, because they had been hurt. . . . They would need her then, if they had been hurt ; they would let themselves be loved then, if they were unhappy.

Well, the child was gone, would never come now ; but perhaps Frederick—some day—when he was old and tired . . .

Such were Mrs. Arbuthnot's reflections and emotions that first day at San Salvatore by herself. She went back to tea dejected as she had not been for years. San Salvatore had taken her carefully built-up semblance of happiness away from her, and given her nothing in exchange. Yes,—it had given her yearnings in exchange, this ache and longing, this queer feeling of bosom ; but that was worse than nothing. And she who had learned balance, who never at home was irritated but always able to be kind, could not, even in her dejection, that afternoon endure Mrs. Fisher's assumption of the position as hostess at tea.

One would have supposed that such a little thing would not have touched her, but it did. Was her nature changing ? Was she to be not only thrown back on long-stifled yearnings after Frederick, but also turned into somebody who wanted to fight over little things ? After tea, when both Mrs. Fisher and Lady Caroline had disappeared again—it was quite evident that nobody wanted her—she was more dejected than ever, overwhelmed by the discrepancy between the

splendour outside her, the warm, teeming beauty and
self-sufficiency of nature, and the blank emptiness of
her heart.

Then came Lotty, back to dinner, incredibly more
freckled, exuding the sunshine she had been collecting
all day, talking, laughing, being tactless, being unwise,
being without reticence ; and Lady Caroline, so quiet
at tea, woke up to animation, and Mrs. Fisher was not
so noticeable, and Rose was beginning to revive a little,
for Lotty's spirits were contagious as she described the
delights of her day, a day which might easily to any
one else have had nothing in it but a very long and
very hot walk and sandwiches, when she suddenly said,
catching Rose's eye, ' Letter gone ? '

Rose flushed. This tactlessness . . .

' What letter ? ' asked Scrap, interested. Both her
elbows were on the table and her chin was supported
in her hands, for the nut-stage had been reached, and
there was nothing for it but to wait in as comfortable
a position as possible till Mrs. Fisher had finished
cracking.

' Asking her husband here,' said Lotty.

Mrs. Fisher looked up. Another husband ? Was
there to be no end to them ? Nor was this one, then,
a widow either ; but her husband was no doubt a decent,
respectable man, following a decent, respectable calling.

She had little hope of Mr. Wilkins; so little, that she had refrained from inquiring what he did.

' Has it ? ' persisted Lotty, as Rose said nothing.

' No,' said, Rose.

' Oh, well—to-morrow then,' said Lotty.

Rose wanted to say No again to this. Lotty would have in her place, and would, besides, have expounded all her reasons. But she could not turn herself inside out like that and invite any and everybody to come and look. How was it that Lotty, who saw so many things, didn't see stuck on her heart, and seeing keep quiet about it, the sore place that was Frederick ?

' Who is your husband ? ' asked Mrs. Fisher, carefully adjusting another nut between the crackers.

' Who should he be,' said Rose quickly, roused at once by Mrs. Fisher to irritation, ' except *Mr.* Arbuthnot ? '

' I mean, of course, what is Mr. Arbuthnot ? '

And Rose, gone painfully red at this, said after a tiny pause, ' My husband.'

Naturally Mrs. Fisher was incensed. She couldn't have believed it of this one, with her decent hair and gentle voice, that she too should be impertinent.

THAT first week the wistaria began to fade, and the flowers of the Judas-tree and peach-trees fell off and carpeted the ground with rose-colour. Then all the freesias disappeared, and the irises grew scarce. And then, while these were clearing themselves away, the double banksia roses came out, and the big summer roses suddenly flaunted gorgeously on the walls and trellises. Fortune's Yellow was one of them ; a very beautiful rose. Presently the tamarisk and the daphnes were at their best, and the lilies at their tallest. By the end of the week the fig-trees were giving shade, the plum-blossom was out among the olives, the modest weigelias appeared in their fresh pink clothes, and on the rocks sprawled masses of thick-leaved, star-shaped flowers, some vivid purple and some a clear, pale lemon.

By the end of the week, too, Mr. Wilkins arrived ; even as his wife had foreseen he would, so he did. And there were signs almost of eagerness about his acceptance of her suggestion, for he had not waited to write a letter in answer to hers, but had telegraphed.

That, surely, was eager. It showed, Scrap thought, a definite wish for reunion; and watching his wife's happy face, and aware of her desire that Mellersh should enjoy his holiday, she told herself that he would be a very unusual fool should he waste his time bothering about anybody else. 'If he isn't nice to her,' Scrap thought, 'he shall be taken to the battlements and tipped over.' For, by the end of the week, she and Mrs. Wilkins had become Caroline and Lotty to each other, and were friends.

Mrs. Wilkins had always been friends, but Scrap had struggled not to be. She had tried hard to be cautious, but how difficult was caution with Mrs. Wilkins! Free herself from every vestige of it, she was so entirely unreserved, so completely expansive, that soon Scrap, almost before she knew what she was doing, was being unreserved too. And nobody could be more unreserved than Scrap, once she let herself go.

The only difficulty about Lotty was that she was nearly always somewhere else. You couldn't catch her; you couldn't pin her down to come and talk. Scrap's fears that she would grab seemed grotesque in retrospect. Why, there was no grab in her. At dinner and after dinner were the only times one really saw her. All day long she was invisible, and would come back in the late afternoon looking a perfect sight, her hair full of bits of moss, and her freckles worse than ever. Perhaps she was making the most of her time before Mellersh arrived to do all the things she wanted to do, and meant to devote herself afterwards to going about with him, tidy and in her best clothes.

Scrap watched her, interested in spite of herself, because it seemed so extraordinary to be as happy as all that on so little. San Salvatore was beautiful, and the weather was divine; but scenery and weather had never been enough for Scrap, and how could they be enough for somebody who would have to leave them quite soon and go back to life in Hampstead? Also, there was the imminence of Mellersh, of that Mellersh from whom Lotty had so lately run. It was all very well to feel one ought to share, and to make a *beau geste* and do it, but the *beaux gestes* Scrap had known hadn't made anybody happy. Nobody really liked being the object of one, and it always meant an effort on the part of the maker. Still, she had to admit there was no effort about Lotty; it was quite plain that everything she did and said was effortless, and that she was just simply, completely happy.

And so Mrs. Wilkins was; for her doubts as to whether she had had time to become steady enough

in serenity to go on being serene in Mellersh's company
when she had it uninterruptedly right round the clock,
had gone by the middle of the week, and she felt that
nothing now could shake her. She was ready for anything. She was firmly grafted, rooted, built into heaven.
Whatever Mellersh said or did, she would not budge
an inch out of heaven, would not rouse herself a single
instant to come outside it and be cross. On the contrary,
she was going to pull him up into it beside her, and
they would sit comfortably together, suffused in light,
and laugh at how much afraid of him she used to be
in Hampstead, and at how deceitful her afraidness had
made her. But he wouldn't need much pulling. He
would come in quite naturally after a day or two,
irresistibly wafted on the scented breezes of that divine
air ; and there he would sit arrayed in stars, thought
Mrs. Wilkins, in whose mind, among much other *débris*,
floated occasional bright shreds of poetry. She laughed
to herself a little at the picture of Mellersh, that top-
hatted, black-coated, respectable family solicitor, arrayed
in stars, but she laughed affectionately, almost with
a maternal pride in how splendid he would look in such
fine clothes. ' Poor lamb,' she murmured to herself
affectionately. And added, ' What he wants is a
thorough airing.'

This was during the first half of the week. By the

beginning of the last half, at the end of which Mr. Wilkins arrived, she left off even assuring herself that she was unshakeable, that she was permeated beyond altering by the atmosphere, she no longer thought of it or noticed it; she took it for granted. If one may say so, and she certainly said so, not only to herself but also to Lady Caroline, she had found her celestial legs.

Contrary to Mrs. Fisher's idea of the seemly—but of course contrary; what else would one expect of Mrs. Wilkins ?—she did not go to meet her husband at Mezzago, but merely walked down to the point where Beppo's fly would leave him and his luggage in the street of Castagneto. Mrs. Fisher disliked the arrival of Mr. Wilkins, and was sure that anybody who could have married Mrs. Wilkins must be at least of an injudicious disposition, but a husband, whatever his disposition, should be properly met. Mr. Fisher had always been properly met. Never once in his married life had he gone unmet at a station, nor had he ever not been seen off. These observances, these courtesies, strengthened the bonds of marriage, and made the husband feel he could rely on his wife's being always there. Always being there was the essential secret for a wife. What would have become of Mr. Fisher if she had neglected to act on this principle she preferred not to think. Enough things became of him as it was; for whatever one's care in stopping up, married life yet seemed to contain chinks.

But Mrs. Wilkins took no pains. She just walked down the hill singing—Mrs. Fisher could hear her—and picked up her husband in the street as casually as if he were a pin. The three others, still in bed, for it was not nearly time to get up, heard her as she passed beneath their windows down the zigzag path to meet Mr. Wilkins, who was coming by the morning train, and Scrap smiled, and Rose sighed, and Mrs. Fisher rang her bell and desired Francesca to bring her her breakfast in her room. All three had breakfast that day in their rooms, moved by a common instinct to take cover.

Scrap always breakfasted in bed, but she had the same instinct for cover, and during breakfast she made plans for spending the whole day where she was. Perhaps, though, it wouldn't be as necessary that day as the next. That day, Scrap calculated, Mellersh would be provided for. He would want to have a bath, and having a bath at San Salvatore was an elaborate business, a real adventure if one had a hot one in the bathroom, and it took a lot of time. It involved the attendance of the entire staff—Domenico and the boy Guiseppe coaxing the patent stove to burn, restraining it when it burnt too fiercely, using the bellows to it when it threatened to go out, relighting it when it did go out;

Francesca anxiously hovering over the tap regulating its trickle, because if it were turned on too full the water instantly ran cold, and if not full enough the stove blew up inside and mysteriously flooded the house; and Costanza and Angela running up and down bringing pails of hot water from the kitchen to eke out what the tap did.

This bath had been put in lately, and was at once the pride and the terror of the servants. It was very patent. Nobody quite understood it. There were long printed instructions as to its right treatment hanging on the wall, in which the word *pericoloso* recurred. When Mrs. Fisher, proceeding on her arrival to the bathroom, saw this word, she went back to her room again and ordered a sponge-bath instead; and when the others found what using the bathroom meant, and how reluctant the servants were to leave them alone with the stove, and how Francesca positively refused to, and stayed with her back turned watching the tap, and how the remaining servants waited anxiously outside the door till the bather came safely out again, they too had sponge-baths brought into their rooms instead.

Mr. Wilkins, however, was a man, and would be sure to want a big bath. Having it, Scrap calculated, would keep him busy for a long while. Then he would unpack, and then, after his night in the train, he would probably sleep till the evening. So would he be provided for the whole of that day, and not be let loose on them till dinner.

Therefore Scrap came to the conclusion she would be quite safe in the garden that day, and got up as usual after breakfast, and dawdled as usual through her dressing, listening with a slightly cocked ear to the sounds of Mr. Wilkins's arrival, of his luggage being carried into Lotty's room on the other side of the landing, of his educated voice as he inquired of Lotty, first, ' Do I give this fellow anything ? ' and immediately afterwards, ' Can I have a hot bath ? '—of Lotty's voice cheerfully assuring him that he needn't give the fellow anything because he was the gardener, and that yes, he could have a hot bath ; and soon after this the landing was filled with the familiar noises of wood being brought, of water being brought, of feet running, of tongues vociferating—in fact, with the preparation of the bath.

Scrap finished dressing, and then loitered at her window, waiting till she should hear Mr. Wilkins go into the bathroom. When he was safely there she would slip out and settle herself in her garden and resume her inquiries into the probable meaning of her life. She was getting on with her inquiries. She dozed much less frequently, and was beginning to be inclined to agree that tawdry was the word to apply to her past. Also she was afraid that her future looked black.

There—she could hear Mr. Wilkins's educated voice again. Lotty's door had opened, and he was coming out of it asking his way to the bathroom.

'It's where you see the crowd,' Lotty's voice answered,—still a cheerful voice, Scrap was glad to notice.

His steps went along the landing, and Lotty's steps seemed to go downstairs, and then there seemed to be a brief altercation at the bathroom door,—hardly so much an altercation as a chorus of vociferations on one side and a wordless determination, Scrap judged, to have a bath by oneself on the other.

Mr. Wilkins knew no Italian, and the expression *pericoloso* left him precisely as it found him,—or would have if he had seen it, but naturally he took no notice of the printed matter on the wall. He firmly closed the door on the servants, resisting Domenico, who tried to the last to press through, and locked himself in as a man should for his bath, judicially considering, as he made his simple preparations for getting in, the singular standard of behaviour of these foreigners who, both male and female, apparently wished to stay with him while he bathed. In Finland, he had heard, the female natives not only were present on such occasions but actually washed the bath-taking traveller. He had not heard, however, that this was true too of Italy, which somehow seemed much nearer civilisation,—perhaps because one went there, and did not go to Finland.

Impartially examining this reflection, and carefully balancing the claims to civilisation of Italy and Finland, Mr. Wilkins got into the bath and turned off the tap. Naturally he turned off the tap. It was what one did. But on the instructions, printed in red letters, was a paragraph saying that the tap should not be turned off as long as there was still fire in the stove. It should be left on—not much on, but on—until the fire was quite out; otherwise, and here again was the word *pericoloso*, the stove would blow up.

Mr. Wilkins got into the bath, turned off the tap, and the stove blew up, exactly as the printed instructions said it would. It blew up, fortunately, only in its inside, but it blew up with a terrific noise, and Mr. Wilkins leapt out of the bath and rushed to the door, and only the instinct born of years of training made him snatch up a towel as he rushed.

Scrap, half-way across the landing on her way out of doors, heard the explosion.

'Good heavens,' she thought, remembering the instructions, ' there goes Mr. Wilkins ! '

And she ran towards the head of the stairs to call the

servants, and as she ran, out ran Mr. Wilkins clutching his towel, and they ran into each other.

'That damned bath!' cried Mr. Wilkins, perhaps for the only time in his life forgetting himself; but he was upset.

Here was an introduction. Mr. Wilkins, imperfectly concealed in his towel, his shoulders exposed at one end and his legs at the other, and Lady Caroline Dester, to meet whom he had swallowed all his anger with his wife and come out to Italy.

For Lotty in her letter had told him who was at San Salvatore besides herself and Mrs. Arbuthnot, and Mr. Wilkins at once had perceived that this was an opportunity which might never recur. Lotty had merely said, 'There are two other women here, Mrs. Fisher and Lady Caroline Dester,' but that was enough. He knew all about the Droitwiches, their wealth, their connections, their place in history, and the power they had, should they choose to exert it, of making yet another solicitor happy by adding him to those they already employed. Some people employed one solicitor for one branch of their affairs, and another for another. The affairs of the Droitwiches must have many branches. He had also heard—for it was, he considered, part of his business to hear, and having heard to remember—of the beauty of their only daughter. Even if the

Droitwiches themselves did not need his services, their daughter might. Beauty led one into strange situations; advice could never come amiss. And should none of them, neither parents nor daughter nor any of their brilliant sons, need him in his professional capacity, it yet was obviously a most valuable acquaintance to make. It opened up vistas. It swelled with possibilities. He might go on living in Hampstead for years, and not again come across such another chance.

Directly his wife's letter reached him he telegraphed and packed. This was business. He was not a man to lose time when it came to business; nor was he a man to jeopardise a chance by neglecting to be amiable. He met his wife perfectly amiably, aware that amiability under such circumstances was wisdom. Besides, he actually felt amiable,—very. For once, Lotty was really helping him. He kissed her affectionately on getting out of Beppo's fly, and was afraid she must have got up extremely early; he made no complaints of the steepness of the walk up; he told her pleasantly of his journey, and, when called upon, obediently admired the views. It was all neatly mapped out in his mind, what he was going to do that first day,—have a shave, have a bath, put on clean clothes, sleep a while, and then would come lunch and the introduction to Lady Caroline.

In the train he had selected the words of his greeting,

going over them with care,—some slight expression of
his gratification in meeting one of whom he, in common
with the whole world, had heard—but of course put
delicately, very delicately ; some slight reference to her
distinguished parents and the part her family had
played in the history of England—made, of course,
with proper tact ; a sentence or two about her eldest
brother Lord Winchcombe, who had won his V.C. in
the late war under circumstances which could only
cause—he might or might not add this—every Englishman's heart to beat higher than ever with pride, and
the first steps towards what might well be the turning-
point in his career would have been taken.

And here he was . . . no, it was too terrible, what
could be more terrible ?   Only a towel on, water running
off his legs, and that exclamation. He knew at once
the lady was Lady Caroline,—the minute the exclama·
tion was out he knew it. Rarely did Mr. Wilkins use
that word, and never, never in the presence of a lady
or a client. While as for the towel—why had he come ?
Why had he not stayed in Hampstead ? It would be
impossible to live this down.

But Mr. Wilkins was reckoning without Scrap.
She, indeed, screwed up her face at the first flash of
him on her astonished sight in an enormous effort not
to laugh, and having choked the laughter down and

got her face serious again, she said as composedly as if he had had all his clothes on, ' How do you do.'

What perfect tact. Mr. Wilkins could have worshipped her. This exquisite ignoring. Blue blood, of course, coming out.

Overwhelmed with gratitude he took her offered hand and said ' How do you do,' in his turn, and merely to repeat the ordinary words seemed magically to restore the situation to the normal. Indeed, he was so much relieved, and it was so natural to be shaking hands, to be conventionally greeting, that he forgot he had only a towel on and his professional manner came back to him. He forgot what he was looking like, but he did not forget that this was Lady Caroline Dester, the lady he had come all the way to Italy to see, and he did not forget that it was in her face, her lovely and important face, that he had flung his terrible exclamation. He must at once entreat her forgiveness. To say such a word to a lady—to any lady, but of all ladies to just this one . . .

' I'm afraid I used unpardonable language,' began Mr. Wilkins very earnestly, as earnestly and ceremoniously as if he had had his clothes on.

' I thought it most appropriate,' said Scrap, who was used to damns.

Mr. Wilkins was incredibly relieved and soothed by

this answer. No offence, then, taken. Blue blood
again. Only blue blood could afford such a liberal,
such an understanding attitude.

' It is Lady Caroline Dester, is it not, to whom I am
speaking ? ' he asked, his voice sounding even more
carefully cultivated than usual, for he had to restrain
too much pleasure, too much relief, too much of
the joy of the pardoned and the shriven from getting
into it.

' Yes,' said Scrap ; and for the life of her she couldn't
help smiling. She couldn't help it. She hadn't meant
to smile at Mr. Wilkins, not ever ; but really he looked
—and then his voice on the top of the rest of him,
oblivious of the towel and his legs, and talking just like
a church.

' Allow me to introduce myself,' said Mr. Wilkins,
with the ceremony of the drawing-room. ' My name is
Mellersh-Wilkins.'

And he instinctively held out his hand a second time
at the words.

' I thought perhaps it was,' said Scrap, a second time
having hers shaken and a second time unable not to
smile.

He was about to proceed to the first of the graceful
tributes he had prepared in the train, oblivious, as he
could not see himself, that he was without his clothes,

when the servants came running up the stairs and, simultaneously, Mrs. Fisher appeared in the doorway of her sitting-room. For all this had happened very quickly, and the servants away in the kitchen, and Mrs. Fisher pacing her battlements, had not had time on hearing the noise to appear before the second hand-shake.

The servants when they heard the dreaded noise knew at once what had happened, and rushed straight into the bathroom to try and staunch the flood, taking no notice of the figure on the landing in the towel, but Mrs. Fisher did not know what the noise could be, and coming out of her room to inquire stood rooted on the door-sill.

It was enough to root anybody. Lady Caroline shaking hands with what evidently, if he had had clothes on, would have been Mrs. Wilkins's husband, and both of them conversing just as if——

Then Scrap became aware of Mrs. Fisher. She turned to her at once. ' Do let me,' she said gracefully, ' introduce Mr. Mellersh-Wilkins. He has just come. This,' she added, turning to Mr. Wilkins, ' is Mrs. Fisher.'

And Mr. Wilkins, nothing if not courteous, reacted at once to the conventional formula. First he bowed to the elderly lady in the doorway, then he crossed over to her, his wet feet leaving footprints as he went, and having got to her he politely held out his hand.

'It is a pleasure,' said Mr. Wilkins in his carefully modulated voice, ' to meet a friend of my wife's.'

Scrap melted away down into the garden.

XV

THE strange effect of this incident was that when they met that evening at dinner both Mrs. Fisher and Lady Caroline had a singular feeling of secret understanding with Mr. Wilkins. He could not be to them as other men. He could not be to them as he would have been if they had met him in his clothes. There was a sense of broken ice ; they felt at once intimate and indulgent ; almost they felt to him as nurses do,—as those feel who have assisted either patients or young children at their baths. They were acquainted with Mr. Wilkins's legs.

What Mrs. Fisher said to him that morning in her first shock will never be known, but what Mr. Wilkins said to her in reply, when reminded by what she was saying of his condition, was so handsome in its apology, so proper in its confusion, that she had ended by being quite sorry for him and completely placated. After all, it was an accident, and nobody could help accidents. And when she saw him next at dinner, dressed, polished,

spotless as to linen and sleek as to hair, she felt this
singular sensation of a secret understanding with him
and, added to it, of a kind of almost personal pride in
his appearance, now that he was dressed, which presently
extended in some subtle way to an almost personal
pride in everything he said.

There was no doubt whatever in Mrs. Fisher's mind
that a man was infinitely preferable as a companion
to a woman.   Mr. Wilkins's presence and conversation
at once raised the standard of the dinner-table from
that of a bear garden—yes, a bear garden—to that of
a civilised social gathering.   He talked as men talk,
about interesting subjects, and, though most courteous
to Lady Caroline, showed no traces of dissolving into
simpers and idiocy whenever he addressed her.   He was,
indeed, precisely as courteous to Mrs. Fisher herself ;
and when for the first time at that table politics were
introduced, he listened to her with the proper seriousness
on her exhibiting a desire to speak, and treated her
opinions with the attention they deserved.   He appeared
to think much as she did about Lloyd George, and in
regard to literature he was equally sound.   In fact
there was real conversation, and he liked nuts.   How
he could have married Mrs. Wilkins was a mystery.

Lotty, for her part, looked on with round eyes.
She had expected Mellersh to take at least two days

before he got to this stage, but the San Salvatore spell had worked instantly. It was not only that he was pleasant at dinner, for she had always seen him pleasant at dinners with other people, but he had been pleasant all day privately,—so pleasant that he had complimented her on her looks while she was brushing out her hair, and kissed her. Kissed her! And it was neither good-morning nor good-night.

Well, this being so, she would put off telling him the truth about her nest-egg, and about Rose not being his hostess after all, till next day. Pity to spoil things. She had been going to blurt it out as soon as he had had a rest, but it did seem a pity to disturb such a very beautiful frame of mind as that of Mellersh this first day. Let him too get more firmly fixed in heaven. Once fixed he wouldn't mind anything.

Her face sparkled with delight at the instantaneous effect of San Salvatore. Even the catastrophe of the bath, of which she had been told when she came in from the garden, had not shaken him. Of course all that he had needed was a holiday. What a brute she had been to him when he wanted to take her himself to Italy. But this arrangement, as it happened, was ever so much better, though not through any merit of hers. She talked and laughed gaily, not a shred of fear of him left in her, and even when she said, struck by his spotlessness, that he looked so clean that one could eat one's dinner off him, and Scrap laughed, Mellersh laughed too. He would have minded that at home, supposing that at home she had had the spirit to say it.

It was a successful evening. Scrap, whenever she looked at Mr. Wilkins, saw him in his towel, dripping water, and felt indulgent. Mrs. Fisher was delighted with him. Rose was a dignified hostess in Mr. Wilkins's eyes, quiet and dignified, and he admired the way she waived her right to preside at the head of the table,— as a graceful compliment, of course, to Mrs. Fisher's age. Mrs. Arbuthnot was, opined Mr. Wilkins, naturally retiring. She was the most retiring of the three ladies. He had met her before dinner alone for a moment in the drawing-room, and had expressed in appropriate language his sense of her kindness in wishing him to join her party, and she had been retiring. Was she shy? Probably. She had blushed, and murmured as if in deprecation, and then the others had come in. At dinner she talked least. He would, of course, become better acquainted with her during the next few days, and it would be a pleasure, he was sure.

Meanwhile Lady Caroline was all and more than all Mr. Wilkins had imagined, and had received his speeches, worked in skilfully between the courses, graciously ; Mrs. Fisher was the exact old lady he had been hoping to come across all his professional life ; and Lotty had not only immensely improved, but was obviously *au mieux*—Mr. Wilkins knew what was necessary in French —with Lady Caroline. He had been much tormented during the day by the thought of how he had stood conversing with Lady Caroline forgetful of his not being dressed, and had at last written her a note most deeply apologising, and beseeching her to overlook his amazing, his incomprehensible obliviousness, to which she had replied in pencil on the back of the envelope, ' Don't worry.' And he had obeyed her commands, and had put it from him. The result was he was now in great contentment. Before going to sleep that night he pinched his wife's ear. She was amazed. These endearments . . .

What is more, the morning brought no relapse in Mr. Wilkins, and he kept up to this high level throughout the day, in spite of its being the first day of the second week, and therefore pay day.

Its being pay day precipitated Lotty's confession, which she had, when it came to the point, been inclined to put off a little longer. She was not afraid, she dared anything, but Mellersh was in such an admirable humour, —why risk clouding it just yet ? When, however, soon after breakfast Costanza appeared with a pile of very dirty little bits of paper covered with sums in pencil,

and having knocked at Mrs. Fisher's door and been
sent away, and at Lady Caroline's door and been sent
away, and at Rose's door and had no answer because
Rose had gone out, she waylaid Lotty, who was showing
Mellersh over the house, and pointed to the bits of paper
and talked very rapidly and loud, and shrugged her
shoulders a great deal, and kept on pointing at the bits
of paper, Lotty remembered that a week had passed
without anybody paying anything to any one, and that
the moment had come to settle up.

'Does this good lady want something?' inquired
Mr. Wilkins mellifluously.

'Money,' said Lotty.

'Money?'

'It's the housekeeping bills.'

'Well, you have nothing to do with those,' said Mr.
Wilkins serenely.

'Oh yes, I have——'

And the confession was precipitated.

It was wonderful how Mellersh took it. One would
have imagined that his sole idea about the nest-egg
had always been that it should be lavished on just this.
He did not, as he would have done at home, cross-
examine her; he accepted everything as it came pouring
out, about her fibs and all, and when she had finished
and said, 'You have every right to be angry, I think,

but I hope you won't be and will forgive me instead,' he merely asked, 'What can be more beneficial than such a holiday?'

Whereupon she put her arm through his and held it tight and said, 'Oh, Mellersh, you really are too sweet!' —her face red with pride in him.

That he should so quickly assimilate the atmosphere, that he should at once become nothing but kindness, showed surely what a real affinity he had with good and beautiful things. He belonged quite naturally in this place of heavenly calm. He was—extraordinary how she had misjudged him—by nature a child of light. Fancy not minding the dreadful fibs she had gone in for before leaving home; fancy passing even those over without comment. Wonderful. Yet not wonderful, for wasn't he in heaven? In heaven nobody minded any of those done-with things, one didn't even trouble to forgive and forget, one was much too happy. She pressed his arm tight in her gratitude and appreciation; and though he did not withdraw his, neither did he respond to her pressure. Mr. Wilkins was of a cool habit, and rarely had any real wish to press.

Meanwhile Costanza, perceiving that she had lost the Wilkinses' ear, had gone back to Mrs. Fisher, who at least understood Italian, besides being clearly in the servants' eyes the one of the party marked down by age and appearance to pay the bills; and to her, while Mrs. Fisher put the final touches to her toilette, for she was preparing, by means of putting on a hat and veil and feather boa and gloves, to go for her first stroll in the lower garden—positively her first since her arrival—she explained that unless she was given money to pay the last week's bills the shops of Castagneto would refuse credit for the current week's food. Not even credit would they give, affirmed Costanza, who had been spending a great deal and was anxious to pay all her relations what was owed them and also to find out how her mistresses took it, for that day's meals. Soon it would be the hour of *colazione*, and how could there be *colazione* without meat, without fish, without eggs, without——

Mrs. Fisher took the bills out of her hand and looked at the total; and she was so much astonished by its size, so much horrified by the extravagance to which it testified, that she sat down at her writing-table to go into the thing thoroughly.

Costanza had a very bad half-hour. She had not supposed it was in the English to be so mercenary. And then *la Vecchia*, as she was called in the kitchen, knew so much Italian, and with a doggedness that filled Costanza with shame on her behalf, for such conduct was the last one expected from the noble English, she went through item after item, requiring, and persisting till she got them, explanations.

There were no explanations, except that Costanza had had one glorious week of doing exactly as she chose, of splendid unbridled licence, and that this was the result.

Costanza, having no explanations, wept. It was miserable to think she would have to cook from now on under watchfulness, under suspicion; and what would her relations say when they found the orders they received were whittled down? They would say she had no influence; they would despise her.

Costanza wept, but Mrs. Fisher was unmoved. In slow and splendid Italian, with the roll of the cantos of the *Inferno*, she informed her that she would pay no bills till the following week, and that meanwhile the food was to be precisely as good as ever, and at a quarter the cost.

Costanza threw up her hands.

Next week, proceeded Mrs. Fisher unmoved, if she found this had been so she would pay the whole. Otherwise—she paused; for what she would do otherwise she did not know herself. But she paused and looked impenetrable, majestic and menacing, and Costanza was cowed.

Then Mrs. Fisher, having dismissed her with a gesture,

went in search of Lady Caroline to complain. She had
been under the impression that Lady Caroline ordered
the meals and therefore was responsible for the prices,
but now it appeared that the cook had been left to do
exactly as she pleased ever since they got there, which
of course was simply disgraceful.

Scrap was not in her bedroom, but the room, on
Mrs. Fisher's opening the door, for she suspected her
of being in it and only pretending not to hear the knock,
was still flowerlike from her presence.

'Scent,' sniffed Mrs. Fisher, shutting it again; and
she wished Carlyle could have had five minutes' straight
talk with this young woman. And yet—perhaps even
he——

She went downstairs to go into the garden in search
of her, and in the hall encountered Mr. Wilkins. He
had his hat on, and was lighting a cigar.

Indulgent as Mrs. Fisher felt towards Mr. Wilkins,
and peculiarly and even mystically related after the
previous morning's encounter, she yet could not like a
cigar in the house. Out of doors she endured it, but
it was not necessary, when out of doors was such a big
place, to indulge the habit indoors. Even Mr. Fisher,
who had been, she should say, a man originally ten-
acious of habits, had quite soon after marriage got out
of this one.

However, Mr. Wilkins, snatching off his hat on seeing her, instantly threw the cigar away. He threw it into the water a great jar of arum lilies presumably contained, and Mrs. Fisher, aware of the value men attach to their newly-lit cigars, could not but be impressed by this immediate and magnificent *amende honorable.*

But the cigar did not reach the water. It got caught in the lilies, and smoked on by itself among them, a strange and depraved-looking object.

'Where are you going to, my prett——' began Mr. Wilkins, advancing towards Mrs. Fisher; but he broke off just in time.

Was it morning spirits impelling him to address Mrs. Fisher in the terms of a nursery rhyme? He wasn't even aware that he knew the thing. Most strange. What could have put it, at such a moment, into his self-possessed head? He felt great respect for Mrs. Fisher, and would not for the world have insulted her by addressing her as a maid, pretty or otherwise. He wished to stand well with her. She was a woman of parts, and also, he suspected, of property. At breakfast they had been most pleasant together, and he had been struck by her apparent intimacy with well-known persons. Victorians, of course; but it was restful to talk about them after the strain of his brother-in-law's Georgian parties on Hampstead Heath. He and she

were getting on famously, he felt.   She already showed
all the symptoms of presently wishing to become a client.
Not for the world would he offend her.   He turned a
little cold at the narrowness of his escape.

She had not, however, noticed.

'You are going out,' he said very politely, all readiness should she confirm his assumption to accompany
her.

'I want to find Lady Caroline,' said Mrs. Fisher,
going towards the glass door leading into the top garden.

'An agreeable quest,' remarked Mr. Wilkins.   'May
I assist in the search ?   Allow me——' he added,
opening the door for her.

'She usually sits over in that corner behind the
bushes,' said Mrs. Fisher.   'And I don't know about
its being an agreeable quest.   She has been letting the
bills run up in the most terrible fashion, and needs a
good scolding.'

'Lady Caroline ? ' said Mr. Wilkins, unable to follow
such an attitude.   'What has Lady Caroline, if I may
inquire, to do with the bills here ? '

'The housekeeping was left to her, and as we all
share alike it ought to have been a matter of honour
with her——'

'But—Lady Caroline housekeeping for the party
here ?   A party which includes my wife ?   My dear

lady, you render me speechless. Do you not know she is the daughter of the Droitwiches ? '

' Oh, is that who she is,' said Mrs. Fisher, scrunching heavily over the pebbles towards the hidden corner. ' Well, that accounts for it. The muddle that man Droitwich made in his department in the war was a national scandal. It amounted to misappropriation of the public funds.'

' But it is impossible, I assure you, to expect the daughter of the Droitwiches——' began Mr. Wilkins earnestly.

' The Droitwiches,' interrupted Mrs. Fisher, ' are neither here nor there. Duties undertaken should be performed. I don't intend my money to be squandered for the sake of any Droitwiches.'

A headstrong old lady. Perhaps not so easy to deal with as he had hoped. But how wealthy. Only the consciousness of great wealth would make her snap her fingers in this manner at the Droitwiches. Lotty, on being questioned, had been vague about her circumstances, and had described her house as a mausoleum with gold-fish swimming about in it ; but now he was sure she was more than very well off. Still, he wished he had not joined her at this moment, for he had no sort of desire to be present at such a spectacle as the scolding of Lady Caroline Dester.

Again, however, he was reckoning without Scrap. Whatever she felt when she looked up and beheld Mr. Wilkins discovering her corner on the very first morning, nothing but angelicness appeared on her face. She took her feet off the parapet on Mrs. Fisher's sitting down on it, and listening gravely to her opening remarks as to her not having any money to fling about in reckless and uncontrolled household expenditure, interrupted her flow by pulling one of the cushions from behind her head and offering it to her.

'Sit on this,' said Scrap, holding it out. 'You'll be more comfortable.'

Mr. Wilkins leapt to relieve her of it.

'Oh, thanks,' said Mrs. Fisher, interrupted.

It was difficult to get into the swing again. Mr. Wilkins inserted the cushion solicitously between the slightly raised Mrs. Fisher and the stone of the parapet, and again she had to say 'Thanks.' It interrupted. Besides, Lady Caroline said nothing in her defence; she only looked at her, and listened with the face of an attentive angel.

It seemed to Mr. Wilkins that it must be difficult to scold a Dester who looked like that and so exquisitely said nothing. Mrs. Fisher, he was glad to see, gradually found it difficult herself, for her severity slackened, and she ended by saying lamely, 'You ought to have told me you were not doing it.'

'I didn't know you thought I was,' said the lovely voice.

'I would now like to know,' said Mrs. Fisher, 'what you propose to do for the rest of the time here.'

'Nothing,' said Scrap, smiling.

'Nothing ? Do you mean to say——'

'If I may be allowed, ladies,' interposed Mr. Wilkins in his suavest professional manner, 'to make a suggestion '—they both looked at him, and remembering him as they first saw him felt indulgent—'I would advise you not to spoil a delightful holiday with worries over housekeeping.'

'Exactly,' said Mrs. Fisher. 'It is what I intend to avoid.'

'Most sensible,' said Mr. Wilkins. 'Why not, then,' he continued, 'allow the cook—an excellent cook, by the way—so much a head *per diem* '—Mr. Wilkins knew what was necessary in Latin—' and tell her that for this sum she must cater for you, and not only cater but cater as well as ever ? One could easily reckon it out. The charges of a moderate hotel, for instance, would do as a basis, halved, or perhaps even quartered.'

'And this week that has just passed ? ' asked Mrs. Fisher. 'The terrible bills of this first week ? What about them ? '

'They shall be my present to San Salvatore,' said

Scrap, who didn't like the idea of Lotty's nest-egg being reduced so much beyond what she was prepared for.

There was a silence. The ground was cut from under Mrs. Fisher's feet.

' Of course if you choose to throw your money about——' she said at last, disapproving but immensely relieved, while Mr. Wilkins was rapt in the contemplation of the precious qualities of blue blood. This readiness, for instance, not to trouble about money, this free-handedness—it was not only what one admired in others, admired in others perhaps more than anything else, but it was extraordinarily useful to the professional classes. When met with it should be encouraged by warmth of reception. Mrs. Fisher was not warm. She accepted— from which he deduced that with her wealth went close-ness—but she accepted grudgingly. Presents were presents, and one did not look them in this manner in the mouth, he felt ; and if Lady Caroline found her pleasure in presenting his wife and Mrs. Fisher with their entire food for a week, it was their part to accept gracefully. One should not discourage gifts.

On behalf of his wife, then, Mr. Wilkins expressed what she would wish to express, and remarking to Lady Caroline—with a touch of lightness, for so should gifts be accepted in order to avoid embarrassing the donor— that she had in that case been his wife's hostess since her arrival, he turned almost gaily to Mrs. Fisher and pointed out that she and his wife must now jointly write Lady Caroline the customary letter of thanks for hospitality. 'A Collins,' said Mr. Wilkins, who knew what was necessary in literature. 'I prefer the name Collins for such a letter to either that of Board and Lodging or Bread and Butter. Let us call it a Collins.'

Scrap smiled, and held out her cigarette case. Mrs. Fisher could not help being mollified. A way out of waste was going to be found, thanks to Mr. Wilkins, and she hated waste quite as much as having to pay for it ; also a way was found out of housekeeping. For a moment she had thought that if everybody tried to force her into housekeeping on her brief holiday by their own indifference (Lady Caroline), or inability to speak Italian (the other two), she would have to send for Kate Lumley after all. Kate could do it. Kate and she had learnt Italian together. Kate would only be allowed to come on condition that she did do it.

But this was much better, this way of Mr. Wilkins's. Really a most superior man. There was nothing like an intelligent, not too young man for profitable and pleasurable companionship. And when she got up, the business for which she had come being settled, and said she now intended to take a little stroll before lunch, Mr. Wilkins did not stay with Lady Caroline, as most of the men she had known would, she was afraid, have wanted to—he asked to be permitted to go and stroll with her; so that he evidently definitely preferred conversation to faces. A sensible, companionable man. A clever, well-read man. A man of the world. A man. She was very glad indeed she had not written to Kate the other day. What did she want with Kate? She had found a better companion.

But Mr. Wilkins did not go with Mrs. Fisher because of her conversation, but because, when she got up and he got up because she got up, intending merely to bow her out of the recess, Lady Caroline had put her feet up on the parapet again, and arranging her head sideways in the cushions had shut her eyes.

The daughter of the Droitwiches desired to go to sleep.

It was not for him, by remaining, to prevent her.

XVI

AND so the second week began, and all was harmony. The arrival of Mr. Wilkins, instead of, as three of the party had feared and the fourth had only been protected from fearing by her burning faith in the effect on him of San Salvatore, disturbing such harmony as there was, increased it. He fitted in. He was determined to please, and he did please. He was most amiable to his wife—not only in public, which she was used to, but in private, when he certainly wouldn't have been if he hadn't wanted to. He did want to. He was so much obliged to her, so much pleased with her, for making him acquainted with Lady Caroline, that he felt really fond of her. Also proud; for there must be, he reflected, a good deal more in her than he had supposed, for Lady Caroline to have become so intimate with her and so affectionate. And the more he treated her as though she were really very nice, the more Lotty expanded and became really very nice, and the more he, affected in his turn, became really very nice himself; so that they

253

went round and round, not in a vicious but in a highly virtuous circle.

Positively, for him, Mellersh petted her. There was at no time much pet in Mellersh, because he was by nature a cool man ; yet such was the influence on him of, as Lotty supposed, San Salvatore, that in this second week he sometimes pinched both her ears, one after the other, instead of only one ; and Lotty, marvelling at such rapidly developing affectionateness, wondered what he would do, should he continue at this rate, in the third week, when her supply of ears would have come to an end.

He was particularly nice about the washstand, and genuinely desirous of not taking up too much of the space in the small bedroom. Quick to respond, Lotty was even more desirous not to be in his way ; and the room became the scene of many an affectionate *combat de générosité*, each of which left them more pleased with each other than ever. He did not again have a bath in the bathroom, though it was mended and ready for him, but got up and went down every morning to the sea, and in spite of the cool nights making the water cold early had his dip as a man should, and came up to breakfast rubbing his hands and feeling, as he told Mrs. Fisher, prepared for anything.

Lotty's belief in the irresistible influence of the

heavenly atmosphere of San Salvatore being thus obviously justified, and Mr. Wilkins, whom Rose knew as alarming and Scrap had pictured as icily unkind, being so evidently a changed man, both Rose and Scrap began to think there might after all be something in what Lotty insisted on, and that San Salvatore did work purgingly on the character.

They were the more inclined to think so in that they too felt a working going on inside themselves : they felt more cleared, both of them, that second week,—Scrap in her thoughts, many of which were now quite nice thoughts, real amiable ones about her parents and relations, with a glimmer in them of recognition of the extraordinary benefits she had received at the hands of—what ? Fate ? Providence ?—anyhow of something, and of how, having received them, she had misused them by failing to be happy ; and Rose in her bosom, which though it still yearned, yearned to some purpose, for she was reaching the conclusion that merely inactively to yearn was no use at all, and that she must either by some means stop her yearning or give it at least a chance—remote, but still a chance—of being quieted by writing to Frederick and asking him to come out.

If Mr. Wilkins could be changed, thought Rose, why not Frederick ? How wonderful it would be, how too

wonderful, if the place worked on him too and were able
to make them even a little understand each other, even
a little be friends.   Rose, so far had loosening and dis-
integration gone on in her character, now was beginning
to think her obstinate strait-lacedness about his books
and her austere absorption in good works had been
foolish and perhaps even wrong.   He was her husband,
and she had frightened him away.   She had frightened
love away, precious love, and that couldn't be good.
Was not Lotty right when she said the other day that
nothing at all except love mattered ?   Nothing certainly seemed much use unless it was built up on love.
But once frightened away, could it ever come back ?
Yes, it might in that beauty, it might in the atmosphere
of happiness Lotty and San Salvatore seemed between
them to spread round like some divine infection.

She had, however, to get him there first, and he
certainly couldn't be got there if she didn't write and
tell him where she was.

She would write.   She must write ; for if she did
there was at least a chance of his coming, and if she
didn't there was manifestly none.   And then, once here
in this loveliness, with everything so soft and kind and
sweet all round, it would be easier to tell him, to try and
explain, to ask for something different, for at least an
attempt at something different in their lives in the

future, instead of the blankness of separation, the cold
—oh, the cold—of nothing at all but the great windiness
of faith, the great bleakness of works. Why, one person
in the world, one single person belonging to one, of one's
very own, to talk to, to take care of, to love, to be
interested in, was worth more than all the speeches on
platforms and the compliments of chairmen in the
world. It was also worth more—Rose couldn't help it,
the thought would come—than all the prayers.

These thoughts were not head thoughts, like Scrap's,
who was altogether free from yearnings, but bosom
thoughts. They lodged in the bosom ; it was in the
bosom that Rose ached, and felt so dreadfully lonely.
And when her courage failed her, as it did on most days,
and it seemed impossible to write to Frederick, she would
look at Mr. Wilkins and revive.

There he was, a changed man. There he was, going
into that small, uncomfortable room every night, that
room whose proximities had been Lotty's only mis-
giving, and coming out of it in the morning, and Lotty
coming out of it too, both of them as unclouded and as
nice to each other as when they went in. And hadn't
he, so critical at home, Lotty had told her, of the least
thing going wrong, emerged from the bath catastrophe
as untouched in spirit as Shadrach, Meshach and
Abed-nego were untouched in body when they emerged

from the fire ?   Miracles were happening in this place.
If they could happen to Mr. Wilkins, why not to
Frederick ?

She got up quickly. Yes, she would write. She
would go and write to him at once.

But suppose——

She paused. Suppose he didn't answer. Suppose
he didn't even answer.

And she sat down again to think a little longer.

In these hesitations did Rose spend most of the
second week.

Then there was Mrs. Fisher. Her restlessness
increased that second week. It increased to such an
extent that she might just as well not have had her
private sitting-room at all, for she could no longer sit.
Not for ten minutes together could Mrs. Fisher sit.
And added to the restlessness, as the days of the second
week proceeded on their way, she had a curious sensation,
which worried her, of rising sap. She knew the feeling,
because she had sometimes had it in childhood in
specially swift springs, when the lilacs and the syringas
seemed to rush out into blossom in a single night, but
it was strange to have it again after over fifty years.
She would have liked to remark on the sensation to
some one, but she was ashamed. It was such an absurd
sensation at her age. Yet oftener and oftener, and

every day more and more, did Mrs. Fisher have a
ridiculous feeling as if she were presently going to
burgeon.

Sternly she tried to frown the unseemly sensation
down. Burgeon, indeed. She had heard of dried staffs,
pieces of mere dead wood, suddenly putting forth fresh
leaves, but only in legend. She was not in legend.
She knew perfectly what was due to herself. Dignity
demanded that she should have nothing to do with
fresh leaves at her age; and yet there it was,—the
feeling that presently, that at any moment now, she
might crop out all green.

Mrs. Fisher was upset. There were many things
she disliked more than anything else, and one was when
the elderly imagined they felt young and behaved
accordingly. Of course they only imagined it, they
were only deceiving themselves; but how deplorable
were the results. She herself had grown old as people
should grow old,—steadily and firmly. No interruptions, no belated after-glows and spasmodic returns.
If, after all these years, she were now going to be
deluded into some sort of unsuitable breaking-out,
how humiliating.

Indeed she was thankful, that second week, that
Kate Lumley was not there. It would be most unpleasant, should anything different occur in her

behaviour, to have Kate looking on. Kate had known
her all her life. She felt she could let herself go—here
Mrs. Fisher frowned at the book she was vainly trying
to concentrate on, for where did that expression come
from ?—much less painfully before strangers than
before an old friend. Old friends, reflected Mrs. Fisher,
who hoped she was reading, compare one constantly
with what one used to be. They are always doing it
if one develops. They are surprised at development.
They hark back ; they expect motionlessness after, say,
fifty, to the end of one's days.

That, thought Mrs. Fisher, her eyes going steadily
line by line down the page and not a word of it getting
through into her consciousness, is foolish of friends.
It is condemning one to a premature death. One should
continue (of course with dignity) to develop, however
old one may be. She had nothing against developing,
against further ripeness, because as long as one was
alive one was not dead,—obviously, decided Mrs. Fisher ;
and development, change, ripening, were life. What
she would dislike would be unripening, going back to
something green. She would dislike it intensely ; and
this is what she felt she was on the brink of doing.

Naturally it made her very uneasy, and only in
constant movement could she find distraction. In-
creasingly restless and no longer able to confine herself

to her battlements, she wandered more and more frequently, and also aimlessly, in and out of the top garden, to the growing surprise of Scrap, especially when she found that all Mrs. Fisher did was to stare for a few minutes at the view, pick a few dead leaves off the rose-bushes, and go away again.

In Mr. Wilkins's conversation she found temporary relief, but though he joined her whenever he could he was not always there, for he spread his attentions judiciously among the three ladies, and when he was somewhere else she had to face and manage her thoughts as best she could by herself. Perhaps it was the excess of light and colour at San Salvatore which made every other place seem dark and black ; and Prince of Wales Terrace did seem a very dark black spot to have to go back to—a dark, narrow street, and her house dark and narrow as the street, with nothing really living or young in it. The goldfish could hardly be called living, or at most not more than half living, and were certainly not young, and except for them there were only the maids, and they were dusty old things.

Dusty old things. Mrs. Fisher paused in her thoughts, arrested by the strange expression. Where had it come from ? How was it possible for it to come at all ? It might have been one of Mrs. Wilkins's, in its levity, its almost slang. Perhaps it was one of hers, and she

had heard her say it and unconsciously caught it from
her.

If so, this was both serious and disgusting. That
the foolish creature should penetrate into Mrs. Fisher's
very mind and establish her personality there, the
personality which was still, in spite of the harmony
apparently existing between her and her intelligent
husband, so alien to Mrs. Fisher's own, so far removed
from what she understood and liked, and infect her with
her undesirable phrases, was most disturbing. Never
in her life before had such a sentence come into Mrs.
Fisher's head. Never in her life before had she thought
of her maids, or of anybody else, as dusty old things.
Her maids were not dusty old things ; they were most
respectable, neat women, who were allowed the use of
the bathroom every Saturday night. Elderly, certainly,
but then so was she, so was her house, so was her
furniture, so were her goldfish. They were all elderly,
as they should be, together. But there was a great
difference between being elderly and being a dusty old
thing.

How true it was what Ruskin said, that evil communications corrupt good manners. But did Ruskin say it ?
On second thoughts she was not sure, but it was just
the sort of thing he would have said if he had said it,
and in any case it was true. Merely hearing Mrs.

Wilkins's evil communications at meals—she did not listen, she avoided listening, yet it was evident she had heard—those communications which, in that they so often were at once vulgar, indelicate and profane, and always, she was sorry to say, laughed at by Lady Caroline, must be classed as evil, was spoiling her own mental manners. Soon she might not only think but say. How terrible that would be. If that were the form her breaking-out was going to take, the form of unseemly speech, Mrs. Fisher was afraid she would hardly with any degree of composure be able to bear it.

At this stage Mrs. Fisher wished more than ever that she were able to talk over her strange feelings with some one who would understand. There was, however, no one who would understand except Mrs. Wilkins herself. She would. She would know at once, Mrs. Fisher was sure, what she felt like. But this was impossible. It would be as abject as begging the very microbe that was infecting one for protection against its disease.

She continued, accordingly, to bear her sensations in silence, and was driven by them into that frequent aimless appearing in the top garden which presently roused even Scrap's attention.

Scrap had noticed it, and vaguely wondered at it, for some time before Mr. Wilkins inquired of her one morning as he arranged her cushions for her—he had established the daily assisting of Lady Caroline into her chair as his special privilege—whether there was anything the matter with Mrs. Fisher.

At that moment Mrs. Fisher was standing by the eastern parapet, shading her eyes and carefully scrutinising the distant white houses of Mezzago. They could see her through the branches of the daphnes.

'I don't know,' said Scrap.

'She is a lady, I take it,' said Mr. Wilkins, 'who would be unlikely to have anything on her mind ?'

'I should imagine so,' said Scrap, smiling.

'If she has, and her restlessness appears to suggest it, I should be more than glad to assist her with advice.'

'I am sure you would be most kind.'

'Of course she has her own legal adviser, but he is not on the spot. I am. And a lawyer on the spot,' said Mr. Wilkins, who endeavoured to make his conversation when he talked to Lady Caroline light, aware that one must be light with young ladies, 'is worth two in—we won't be ordinary and complete the proverb, but say London.'

'You should ask her.'

'Ask her if she needs assistance ? Would you advise

it ? Would it not be a little—a little delicate to touch on such a question, the question whether or no a lady has something on her mind ? '

' Perhaps she will tell you if you go and talk to her. I think it must be lonely to be Mrs. Fisher.'

' You are all thoughtfulness and consideration,' declared Mr. Wilkins, wishing, for the first time in his life, that he were a foreigner so that he might respectfully kiss her hand on withdrawing to go obediently and relieve Mrs. Fisher's loneliness.

It was wonderful what a variety of exits from her corner Scrap contrived for Mr. Wilkins. Each morning she found a different one, which sent him off pleased after he had arranged her cushions for her. She allowed him to arrange the cushions because she instantly had discovered, the very first five minutes of the very first evening, that her fears lest he should cling to her and stare in dreadful admiration were baseless. Mr. Wilkins did not admire like that. It was not only, she instinctively felt, not in him, but if it had been he would not have dared to in her case. He was all respectfulness. She could direct his movements in regard to herself with the raising of an eyelash. His one concern was to obey. She had been prepared to like him if he would only be so obliging as not to admire her, and she did like him. She did not forget his moving defencelessness the first morning in his towel, and he amused her, and he was kind to Lotty. It is true she liked him most when he wasn't there, but then she usually liked everybody most when they weren't there. Certainly he did seem to be one of those men, rare in her experience, who never looked at a woman from the predatory angle. The comfort of this, the simplification it brought into the relations of the party, was immense. From this point of view Mr. Wilkins was simply ideal; he was unique and precious. Whenever she thought of him, and was perhaps inclined to dwell on the aspects of him that were a little boring, she remembered this and murmured, ' But what a treasure.'

Indeed it was Mr. Wilkins's one aim during his stay at San Salvatore to be a treasure. At all costs the three ladies who were not his wife must like him and trust him. Then presently when trouble arose in their lives—and in what lives did not trouble sooner or later arise ?—they would recollect how reliable he was and how sympathetic, and turn to him for advice. Ladies with something on their minds were exactly what he wanted. Lady Caroline, he judged, had nothing on hers at the moment, but so much beauty—for he could not but see what was evident—must have had its difficulties in the past and would have more of them before it had done. In the past he had not been at hand; in the future he hoped to be. And meanwhile the behaviour of Mrs. Fisher, the next in importance of the ladies from the professional point of view, showed definite promise. It was almost certain that Mrs. Fisher had something on her mind. He had been observing her attentively, and it was almost certain.

With the third, with Mrs. Arbuthnot, he had up to this made least headway, for she was so very retiring and quiet. But might not this very retiringness, this tendency to avoid the others and spend her time alone, indicate that she too was troubled? If so, he was her man. He would cultivate her. He would follow her and sit with her, and encourage her to tell him about herself. Arbuthnot, he understood from Lotty, was a British Museum official,—nothing specially important at present, but Mr. Wilkins regarded it as his business to know all sorts and kinds. Besides, there was promotion. Arbuthnot, promoted, might become very much worth while.

As for Lotty, she was charming. She really had all the qualities he had credited her with during his courtship, and they had been, it appeared, merely in abeyance since. His early impressions of her were now being endorsed by the affection and even admiration Lady Caroline showed for her. Lady Caroline Dester was the last person, he was sure, to be mistaken on such

a subject. Her knowledge of the world, her constant
association with only the best, must make her quite
unerring. Lotty was evidently, then, that which before
marriage he had believed her to be,—she was valuable.
She certainly had been most valuable in introducing
him to Lady Caroline and Mrs. Fisher. A man in his
profession could be immensely helped by a clever and
attractive wife. Why had she not been attractive
sooner ? Why this sudden flowering ?

Mr. Wilkins began too to believe there was something peculiar, as Lotty had almost at once informed
him, in the atmosphere of San Salvatore. It promoted
expansion. It brought out dormant qualities. And
feeling more and more pleased, and even charmed, by
his wife, and very content with the progress he was
making with the two others, and hopeful of progress
to be made with the retiring third, Mr. Wilkins could
not remember ever having had such an agreeable holiday. The only thing that might perhaps be bettered
was the way they would call him Mr. Wilkins. Nobody
said Mr. Mellersh-Wilkins. Yet he had introduced himself to Lady Caroline—he flinched a little on remembering
the circumstances—as Mellersh-Wilkins.

Still, this was a small matter, not enough to worry
about. He would be foolish if in such a place and such
society he worried about anything. He was not even

worrying about what the holiday was costing, and had made up his mind to pay not only his own expenses but his wife's as well, and surprise her at the end by presenting her with her nest-egg as intact as when she started ; and just the knowledge that he was preparing a happy surprise for her made him feel warmer than ever towards her.

In fact Mr. Wilkins, who had begun by being consciously and according to plan on his best behaviour, remained on it unconsciously, and with no effort at all.

And meanwhile the beautiful golden days were dropping gently from the second week one by one, equal in beauty with those of the first, and the scent of beanfields in flower on the hillside behind the village came across to San Salvatore whenever the air moved. In the garden that second week the poet's eyed narcissus disappeared out of the long grass at the edge of the zigzag path, and wild gladiolus, slender and rose-coloured, came in their stead, white pinks bloomed in the borders, filling the whole place with their smoky-sweet smell, and a bush nobody had noticed burst into glory and fragrance, and it was a purple lilac bush. Such a jumble of spring and summer was not to be believed in, except by those who dwelt in those gardens. Everything seemed to be out together,—all the things crowded into one month which in England are spread penuriously over six. Even primroses were found one day by Mrs. Wilkins in a cold corner up in the hills; and when she brought them down to the geraniums and heliotrope of San Salvatore they looked quite shy.

XVII

On the first day of the third week Rose wrote to Frederick.

In case she should again hesitate and not post the letter, she gave it to Domenico to post; for if she did not write now there would be no time left at all. Half the month at San Salvatore was over. Even if Frederick started directly he got the letter, which of course he wouldn't be able to do, what with packing and passport, besides not being in a hurry to come, he couldn't arrive for five days.

Having done it, Rose wished she hadn't. He wouldn't come. He wouldn't bother to answer. And if he did answer, it would just be giving some reason which was not true, about being too busy to get away; and all that had been got by writing to him would be that she would be more unhappy than before.

What things one did when one was idle. This resurrection of Frederick, or rather this attempt to resurrect him, what was it but the result of having

271

nothing whatever to do ? She wished she had never
come away on a holiday. What did she want with
holidays ? Work was her salvation; work was the
only thing that protected one, that kept one steady
and one's values true. At home in Hampstead, absorbed
and busy, she had managed to get over Frederick,
thinking of him latterly only with the gentle melancholy
with which one thinks of some one once loved but long
since dead; and now this place, idleness in this soft
place, had thrown her back to the wretched state she
had climbed so carefully out of years ago. Why, if
Frederick did come she would only bore him. Hadn't
she seen in a flash quite soon after getting to San
Salvatore that that was really what kept him away from
her ? And why should she suppose that now, after such a
long estrangement, she would be able not to bore him, be
able to do anything but stand before him like a tongue-
tied idiot, with all the fingers of her spirit turned into
thumbs ? Besides, what a hopeless position, to have
as it were to beseech : Please wait a little—please
don't be impatient—I think perhaps I shan't be a bore
presently.

A thousand times a day Rose wished she had let
Frederick alone. Lotty, who asked her every evening
whether she had sent her letter yet, exclaimed with
delight when the answer at last was yes, and threw

her arms round her. ' Now we shall be *completely* happy ! ' cried the enthusiastic Lotty.

But nothing seemed less certain to Rose, and her expression became more and more the expression of one who has something on her mind.

Mr. Wilkins, wanting to find out what it was, strolled in the sun in his Panama hat, and began to meet her accidentally.

' I did not know,' said Mr. Wilkins the first time, courteously raising his hat, ' that you too liked this particular spot.' And he sat down beside her.

In the afternoon she chose another spot ; and she had not been in it half an hour before Mr. Wilkins, lightly swinging his cane, came round the corner.

' We are destined to meet in our rambles,' said Mr. Wilkins pleasantly. And he sat down beside her.

Mr. Wilkins was very kind, and she had, she saw, misjudged him in Hampstead, and this was the real man, ripened like fruit by the beneficent sun of San Salvatore, but Rose did want to be alone. Still, she was grateful to him for proving to her that though she might bore Frederick she did not bore everybody ; if she had, he would not have sat talking to her on each occasion till it was time to go in. True he bored her, but that wasn't anything like so dreadful as if she bored him. Then indeed her vanity would have been

sadly ruffled. For now that Rose was not able to say
her prayers she was being assailed by every sort of
weakness : vanity, sensitiveness, irritability, pugnacity,
—strange, unfamiliar devils to have coming crowding
on one and taking possession of one's swept and empty
heart. She had never been vain or irritable or pugnacious
in her life before. Could it be that San Salvatore was
capable of opposite effects, and the same sun that
ripened Mr. Wilkins made her go acid ?

The next morning, so as to be sure of being alone,
she went down, while Mr. Wilkins was still lingering
pleasantly with Mrs. Fisher over breakfast, to the rocks
by the water's edge where she and Lotty had sat the
first day. Frederick by now had got her letter. To-day,
if he were like Mr. Wilkins, she might get a telegram
from him.

She tried to silence the absurd hope by jeering at
it. Yet—if Mr. Wilkins had telegraphed, why not
Frederick ? The spell of San Salvatore lurked even,
it seemed, in notepaper. Lotty had not dreamed of
getting a telegram, and when she came in at lunch-
time there it was. It would be too wonderful if when
she went back at lunch-time she found one there for
her too. . . .

Rose clasped her hands tight round her knees. How
passionately she longed to be important to somebody

again,—not important on platforms, not important as
an asset in an organisation, but privately important,
just to one other person, quite privately, nobody else
to know or notice. It didn't seem much to ask in a
world so crowded with people, just to have one of them,
only one out of all the millions, to oneself. Somebody
who needed one, who thought of one, who was eager
to come to one—oh, *oh* how dreadfully one wanted to
be precious !

All the morning she sat beneath the pine-tree by the
sea. Nobody came near her. The great hours passed
slowly ; they seemed enormous. But she wouldn't go
up before lunch, she would give the telegram time to
arrive. . . .

That day Scrap, egged on by Lotty's persuasions
and also thinking that perhaps she had sat long enough,
had arisen from her chair and cushions and gone off
with Lotty and sandwiches up into the hills till evening.
Mr. Wilkins, who wished to go with them, stayed on
Lady Caroline's advice with Mrs. Fisher in order to
cheer her solitude, and though he left off cheering her
about eleven to go and look for Mrs. Arbuthnot, so as
for a space to cheer her too, thus dividing himself
impartially between these solitary ladies, he came back
again presently mopping his forehead and continued
with Mrs. Fisher where he had left off, for this time

Mrs. Arbuthnot had hidden successfully. There was a telegram, too, for her he noticed when he came in. Pity he did not know where she was.

'Ought we to open it ? ' he said to Mrs. Fisher.

' No,' said Mrs. Fisher.

' It may require an answer.'

' I don't approve of tampering with other people's correspondence.'

' Tampering ! My dear lady——'

Mr. Wilkins was shocked. Such a word. Tampering. He had the greatest possible esteem for Mrs. Fisher, but he did at times find her a little difficult. She liked him, he was sure, and she was in a fair way, he felt, to become a client, but he feared she would be a headstrong and secretive client. She was certainly secretive, for though he had been skilful and sympathetic for a whole week, she had as yet given him no inkling of what was so evidently worrying her.

' Poor old thing,' said Lotty, on his asking her if she perhaps could throw light on Mrs. Fisher's troubles. ' She hasn't got love.'

' Love ? ' Mr. Wilkins could only echo, genuinely scandalised. ' But surely, my dear—at her age——'

' *Any* love,' said Lotty.

That very morning he had asked his wife, for he now sought and respected her opinion, if she could tell him what was the matter with Mrs. Arbuthnot, for she too, though he had done his best to thaw her into confidences, had remained persistently retiring.

' She wants her husband,' said Lotty.

' Ah,' said Mr. Wilkins, a new light shed on Mrs. Arbuthnot's shy and modest melancholy. And he added, ' Very proper.'

And Lotty said, smiling at him, ' One does.'

And Mr. Wilkins said, smiling at her, ' Does one ? '

And Lotty said, smiling at him, ' Of course.'

And Mr. Wilkins, much pleased with her, though it was still quite early in the day, a time when caresses are sluggish, pinched her ear.

Just before half-past twelve Rose came slowly up through the pergola and between the camellias ranged on either side of the old stone steps. The rivulets of periwinkles that flowed down them when first she arrived were gone, and now there were these bushes, incredibly rosetted. Pink, white, red, striped,—she fingered and smelt them one after the other, so as not to get to her disappointment too quickly. As long as she hadn't seen for herself, seen the table in the hall quite empty except for its bowl of flowers, she still could hope, she still could have the joy of imagining the telegram lying on it waiting for her. But there is no smell in a camellia, as Mr. Wilkins, who was stand-

ing in the doorway on the look-out for her and knew
what was necessary in horticulture, reminded her.

She started at his voice and looked up.

'A telegram has come for you,' said Mr. Wilkins.

She stared at him, her mouth open.

'I searched for you everywhere, but failed——'

Of course. She knew it. She had been sure of it
all the time. Bright and burning, Youth in that instant
flashed down again on Rose. She flew up the steps,
red as the camellia she had just been fingering, and was
in the hall and tearing open the telegram before Mr.
Wilkins had finished his sentence. Why, but if things
could happen like this—why, but there was no end to—
why, she and Frederick—they were going to be—again
—at last——

'No bad news, I trust ?' said Mr. Wilkins who had
followed her, for when she had read the telegram she
stood staring at it and her face went slowly white.
Curious to watch how her face went slowly white.

She turned and looked at Mr. Wilkins as if trying to
remember him.

'Oh no. On the contrary——'

She managed to smile. 'I'm going to have a visitor,'
she said, holding out the telegram ; and when he had
taken it she walked away towards the dining-room,
murmuring something about lunch being ready.

Mr. Wilkins read the telegram. It had been sent that morning from Mezzago, and was :

Am passing through on way to Rome. May I pay my respects this afternoon ?   THOMAS BRIGGS.

Why should such a telegram make the interesting lady turn pale ? For her pallor on reading it had been so striking as to convince Mr. Wilkins she was receiving a blow.

' Who is Thomas Briggs ? ' he asked, following her into the dining-room.

She looked at him vaguely. ' Who is—— ? ' she repeated, getting her thoughts together again.

' Thomas Briggs.'

' Oh. Yes. He is the owner. This is his house. He is very nice. He is coming this afternoon.'

Thomas Briggs was at that very moment coming. He was jogging along the road between Mezzago and Castagneto in a fly, sincerely hoping that the dark-eyed lady would grasp that all he wanted was to see her, and not at all to see if his house were still there. He felt that an owner of delicacy did not intrude on a tenant. But—he had been thinking so much of her since that day. Rose Arbuthnot. Such a pretty name. And such a pretty creature,—mild, milky, mothery in the best sense ; the best sense being that she wasn't his

mother and couldn't have been if she had tried, for
parents were the only things impossible to have younger
than oneself. Also, he was passing so near. It seemed
absurd not just to look in and see if she were comfortable. He longed to see her in his house. He longed to
see it as her background, to see her sitting in his chairs,
drinking out of his cups, using all his things. Did she
put the big crimson brocade cushion in the drawing-
room behind her little dark head ? Her hair and the
whiteness of her skin would look lovely against it. Had
she seen the portrait of herself on the stairs ? He
wondered if she liked it. He would explain it to her.
If she didn't paint, and she had said nothing to suggest
it, she wouldn't perhaps notice how exactly the moulding
of the eyebrows and the slight hollow of the cheek——

He told the fly to wait in Castagneto, and crossed the
piazza, hailed by children and dogs, who all knew him
and sprang up suddenly from nowhere, and walking
quickly up the zigzag path, for he was an active young
man not much more than thirty, he pulled the ancient
chain that rang the bell, and waited decorously on the
proper side of the open door to be allowed to come in.

At the sight of him Francesca flung up every bit of
her that would fling up,—eyebrows, eyelids, and hands,
and volubly assured him that all was in perfect order
and that she was doing her duty.

' Of course, of course,' said Briggs, cutting her short. ' No one doubts it.'

And he asked her to take in his card to her mistress.

' Which mistress ? ' asked Francesca.

' Which mistress ? '

' There are four,' said Francesca, scenting an irregularity on the part of the tenants, for her master looked surprised ; and she felt pleased, for life was dull and irregularities helped it along at least a little.

' Four ? ' he repeated surprised. ' Well, take it to the lot then,' he said, recovering himself, for he noticed her expression.

Coffee was being drunk in the top garden in the shade of the umbrella pine. Only Mrs. Fisher and Mr. Wilkins were drinking it, for Mrs. Arbuthnot, after eating nothing and being completely silent during lunch, had disappeared immediately afterwards.

While Francesca went away into the garden with his card, her master stood examining the picture on the staircase of that Madonna by an early Italian painter, name unknown, picked up by him at Orvieto, who was so much like his tenant. It really was remarkable, the likeness. Of course his tenant that day in London had had her hat on, but he was pretty sure her hair grew just like that off her forehead. The expression of the eyes, grave and sweet, was exactly the same. He rejoiced to think that he would always have her portrait.

He looked up at the sound of footsteps, and there she was, coming down the stairs just as he had imagined her in that place, dressed in white.

She was astonished to see him so soon. She had supposed he would come about tea-time, and till then she had meant to sit somewhere out of doors where she could be by herself.

He watched her coming down the stairs with the utmost eager interest. In a moment she would be level with her portrait.

'It really is extraordinary,' said Briggs.

'How do you do,' said Rose, intent only on a decent show of welcome.

She did not welcome him. He was here, she felt, the telegram bitter in her heart, instead of Frederick, doing what she had longed Frederick would do, taking his place.

'Just stand still a moment——'

She obeyed automatically.

'Yes—quite astonishing. Do you mind taking off your hat ? '

Rose, surprised, took it off obediently.

'Yes—I thought so—I just wanted to make sure. And look—have you noticed——'

He began to make odd swift passes with his hand over the face in the picture, measuring it, looking from it to her.

Rose's surprise became amusement, and she could not help smiling. 'Have you come to compare me with my original ? ' she asked.

' You do see how extraordinarily alike——'

' I didn't know I looked so solemn.'

' You don't. Not now. You did a minute ago, quite as solemn. Oh yes—how do you do,' he finished suddenly, noticing her outstretched hand. And he laughed and shook it, flushing—a trick of his—to the roots of his fair hair.

Francesca came back. ' The Signora Fisher,' she said, ' will be pleased to see Him.'

' Who is the Signora Fisher ? ' he asked Rose.

' One of the four who are sharing your house.'

' Then there are four of you ? '

' Yes. My friend and I found we couldn't afford it by ourselves.'

' Oh, I say——' began Briggs in confusion, for he would best have liked Rose Arbuthnot—pretty name—not to have to afford anything, but to stay at San Salvatore as long as she liked as his guest.

' Mrs. Fisher is having coffee in the top garden,' said Rose. ' I'll take you to her and introduce you.'

'I don't want to go. You've got your hat on, so you were going for a walk. Mayn't I come too ? I'd immensely like being shown round by you.'

'But Mrs. Fisher is waiting for you.'

'Won't she keep ? '

'Yes,' said Rose, with the smile that had so much attracted him the first day. ' I think she will keep quite well till tea.'

'Do you speak Italian ? '

'No,' said Rose. ' Why ? '

On that he turned to Francesca, and told her at a great rate, for in Italian he was glib, to go back to the Signora in the top garden and tell her he had encountered his old friend the Signora Arbuthnot, and was going for a walk with her and would present himself to her later.

'Do you invite me to tea ? ' he asked Rose, when Francesca had gone.

'Of course. It's your house.'

'It isn't. It's yours.'

'Till Monday week,' she smiled.

'Come and show me all the views,' he said eagerly ; and it was plain, even to the self-depreciatory Rose, that she did not bore Mr. Briggs.

XVIII

THEY had a very pleasant walk, with a great deal of
sitting down in warm, thyme-fragrant corners, and if
anything could have helped Rose to recover from the
bitter disappointment of the morning it would have
been the company and conversation of Mr. Briggs. He
did help her to recover, and the same process took place
as that which Lotty had undergone with her husband,
and the more Mr. Briggs thought Rose charming the
more charming she became.

Briggs was a man incapable of concealments, who
never lost time if he could help it. They had not got
to the end of the headland where the lighthouse is—
Briggs asked her to show him the lighthouse, because
the path to it, he knew, was wide enough for two to
walk abreast and fairly level—before he had told her
of the impression she had made on him in London

Since even the most religious, sober women like to
know they have made an impression, particularly the
kind that has nothing to do with character or merits,

Rose was pleased. Being pleased, she smiled. Smiling, she was more attractive than ever. Colour came into her cheeks, and brightness into her eyes. She heard herself saying things that really sounded quite interesting and even amusing. If Frederick were listening now, she thought, perhaps he would see that she couldn't after all be such a hopeless bore ; for here was a man, nice-looking, young, and surely clever—he seemed clever, and she hoped he was, for then the compliment would be still greater—who was evidently quite happy to spend the afternoon just talking to her.

And indeed Mr. Briggs seemed very much interested. He wanted to hear all about everything she had been doing from the moment she got there. He asked her if she had seen this, that, and the other in the house, what she liked best, which room she had, if she were comfortable, if Francesca was behaving, if Domenico took care of her, and whether she didn't enjoy using the yellow sitting-room—the one that got all the sun and looked out towards Genoa.

Rose was ashamed how little she had noticed in the house, and how few of the things he spoke of as curious or beautiful in it she had even seen. Swamped in thoughts of Frederick, she appeared to have lived in San Salvatore blindly, and more than half the time had gone, and what had been the good of it ? She might just as well have been sitting hankering on Hampstead Heath. No, she mightn't; through all her hankerings she had been conscious that she was at least in the very heart of beauty; and indeed it was this beauty, this longing to share it, that had first started her off hankering.

Mr. Briggs, however, was too much alive for her to be able to spare any attention at this moment for Frederick, and she praised the servants in answer to his questions, and praised the yellow sitting-room without telling him she had only been in it once and then was ignominiously ejected, and she told him she knew hardly anything about art and curiosities, but thought perhaps if somebody would tell her about them she would know more, and she said she had spent every day since her arrival out-of-doors, because out-of-doors there was so very wonderful and different from anything she had ever seen.

Briggs walked by her side along his paths that were yet so happily for the moment her paths, and felt all the innocent glows of family life. He was an orphan and an only child, and had a warm, domestic disposition. He would have adored a sister and spoilt a mother, and was beginning at this time to think of marrying; for though he had been very happy with his various loves, each of whom, contrary to the usual experience,

turned ultimately into his devoted friend, he was fond
of children and thought he had perhaps now got to the
age of settling if he did not wish to·be too old by the
time his eldest son was twenty. San Salvatore had
latterly seemed a little forlorn. He fancied it echoed
when he walked about it. He had felt lonely there ;
so lonely that he had preferred this year to miss out a
spring and let it. It wanted a wife in it. It wanted
that final touch of warmth and beauty, for he never
thought of his wife except in terms of warmth and
beauty,—she would of course be beautiful and kind.
It amused him how much in love with this vague wife
he was already.

At such a rate was he making friends with the lady
with the sweet name as he walked along the path towards
the lighthouse, that he was sure presently he would be
telling her everything about himself and his past doings
and his future hopes ; and the thought of such a swiftly
developing confidence made him laugh.

' Why are you laughing ? ' she asked, looking at him
and smiling.

' It's so like coming home,' he said.

' But it *is* coming home for you to come here.'

' I mean *really* like coming home. To one's—one's
family. I never had a family. I'm an orphan.'

' Oh, are you ? ' said Rose with the proper sympathy.

'I hope you've not been one very long. No, I mean I hope you have been one very long. No—I don't know what I mean, except that I'm sorry.'

He laughed again. 'Oh I'm used to it. I haven't anybody. No sisters or brothers.'

'Then you're an only child,' she observed intelligently.

'Yes. And there's something about you that's exactly my idea of a—of a family.'

She was amused.

'So—cosy,' he said, looking at her and searching for a word.

'You wouldn't think so if you saw my house in Hampstead,' she said, a vision of that austere and hardseated dwelling presenting itself to her mind, with nothing soft in it except the shunned and neglected Du Barri sofa. No wonder, she thought, for a moment clear-brained, that Frederick avoided it. There was nothing cosy about *his* family.

'I don't believe any place you lived in could be anything but exactly like you,' he said.

'You're not going to pretend San Salvatore is like me ?'

'Indeed I do pretend it. Surely you admit that it is beautiful ? '

He said several things like that. She enjoyed her

walk. She could not recollect any walk so pleasant since her courting days.

She came back to tea, bringing Mr. Briggs, and looking quite different, Mr. Wilkins noticed, from what she had looked till then. Trouble here, trouble here, thought Mr. Wilkins, mentally rubbing his professional hands. He could see himself being called in presently to advise. On the one hand there was Arbuthnot, on the other hand here was Briggs. Trouble brewing, trouble sooner or later. But why had Briggs's telegram acted on the lady like a blow ? If she had turned pale from excess of joy, then trouble was nearer than he had supposed. She was not pale now ; she was more like her name than he had yet seen her. Well, he was the man for trouble. He regretted, of course, that people should get into it, but being in he was their man.

And Mr. Wilkins, invigorated by these thoughts, his career being very precious to him, proceeded to assist in doing the honours to Mr. Briggs, both in his quality of sharer in the temporary ownership of San Salvatore and of probable helper out of difficulties, with great hospitality, and pointed out the various features of the place to him, and led him to the parapet and showed him Mezzago across the bay.

Mrs. Fisher too was gracious. This was this young

man's house. He was a man of property. She liked
property, and she liked men of property. Also there
seemed a peculiar merit in being a man of property so
young. Inheritance, of course ; and inheritance was
more respectable than acquisition. It did indicate
fathers ; and in an age where most people appeared
neither to have them nor to want them she liked this
too.

Accordingly it was a pleasant meal, with everybody
amiable and pleased. Briggs thought Mrs. Fisher a
dear old lady, and showed he thought so ; and again
the magic worked, and she became a dear old lady.
She developed benignity with him, and a kind of benignity which was almost playful—actually before tea
was over including in some observation she made him
the words ' My dear boy.'

Strange words in Mrs. Fisher's mouth. It is doubtful
whether in her life she had used them before. Rose
was astonished. How nice people really were. When
would she leave off making mistakes about them ? She
hadn't suspected this side of Mrs. Fisher, and she began
to wonder whether those other sides of her with which
alone she was acquainted had not perhaps after all
been the effect of her own militant and irritating behaviour. Probably they were. How horrid, then, she
must have been. She felt very penitent when she saw

Mrs. Fisher beneath her eyes blossoming out into real amiability the moment some one came along who was charming to her, and she could have sunk into the ground with shame when Mrs. Fisher presently laughed, and she realised by the shock it gave her that the sound was entirely new. Not once before had she or any one else there heard Mrs. Fisher laugh. What an indictment of the lot of them! For they had all laughed, the others, some more and some less, at one time or another since their arrival, and only Mrs. Fisher had not. Clearly, since she could enjoy herself as she was now enjoying herself, she had not enjoyed herself before. Nobody had cared whether she did or not, except perhaps Lotty. Yes; Lotty had cared, and had wanted her to be happy; but Lotty seemed to produce a bad effect on Mrs. Fisher, while as for Rose herself she had never been with her for five minutes without wanting, really wanting, to provoke and oppose her.

How very horrid she had been. She had behaved unpardonably. Her penitence showed itself in a shy and deferential solicitude towards Mrs. Fisher which made the observant Briggs think her still more angelic, and wish for a moment that he were an old lady himself in order to be behaved to by Rose Arbuthnot just like that. There was evidently no end, he thought, to the things she could do sweetly. He would even not mind taking medicine, really nasty medicine, if it were Rose Arbuthnot bending over him with the dose.

She felt his bright blue eyes, the brighter because he was so sunburnt, fixed on her with a twinkle in them, and smiling asked him what he was thinking about.

But he couldn't very well tell her that, he said ; and added, ' Some day.'

' Trouble, trouble,' thought Mr. Wilkins at this, again mentally rubbing his hands. ' Well, I'm their man.'

' I'm sure,' said Mrs. Fisher benignly, ' you have no thoughts we may not hear.'

' I'm sure,' said Briggs, ' I would be telling you every one of my secrets in a week.'

' You would be telling somebody very safe, then,' said Mrs. Fisher benevolently,—just such a son would she have liked to have had. ' And in return,' she went on, ' I daresay I would tell you mine.'

' Ah no,' said Mr. Wilkins, adapting himself to this tone of easy *badinage*, ' I must protest. I really must. I have a prior claim, I am the older friend. I have known Mrs. Fisher ten days, and you, Briggs, have not yet known her one. I assert my right to be told her secrets first. That is,' he added, bowing gallantly, ' if she has any—which I beg leave to doubt.'

' Oh, haven't I ! ' exclaimed Mrs. Fisher, thinking of those green leaves. That she should exclaim at all was surprising, but that she should do it with gaiety was miraculous. Rose could only watch her in wonder.

' Then I shall worm them out,' said Briggs with equal gaiety.

' They won't need much worming out,' said Mrs. Fisher. ' My difficulty is to keep them from bursting out.'

It might have been Lotty talking. Mr. Wilkins adjusted the single eyeglass he carried with him for occasions like this, and examined Mrs. Fisher carefully. Rose looked on, unable not to smile too since Mrs. Fisher seemed so much amused, though Rose did not quite know why, and her smile was a little uncertain, for Mrs. Fisher amused was a new sight, not without its awe-inspiring aspects, and had to be got accustomed to.

What Mrs. Fisher was thinking was how much surprised they would be if she told them of her very odd and exciting sensation of going to come out all over buds. They would think she was an extremely silly old woman, and so would she have thought as lately as two days ago; but the bud idea was becoming

familiar to her, she was more *apprivoisée* now, as dear
Matthew Arnold used to say, and though it would
undoubtedly be best if one's appearance and sensations
matched, yet supposing they did not—and one couldn't
have everything—was it not better to feel young somewhere rather than old everywhere ? Time enough to
be old everywhere again, inside as well as out, when
she got back to her sarcophagus in Prince of Wales
Terrace.

Yet it is probable that without the arrival of Briggs
Mrs. Fisher would have gone on secretly fermenting in
her shell. The others only knew her as severe. It
would have been more than her diginity could bear
suddenly to relax,—especially towards the three young
women. But now came the stranger Briggs, a stranger
who at once took to her as no young man had taken
to her in her life, and it was the coming of Briggs and
his real and manifest appreciation—for just such a
grandmother, thought Briggs, hungry for home life and
its concomitants, would he have liked to have—that
released Mrs. Fisher from her shell ; and here she was
at last, as Lotty had predicted, pleased, good-humoured
and benevolent.

Lotty, coming back half an hour later from her
picnic, and following the sound of voices into the top
garden in the hope of still finding tea, saw at once

what had happened, for Mrs. Fisher at that very moment
was laughing.

'She's burst her cocoon,' thought Lotty; and swift
as she was in all her movements, and impulsive, and
also without any sense of propriety to worry and delay
her, she bent over the back of Mrs. Fisher's chair and
kissed her.

'Good gracious!' cried Mrs. Fisher, starting violently,
for such a thing had not happened to her since Mr.
Fisher's earlier days, and then only gingerly. This kiss
was a real kiss, and rested on Mrs. Fisher's cheek a
moment with a strange, soft sweetness.

When she saw whose it was, a deep flush spread over
her face. Mrs. Wilkins kissing her and the kiss feeling
so affectionate. . . . Even if she had wanted to she
could not in the presence of the appreciative Mr. Briggs
resume her cast-off severity and begin rebuking again;
but she did not want to. Was it possible Mrs. Wilkins
liked her,—had liked her all this time, while she had
been so much disliking her herself? A queer little
trickle of warmth filtered through the frozen defences
of Mrs. Fisher's heart. Somebody young kissing her—
somebody young *wanting* to kiss her. . . . Very much
flushed, she watched the strange creature, apparently
quite unconscious she had done anything extraordinary,
shaking hands with Mr. Briggs, on her husband's intro-

ducing him, and immediately embarking on the friendliest conversation with him, exactly as if she had known him all her life. What a strange creature; what a very strange creature. It was natural, she being so strange, that one should have, perhaps, misjudged her. . . .

'I'm sure you want some tea,' said Briggs with eager hospitality to Lotty. He thought her delightful,—freckles, picnic-untidiness and all. Just such a sister would he——

'This is cold,' he said, feeling the teapot. 'I'll tell Francesca to make you some fresh——'

He broke off and blushed. 'Aren't I forgetting myself,' he said, laughing and looking round at them.

'Very natural, very natural,' Mr. Wilkins reassured him.

'I'll go and tell Francesca,' said Rose, getting up.

'No, no,' said Briggs. 'Don't go away.' And he put his hands to his mouth and shouted.

'Francesca!' shouted Briggs.

She came running. No summons in their experience had been answered by her with such celerity.

'"Her Master's Voice,"' remarked Mr. Wilkins; aptly, he considered.

'Make fresh tea,' ordered Briggs in Italian. 'Quick —quick——' And then remembering himself he blushed again, and begged everybody's pardon.

'Very natural, very natural,' Mr. Wilkins reassured him.

Briggs then explained to Lotty what he had explained twice already, once to Rose and once to the other two, that he was on his way to Rome and thought he would get out at Mezzago and just look in to see if they were comfortable and continue his journey the next day, staying the night in an hotel at Mezzago.

'But how ridiculous,' said Lotty. 'Of course you must stay here. It's your house. There's Kate Lumley's room,' she added, turning to Mrs. Fisher. 'You wouldn't mind Mr. Briggs having it for one night? Kate Lumley isn't *in* it, you know,' she said turning to Briggs again and laughing.

And Mrs. Fisher to her immense surprise laughed too. She knew that at any other time this remark would have struck her as excessively unseemly, and yet now she only thought it funny.

No indeed, she assured Briggs, Kate Lumley was not in that room. Very fortunately, for she was an excessively wide person and the room was excessively narrow. Kate Lumley might get into it, but that was about all. Once in, she would fit it so tightly that probably she would never be able to get out again. It was entirely at Mr. Briggs's disposal, and she hoped he would do nothing so absurd as go to an hotel,—he, the owner of the whole place.

Rose listened to this speech wide-eyed with amazement. Mrs. Fisher laughed very much as she made it. Lotty laughed very much too, and at the end of it bent down and kissed her again,—kissed her several times.

' So you see, my dear boy,' said Mrs. Fisher, ' you must stay here and give us all a great deal of pleasure.'

' A great deal indeed,' corroborated Mr. Wilkins heartily.

' A very great deal,' repeated Mrs. Fisher, looking exactly like a pleased mother.

' Do,' said Rose, on Briggs's turning inquiringly to her.

' How kind of you all,' he said, his face broad with smiles. ' I'd love to be a guest here. What a new sensation. And with three such——'

He broke off and looked round. ' I say,' he asked, ' oughtn't I to have a fourth hostess ? Francesca said she had four mistresses.'

' Yes. There's Lady Caroline,' said Lotty.

' Then hadn't we better find out first if she invites me too ? '

' Oh, but she's sure——' began Lotty.

' The daughter of the Droitwiches, Briggs,' said Mr. Wilkins, ' is not likely to be wanting in the proper hospitable impulses.'

' The daughter of the——' repeated Briggs ; but he
stopped dead, for there in the doorway was the daughter
of the Droitwiches herself ; or rather, coming towards
him out of the dark doorway into the brightness of the
sunset, was that which he had not in his life yet seen
but only dreamed of, his ideal of absolute loveliness.

AND then when she spoke . . . what chance was there
for poor Briggs ?   He was undone.   All Scrap said was,
'How do you do,' on Mr. Wilkins presenting him, but
it was enough : it undid Briggs.

From a cheerful, chatty, happy young man, overflowing with life and friendliness, he became silent,
solemn, and with little beads on his temples.   Also he
became clumsy, dropping the teaspoon as he handed
her her cup, mismanaging the macaroons, so that one
rolled on the ground.   His eyes could not keep off the
enchanting face for a moment ; and when Mr. Wilkins,
elucidating him, for he failed to elucidate himself,
informed Lady Caroline that in Mr. Briggs she beheld
the owner of San Salvatore, who was on his way to
Rome, but had got out at Mezzago, etc. etc., and that
the other three ladies had invited him to spend the night
in what was to all intents and purposes his own house
rather than an hotel, and Mr. Briggs was only waiting
for the seal of her approval to this invitation, she being
the fourth hostess,—when Mr. Wilkins, balancing his

sentences and being admirably clear and enjoying the sound of his own cultured voice, explained the position in this manner to Lady Caroline, Briggs sat and said never a word.

A deep melancholy invaded Scrap. The symptoms of the incipient grabber were all there and only too familiar, and she knew that if Briggs stayed her rest-cure might be regarded as over.

Then Kate Lumley occurred to her. She caught at Kate as at a straw.

'It would have been delightful,' she said, faintly smiling at Briggs—she could not in decency not smile, at least a little, but even a little betrayed the dimple, and Briggs's eyes became more fixed than ever—' I'm only wondering if there is room.'

' Yes, there is,' said Lotty. ' There's Kate Lumley's room.'

' I thought,' said Scrap to Mrs. Fisher, and it seemed to Briggs that he had never heard music till now, ' your friend was expected immediately.'

' Oh no,' said Mrs. Fisher,—with an odd placidness, Scrap thought.

' Miss Lumley,' said Mr. Wilkins, ' —or should I,' he inquired of Mrs. Fisher, ' say Mrs. ? '

' Nobody has ever married Kate,' said Mrs. Fisher complacently.

'Quite so. Miss Lumley does not arrive to-day in any case, Lady Caroline, and Mr. Briggs has—unfortunately, if I may say so—to continue his journey to-morrow, so that his staying would in no way interfere with Miss Lumley's possible movements.'

'Then of course I join in the invitation,' said Scrap, with what was to Briggs the most divine cordiality.

He stammered something, flushing scarlet, and Scrap thought, '*Oh*,' and turned her head away; but that merely made Briggs acquainted with her profile, and if there existed anything more lovely than Scrap's full face it was her profile.

Well, it was only for this one afternoon and evening. He would leave, no doubt, the first thing in the morning. It took hours to get to Rome. Awful if he hung on till the night train. She had a feeling that the principal express to Rome passed through at night. Why hadn't that woman Kate Lumley arrived yet? She had forgotten all about her, but now she remembered she was to have been invited a fortnight ago. What had become of her? This man, once let in, would come and see her in London, would haunt the places she was likely to go to. He had the makings, her experienced eye could see, of a passionately persistent grabber.

'If,' thought Mr. Wilkins, observing Briggs's face

and sudden silence, ' any understanding existed between this young fellow and Mrs. Arbuthnot, there is now going to be trouble. Trouble of a different nature from the kind I feared, in which Arbuthnot would have played a leading part, in fact the part of petitioner, but trouble that may need help and advice none the less for its not being publicly scandalous. Briggs, impelled by his passions and her beauty, will aspire to the daughter of the Droitwiches. She, naturally and properly, will repel him. Mrs. Arbuthnot, left in the cold, will be upset and show it. Arbuthnot on his arrival will find his wife in enigmatic tears. Inquiring into their cause, he will be met with an icy reserve. More trouble may then be expected, and in me they will seek and find their adviser. When Lotty said Mrs. Arbuthnot wanted her husband, she was wrong. What Mrs. Arbuthnot wants is Briggs, and it looks uncommonly as if she were not going to get him. Well, I'm their man.'

' Where are your things, Mr. Briggs ? ' asked Mrs. Fisher, her voice round with motherliness. ' Oughtn't they to be fetched ? ' For the sun was nearly in the sea now, and the sweet-smelling April dampness that followed immediately on its disappearance was beginning to steal into the garden.

Briggs started. ' My things ? ' he repeated. ' Oh yes—I must fetch them. They're in Mezzago. I'll send Domenico. My fly is waiting in the village. He can go back in it. I'll go and tell him.'

He got up. To whom was he talking? To Mrs. Fisher, ostensibly, yet his eyes were fixed on Scrap, who said nothing and looked at no one.

Then, recollecting himself, he stammered, 'I'm awfully sorry—I keep on forgetting—I'll go down and fetch them myself.'

'We can easily send Domenico,' said Rose; and at her gentle voice he turned his head.

Why, there was his friend, the sweet-named lady,— but how had she not in this short interval changed! Was it the failing light making her so colourless, so vague-featured, so dim, so much like a ghost? A nice, good ghost, of course, and still with a pretty name, but only a ghost.

He turned from her to Scrap again, and forgot Rose Arbuthnot's existence. How was it possible for him to bother about anybody or anything else in this first moment of being face to face with his dream come true?

Briggs had not supposed or hoped that any one as beautiful as his dream of beauty existed. He had never till now met even an approximation. Pretty women, charming women by the score he had met and properly appreciated, but never the real, the godlike thing itself. He used to think, 'If ever I saw a perfectly beautiful

woman I should die '; and though, having now met what
to his ideas was a perfectly beautiful woman, he did
not die, he became very nearly as incapable of managing
his own affairs as if he had.

The others were obliged to arrange everything for
him. By questions they extracted from him that his
luggage was in the station cloakroom at Mezzago, and
they sent for Domenico, and, urged and prompted by
everybody except Scrap, who sat in silence and looked
at no one, Briggs was induced to give him the necessary
instructions for going back in the fly and bringing out
his things.

It was a sad sight to see the collapse of Briggs.
Everybody noticed it, even Rose.

' Upon my word,' thought Mrs. Fisher, ' the way one
pretty face can turn a delightful man into an idiot is
past all patience.'

And feeling the air getting chilly, and the sight of
the enthralled Briggs painful, she went in to order his
room to be got ready, regretting now that she had
pressed the poor boy to stay. She had forgotten Lady
Caroline's kill-joy face for the moment, and the more
completely owing to the absence of any ill effects produced by it on Mr. Wilkins. Poor boy. Such a charming boy too, left to himself. It was true she could not
accuse Lady Caroline of not leaving him to himself,

for she was taking no notice of him at all, but that did not help.   Exactly like foolish moths did men, in other respects intelligent, flutter round the impassive lighted candle of a pretty face.   She had seen them doing it. She had looked on only too often.   Almost she laid a motherly hand on Briggs's fair head as she passed him. Poor boy.

Then Scrap, having finished her cigarette, got up and went indoors too.   She saw no reason why she should sit there in order to gratify Mr. Briggs's desire to stare.   She would have liked to stay out longer, to go to her corner behind the daphne bushes and look at the sunset sky and watch the lights coming out one by one in the village below and smell the sweet moistness of the evening, but if she did Mr. Briggs would certainly follow her.

The old familiar tyranny had begun again.   Her holiday of peace and liberation was interrupted,— perhaps over, for who knew if he would go away, after all, to-morrow ?   He might leave the house, driven out of it by Kate Lumley, but there was nothing to prevent his taking rooms in the village and coming up every day.   This tyranny of one person over another !   And she was so miserably constructed that she wouldn't even be able to frown him down without being mis-understood.

Scrap, who loved this time of the evening in her corner, felt indignant with Mr. Briggs who was doing her out of it, and she turned her back on the garden and him and went towards the house without a look or a word. But Briggs, when he realised her intention, leapt to his feet, snatched chairs which were not in her way out of it, kicked a footstool which was not in her path on one side, hurried to the door, which stood wide open, in order to hold it open, and followed her through it, walking by her side along the hall.

What was to be done with Mr. Briggs ? Well, it was his hall ; she couldn't prevent his walking along it.

' I hope,' he said, not able while walking to take his eyes off her, so that he knocked against several things he would otherwise have avoided—the corner of a bookcase, an ancient carved cupboard, the table with the flowers on it, shaking the water over—' that you are quite comfortable here ? If you're not I'll—I'll flay them alive.'

His voice vibrated. What was to be done with Mr. Briggs ? She could of course stay in her room the whole time, say she was ill, not appear at dinner ; but again, the tyranny of this . . .

' I'm very comfortable indeed,' said Scrap.

' If I had dreamed you were coming——' he began.

' It's a wonderful old place,' said Scrap, doing her

utmost to sound detached and forbidding, but with
little hope of success.

The kitchen was on this floor, and passing its door,
which was open a crack, they were observed by the
servants, whose thoughts, communicated to each other
by looks, may be roughly reproduced by such rude
symbols as Aha and Oho,—symbols which represented
and included their appreciation of the inevitable, their
foreknowledge of the inevitable, and their complete
understanding and approval.

' Are you going upstairs ? ' asked Briggs, as she paused
at the foot of them.

' Yes.'

' Which room do you sit in ?   The drawing-room,
or the small yellow room ? '

' In my own room.'

So then he couldn't go up with her ; so then all
he could do was to wait till she came out again.

He longed to ask her which was her own room—it
thrilled him to hear her call any room in his house her
own room—that he might picture her in it.   He longed
to know if by any happy chance it was his room, for ever
after to be filled with her wonder ; but he didn't dare.
He would find that out later from some one else,—
Francesca, anybody.

' Then I shan't see you again till dinner ? '

'Dinner is at eight,' was Scrap's evasive answer as she went upstairs.

He watched her go.

She passed the Madonna, the portrait of Rose Arbuthnot, and the dark-eyed figure he had thought so sweet seemed to turn pale, to shrivel into insignificance as she passed.

She turned the bend of the stairs, and the setting sun, shining through the west window a moment on her face, turned her to glory.

She disappeared, and the sun went out too, and the stairs were dark and empty.

He listened till her footsteps were silent, trying to tell from the sound of the shutting door which room she had gone into, then wandered aimlessly away through the hall again, and found himself back in the top garden.

Scrap from her window saw him there. She saw Lotty and Rose sitting on the end parapet, where she would have liked to have been, and she saw Mr. Wilkins buttonholing Briggs and evidently telling him the story of the oleander tree in the middle of the garden.

Briggs was listening with a patience she thought rather nice, seeing that it was his oleander and his own father's story. She knew Mr. Wilkins was telling him the story by his gestures. Domenico had told it her soon after her arrival, and he had also told Mrs.

Fisher, who had told Mr. Wilkins. Mrs. Fisher thought highly of this story, and often spoke of it. It was about a cherrywood walking-stick. Briggs's father had thrust this stick into the ground at that spot, and said to Domenico's father, who was then the gardener, ' Here we will have an oleander.' And Briggs's father left the stick in the ground as a reminder to Domenico's father, and presently—how long afterwards nobody remembered—the stick began to sprout, and it was an oleander.

There stood poor Mr. Briggs being told all about it, and listening to the story he must have known from infancy with patience.

Probably he was thinking of something else. She was afraid he was. How unfortunate, how extremely unfortunate, the determination that seized people to get hold of and engulf other people. If only they could be induced to stand more on their own feet. Why couldn't Mr. Briggs be more like Lotty, who never wanted anything of anybody, but was complete in herself and respected other people's completeness ? One loved being with Lotty. With her one was free, and yet befriended. Mr. Briggs looked so really nice, too. She thought she might like him if only he wouldn't so excessively like her.

Scrap felt melancholy. Here she was. shut up in

her bedroom, which was stuffy from the afternoon sun that had been pouring into it, instead of out in the cool garden, and all because of Mr. Briggs.

Intolerable tyranny, she thought, flaring up. She wouldn't endure it; she would go out all the same; she would run downstairs while Mr. Wilkins—really that man was a treasure—held Mr. Briggs down telling him about the oleander, and get out of the house by the front door, and take cover in the shadows of the zigzag path. Nobody could see her there; nobody would think of looking for her there.

She snatched up a wrap, for she did not mean to come back for a long while, perhaps not even to dinner —it would be all Mr. Briggs's fault if she went dinnerless and hungry—and with another glance out of the window to see if he were still safe, she stole out and got away to the sheltering trees of the zigzag path, and there sat down on one of the seats placed at each bend to assist the upward journey of those who were breathless.

Ah, this was lovely, thought Scrap with a sigh of relief. How cool. How good it smelt. She could see the quiet water of the little harbour through the pine trunks, and the lights coming out in the houses on the other side, and all round her the green dusk was splashed by the rose-pink of the gladioluses in the grass and the white of the crowding daisies.

Ah, this was lovely. So still. Nothing moving —not a leaf, not a stalk. The only sound was a dog barking, far away somewhere up on the hills, or when the door of the little restaurant in the piazza below was opened and there was a burst of voices, silenced again immediately by the swinging to of the door.

She drew in a deep breath of pleasure. Ah, this was——

Her deep breath was arrested in the middle. What was that ?

She leaned forward listening, her body tense.

Footsteps. On the zigzag path. Briggs. Finding her out.

Should she run ?

No—the footsteps were coming up, not down. Some one from the village. Perhaps Angelo, with provisions.

She relaxed again. But the steps were not the steps of Angelo, that swift and springy youth ; they were slow and considered, and they kept on pausing.

' Some one who isn't used to hills,' thought Scrap.

The idea of going back to the house did not occur to her. She was afraid of nothing in life except love. Brigands or murderers as such held no terrors for the daughter of the Droitwiches ; she only would have been afraid of them if they left off being brigands and murderers and began instead to try and make love.

The next moment the footsteps turned the corner of her bit of path, and stood still.

'Getting his wind,' thought Scrap, not looking round.

Then as he—from the sounds of the steps she took them to belong to a man—did not move, she turned her head, and beheld with astonishment a person she had seen a good deal of lately in London, the well-known writer of amusing memoirs, Mr. Ferdinand Arundel.

She stared. Nothing in the way of being followed surprised her any more, but that he should have dis-covered where she was surprised her. Her mother had promised faithfully to tell no one.

'You ? ' she said, feeling betrayed. 'Here ? '

He came up to her and took off his hat. His fore-head beneath the hat was wet with the beads of un-accustomed climbing. He looked ashamed and entreat-ing, like a guilty but devoted dog.

'You must forgive me,' he said. 'Lady Droitwich told me where you were, and as I happened to be passing through on my way to Rome I thought I would get out at Mezzago and just look in and see how you were.'

'But—didn't my mother tell you I was doing a rest-cure ? '

' Yes. She did. And that's why I haven't intruded on you earlier in the day. I thought you would probably sleep all day, and wake up about now so as to be fed.'

' But——'

' I know. I've got nothing to say in excuse. I couldn't help myself.'

' This,' thought Scrap, ' comes of mother insisting on having authors to lunch, and me being so much more amiable in appearance than I really am.'

She had been amiable to Ferdinand Arundel; she liked him,—or rather she did not dislike him. He seemed a jovial, simple man, and had the eyes of a nice dog. Also, though it was evident that he admired her, he had not in London grabbed. There he had merely been a good-natured, harmless person of entertaining conversation, who helped to make luncheons agreeable. Now it appeared that he too was a grabber. Fancy following her out there,—daring to. Nobody else had. Perhaps her mother had given him the address because she considered him so absolutely harmless, and thought he might be useful and see her home.

Well, whatever he was he couldn't possibly give her the trouble an active young man like Mr. Briggs might give her. Mr. Briggs, infatuated, would be reckless, she felt, would stick at nothing, would lose his head publicly. She could imagine Mr. Briggs doing things with ropeladders, and singing all night under her window,—being really difficult and uncomfortable. Mr. Arundel hadn't the figure for any kind of recklessness. He had lived too long and too well. She was sure he couldn't sing, and wouldn't want to. He must be at least forty. How many good dinners could not a man have eaten by the time he was forty ? And if during that time instead of taking exercise he had sat writing books, he would quite naturally acquire the figure Mr. Arundel had in fact acquired—the figure rather for conversation than adventure.

Scrap, who had become melancholy at the sight of Briggs, became philosophical at the sight of Arundel. Here he was. She couldn't send him away till after dinner. He must be nourished.

This being so, she had better make the best of it, and do that with a good grace which anyhow wasn't to be avoided. Besides, he would be a temporary shelter from Mr. Briggs. She was at least acquainted with Ferdinand Arundel, and could hear news from him of her mother and her friends, and such talk would put up a defensive barrier at dinner between herself and the approaches of the other one. And it was only for one dinner, and he couldn't eat *her*.

She therefore prepared herself for friendliness. ' I'm to be fed,' she said, ignoring his last remark, ' at eight, and you must come up and be fed too. Sit down and get cool and tell me how everybody is.'

'May I really dine with you ? In these travelling things ? ' he said, wiping his forehead before sitting down beside her.

She was too lovely to be true, he thought. Just to look at her for an hour, just to hear her voice, was enough reward for his journey and his fears.

'Of course. I suppose you've left your fly in the village, and will be going on from Mezzago by the night train.'

'Or stay in Mezzago in an hotel and go on to-morrow. But tell me,' he said, gazing at the adorable profile, ' about yourself. London has been extraordinarily dull and empty. Lady Droitwich said you were with people here she didn't know. I hope they've been kind to you ? You look—well, as if your cure had done everything a cure should.'

'They've been very kind,' said Scrap. 'I got them out of an advertisement.'

'An advertisement ? '

'It's a good way, I find, to get friends. I'm fonder of one of these than I've been of anybody for years.'

'Really ? Who is it ? '

'You shall guess which of them it is when you see them. Tell me about mother. When did you see her

last ? We arranged not to write to each other unless
there was something special. I wanted to have a
month that was perfectly blank.'

'And now I've come and interrupted. I can't tell
you how ashamed I am—both of having done it and of
not having been able to help it.'

'Oh, but,' said Scrap quickly, for he could not have
come on a better day, when up there waiting and watching for her was, she knew, the enamoured Briggs, 'I'm
really very glad indeed to see you. Tell me about
mother.'

XX

SCRAP wanted to know so much about her mother that
Arundel had presently to invent. He would talk about
anything she wished if only he might be with her for a
while and see her and hear her, but he knew very little
of the Droitwiches and their friends really,—beyond
meeting them at those bigger functions where literature
is also represented, and amusing them at luncheons and
dinners, he knew very little of them really. To them
he had always remained Mr. Arundel ; no one called him
Ferdinand ; and he only knew the gossip also available
to the evening papers and the frequenters of clubs.   But
he was, however, good at inventing ; and as soon as he
had come to an end of first-hand knowledge, in order to
answer her inquiries and keep her there to himself he
proceeded to invent.   It was quite easy to fasten some
of the entertaining things he was constantly thinking
on to other people and pretend they were theirs.
Scrap, who had that affection for her parents which
warms in absence, was athirst for news, and became

more and more interested by the news he gradually imparted.

At first it was ordinary news.   He had met her mother here, and seen her there.   She looked very well ; she said so and so.   But presently the things Lady Droitwich had said took on an unusual quality : they became amusing.

' Mother said *that* ? ' Scrap interrupted, surprised.

And presently Lady Droitwich began to do amusing things as well as say them.

' *Mother* did that ? ' Scrap inquired, wide-eyed.

Arundel warmed to his work.   He fathered some of the most entertaining ideas he had lately had on to Lady Droitwich, and also any charming funny things that had been done—or might have been done, for he could imagine almost anything.

Scrap's eyes grew round with wonder and affectionate pride in her mother.   Why, but how funny—fancy mother.   What an old darling.   Did she really do that ?   How perfectly adorable of her.   And did she really say—but how wonderful of her to think of it.   What sort of a face did Lloyd George make ?

She laughed and laughed, and had a great longing to hug her mother, and the time flew, and it grew quite dusk, and it grew nearly dark, and Mr. Arundel still went on amusing her, and it was a quarter to eight before she suddenly remembered dinner.

' Oh, good heavens ! ' she exclaimed, jumping up.

' Yes.   It's late,' said Arundel.

' I'll go on quickly and send the maid to you.   I must run, or I'll never be ready in time——'

And she was gone up the path with the swiftness of a young, slender deer.

Arundel followed. He did not wish to arrive too hot, so had to go slowly. Fortunately he was near the top, and Francesca came down the pergola to pilot him indoors, and having shown him where he could wash she put him in the empty drawing-room to cool himself by the crackling wood fire.

He got as far away from the fire as he could, and stood in one of the deep window-recesses looking out at the distant lights of Mezzago. The drawing-room door was open, and the house was quiet with the hush that precedes dinner, when the inhabitants are all shut up in their rooms dressing. Briggs in his room was throwing away spoilt tie after spoilt tie ; Scrap in hers was hurrying into a black frock with a vague notion that Mr. Briggs wouldn't be able to see her so clearly in black ; Mrs. Fisher was fastening the lace shawl, which nightly transformed her day dress into her evening dress, with the brooch Ruskin had given her on her marriage, formed of two pearl lilies tied together by a blue enamel ribbon on which was written in gold letters *Esto perpetua* ; Mr. Wilkins was sitting on the edge of his bed brushing his wife's hair—thus far in this third week had he progressed in demonstrativeness—while she, for her part, sitting on a chair in front of him, put his studs in a clean shirt ; and Rose, ready dressed, sat at her window considering her day.

Rose was quite aware of what had happened to Mr. Briggs. If she had had any difficulty about it, Lotty would have removed it by the frank comments she made while she and Rose sat together after tea on the wall. Lotty was delighted at more love being introduced into San Salvatore, even if it were only one-sided, and said that when once Rose's husband was there she didn't suppose, now that Mrs. Fisher too had at last come unglued,—Rose protested at the expression, and Lotty retorted that it was in Keats,—there would be another place in the world more swarming with happiness than San Salvatore.

'Your husband,' said Lotty, swinging her feet, 'might be here quite soon, perhaps to-morrow evening if he starts at once, and there'll be a glorious final few days before we all go home refreshed for life. I don't believe any of us will ever be the same again—and I wouldn't be a bit surprised if Caroline doesn't end by

getting fond of the young man Briggs.   It's in the air.
You *have* to get fond of people here.'

Rose sat at her window thinking of these things.
Lotty's optimism . . . yet it had been justified by
Mr. Wilkins ; and look, too, at Mrs. Fisher.   If only it
would come true as well about Frederick !   For Rose,
who between lunch and tea had left off thinking about
Frederick, was now, between tea and dinner, thinking
of him harder than ever.

It had been funny and delightful, that little interlude
of admiration, but of course it couldn't go on once
Caroline appeared.   Rose knew her place.   She could
see as well as any one the unusual, the unique loveliness
of Lady Caroline.   How warm, though, things like
admiration and appreciation made one feel, how capable
of really deserving them, how different, how glowing.
They seemed to quicken unsuspected faculties into life.
She was sure she had been a thoroughly amusing woman
between lunch and tea, and a pretty one too.   She was
quite certain she had been pretty ; she saw it in Mr.
Briggs's eyes as clearly as in a looking-glass.   For a
brief space, she thought, she had been like a torpid fly
brought back to gay buzzing by the lighting of a fire
in a wintry room.   She still buzzed, she still tingled,
just at the remembrance.   What fun it had been, having
an admirer even for that little while.   No wonder people

liked admirers. They seemed, in some strange way, to make one come alive.

Although it was all over she still glowed with it and felt more exhilarated, more optimistic, more as Lotty probably constantly felt, than she had done since she was a girl. She dressed with care, though she knew Mr. Briggs would no longer see her, but it gave her pleasure to see how pretty, while she was about it, she could make herself look; and very nearly she stuck a crimson camellia in her hair down by her ear. She did hold it there for a minute, and it looked almost sinfully attractive and was exactly the colour of her mouth, but she took it out again with a smile and a sigh and put it in the proper place for flowers, which is water. She mustn't be silly, she thought. Think of the poor. Soon she would be back with them again, and what would a camellia behind her ear seem like then? Simply fantastic.

But on one thing she was determined : the first thing she would do when she got home would be to have it out with Frederick. If he didn't come to San Salvatore that is what she would do—the very first thing. Long ago she ought to have done this, but always she had been handicapped, when she tried to, by being so dreadfully fond of him and so much afraid that fresh wounds were going to be given her wretched, soft heart. But now let him wound her as much as he chose, as much as he possibly could, she would still have it out with him. Not that he ever intentionally wounded her ; she knew he never meant to, she knew he often had no idea of having done it. For a person who wrote books, thought Rose, Frederick didn't seem to have much imagination. Anyhow, she said to herself, getting up from the dressing-table, things couldn't go on like this. She would have it out with him. This separate life, this freezing loneliness, she had had enough of it. Why shouldn't she too be happy ? Why on earth —the energetic expression matched her mood of rebelliousness—shouldn't she too be loved and allowed to love ?

She looked at her little clock. Still ten minutes before dinner. Tired of staying in her bedroom she thought she would go on to Mrs. Fisher's battlements, which would be empty at this hour, and watch the moon rise out of the sea.

She went into the deserted upper hall with this intention, but was attracted on her way along it by the firelight shining through the open door of the drawing-room.

How gay it looked. The fire transformed the room. A dark, ugly room in the daytime, it was transformed just as she had been transformed by the warmth of—

no, she wouldn't be silly ; she would think of the poor ; the thought of them always brought her down to sobriety at once.

She peeped in. Firelight and flowers ; and outside the deep slits of windows hung the blue curtain of the night. How pretty. What a sweet place San Salvatore was. And that gorgeous lilac on the table— she must go and put her face in it . . .

But she never got to the lilac. She went one step towards it, and then stood still, for she had seen the figure looking out of the window in the farthest corner, and it was Frederick.

All the blood in Rose's body rushed to her heart and seemed to stop its beating.

Frederick. Come.

She stood quite still. He had not heard her. He did not turn round. She stood looking at him. The miracle had happened, and he had come.

She stood holding her breath. So he needed her, for he had come instantly. So he too must have been thinking, longing . . .

Her heart, which had seemed to stop beating, was suffocating her now, the way it raced along. Frederick did love her then,—he must love her, or why had he come ? Something, perhaps her absence, had made him turn to her, want her . . . and now the under-

standing she had made up her mind to have with him
would be quite—would be quite—easy——

Her thoughts wouldn't go on. Her mind stammered.
She couldn't think. She could only see and feel. She
didn't know how it had happened. It was a miracle.
God could do miracles. God had done this one. God
could—God could—could——

Her mind stammered again, and broke off.

'Frederick——' she tried to say; but no sound
came, or if it did the crackling of the fire covered
it up.

She must go nearer. She began to creep towards
him—softly, softly.

He did not move. He had not heard.

She stole nearer and nearer, and the fire crackled
and he heard nothing.

She stopped a moment, unable to breathe. She was
afraid. Suppose he—suppose he—oh, but he had come,
he had come.

She went on again, close up to him, and her heart
beat so loud that she thought he must hear it. And
couldn't he feel—didn't he know——

'Frederick,' she whispered, hardly able even to
whisper, choked by the beating of her heart.

He spun round on his heels.

'Rose!' he exclaimed, staring blankly.

But she did not see his stare, for her arms were round his neck, and her cheek was against his, and she was murmuring, her lips on his ear, 'I knew you would come—in my very heart I always, always knew you would come——'

XXI

Now Frederick was not the man to hurt anything if he could help it; besides, he was completely bewildered. Not only was his wife here—here, of all places in the world—but she was clinging to him as she had not clung for years, and murmuring love, and welcoming him. If she welcomed him she must have been expecting him. Strange as this was, it was the only thing in the situation which was evident,—that, and the softness of her cheek against his, and the long-forgotten sweet smell of her.

Frederick was bewildered. But not being the man to hurt anything if he could help it he too put his arms round her, and having put them round her he also kissed her; and presently he was kissing her almost as tenderly as she was kissing him; and presently he was kissing her quite as tenderly; and again presently he was kissing her more tenderly, and just as if he had never left off.

He was bewildered, but he still could kiss. It seemed curiously natural to be doing it. It made him feel as

329

if he were thirty again instead of forty, and Rose were
his Rose of twenty, the Rose he had so much adored
before she began to weigh what he did with her idea of
right, and the balance went against him, and she had
turned strange, and stony, and more and more shocked,
and oh, so lamentable. He couldn't get at her in those
days at all; she wouldn't, she couldn't understand.
She kept on referring everything to what she called
God's eyes—in God's eyes it couldn't be right, it wasn't
right. Her miserable face,—whatever her principles did
for her they didn't make her happy,—her little miserable
face, twisted with effort to be patient, had been at last
more than he could bear to see, and he had kept away
as much as he could. She never ought to have been the
daughter of a low-church rector—narrow devil; she
was quite unfitted to stand up against such an up-
bringing.

What had happened, why she was here, why she was
his Rose again, passed his comprehension; and meanwhile, and until such time as he understood, he still
could kiss. In fact he could not stop kissing; and it
was he now who began to murmur, to say love things
in her ear under the hair that smelt so sweet and tickled
him just as he remembered it used to tickle him.

And as he held her close to his heart and her arms
were soft round his neck, he felt stealing over him a

delicious sense of—at first he didn't know what it was, this delicate, pervading warmth, and then he recognised it as security. Yes; security. No need now to be ashamed of his figure, and to make jokes about it so as to forestall other people's and show he didn't mind it; no need now to be ashamed of getting hot going up hills, or to torment himself with pictures of how he probably appeared to beautiful young women,—how middle-aged, how absurd in his inability to keep away from them. Rose cared nothing for such things. With her he was safe. To her he was her lover, as he used to be; and she would never notice or mind any of the ignoble changes that getting older had made in him and would go on making more and more.

Frederick continued, therefore, with greater and greater warmth and growing delight to kiss his wife, and the mere holding of her in his arms caused him to forget everything else. How could he, for instance, remember or think of Lady Caroline, to mention only one of the complications with which his situation bristled, when here was his sweet wife, miraculously restored to him, whispering with her cheek against his in the dearest, most romantic words how much she loved him, how terribly she had missed him? He did for one brief instant, for even in moments of love there are brief instants of lucid thought, recognise the immense

power of the woman present and being actually held
compared to that of the woman, however beautiful, who
is somewhere else, but that is as far as he got towards
remembering Scrap ; no farther.   She was like a dream,
fleeing before the morning light.

'When did you start ? ' murmured Rose, her mouth
on his ear.   She couldn't let him go ; not even to talk
she couldn't let him go.

'Yesterday morning,' murmured Frederick, holding
her close.   He couldn't let her go either.

'Oh—the very instant then,' murmured Rose.

This was cryptic, but Frederick said, 'Yes, the very
instant,' and kissed her neck.

'How quickly my letter got to you,' murmured Rose,
whose eyes were shut in the excess of her happiness.

'Didn't it,' said Frederick, who felt like shutting
his eyes himself.

So there had been a letter.   Soon, no doubt, light
would be vouchsafed him, and meanwhile this was so
strangely, touchingly sweet, this holding his Rose to
his heart again after all the years, that he couldn't
bother to try to guess anything.   Oh, he had been happy
during these years, because it was not in him to be
unhappy ; besides, how many interests life had had to
offer him, how many friends, how much success, how
many women only too willing to help him to blot out

the thought of the altered, petrified, pitiful little wife at home who wouldn't spend his money, who was appalled by his books, who drifted away and away from him, and always if he tried to have it out with her asked him with patient obstinacy what he thought the things he wrote and lived by looked in the eyes of God. 'No one,' she said once, 'should ever write a book God wouldn't like to read. That is the test, Frederick.' And he had laughed hysterically, burst into a great shriek of laughter, and rushed out of the house, away from her solemn little face—away from her pathetic, solemn little face. . . .

But this Rose was his youth again, the best part of his life, the part of it that had had all the visions in it and all the hopes. How they had dreamed together, he and she, before he struck that vein of memoirs ; how they had planned, and laughed, and loved. They had lived for a while in the very heart of poetry. After the happy days came the happy nights, the happy, happy nights, with her asleep close against his heart, with her when he woke in the morning still close against his heart, for they hardly moved in their deep, happy sleep. It was wonderful to have it all come back to him at the touch of her, at the feel of her face against his,—wonderful that she should be able to give him back his youth.

'Sweetheart—sweetheart,' he murmured, overcome by remembrance, clinging to her now in his turn.

'Beloved husband,' she breathed,—the bliss of it —the sheer bliss . . .

Briggs, coming in a few minutes before the gong went on the chance that Lady Caroline might be there, was much astonished. He had supposed Rose Arbuthnot was a widow, and he still supposed it; so that he was much astonished.

'Well I'm damned,' thought Briggs, quite clearly and distinctly, for the shock of what he saw in the window startled him so much that for a moment he was shaken free of his own confused absorption.

Aloud he said, very red, 'Oh I say—I beg your pardon'—and then stood hesitating, and wondering whether he oughtn't to go back to his bedroom again.

If he had said nothing they would not have noticed he was there, but when he begged their pardon Rose turned and looked at him as one looks who is trying to remember, and Frederick looked at him too without at first quite seeing him.

They didn't seem, thought Briggs, to mind or to be at all embarrassed. He couldn't be her brother; no brother ever brought that look into a woman's face. It was very awkward. If they didn't mind, he did. It upset him to come across his Madonna forgetting herself.

' Is this one of your friends ? ' Frederick was able after an instant to ask Rose, who made no attempt to introduce the young man standing awkwardly in front of them but continued to gaze at him with a kind of abstracted, radiant goodwill.

' It's Mr. Briggs,' said Rose, recognising him.   ' This is my husband,' she added.

And Briggs, shaking hands, just had time to think how surprising it was to have a husband when you were a widow before the gong sounded, and Lady Caroline would be there in a minute, and he ceased to be able to think at all, and merely became a thing with its eyes fixed on the door.

Through the door immediately entered, in what seemed to him an endless procession, first Mrs. Fisher, very stately in her evening lace shawl and brooch, who when she saw him at once relaxed into smiles and benignity, only to stiffen, however, when she caught sight of the stranger ;   then Mr. Wilkins, cleaner and neater and more carefully dressed and brushed than any man on earth ;   and then, tying something hurriedly as she came, Mrs. Wilkins ;   and then nobody.

Lady Caroline was late.   Where was she ?   Had she heard the gong ?   Oughtn't it to be beaten again ?   Suppose she didn't come to dinner after all. . . .

Briggs went cold.

'Introduce me,' said Frederick on Mrs. Fisher's entrance, touching Rose's elbow.

'My husband,' said Rose, holding him by the hand,
her face exquisite.

'This,' thought Mrs. Fisher, 'must now be the last
of the husbands, unless Lady Caroline produces one
from up her sleeve.'

But she received him graciously, for he certainly
looked exactly like a husband, not at all like one of
those people who go about abroad pretending they are
husbands when they are not, and said she supposed
he had come to accompany his wife home at the end of
the month, and remarked that now the house would be
completely full. 'So that,' she added, smiling at
Briggs, 'we shall at last really be getting our money's
worth.'

Briggs grinned automatically, because he was just
able to realise that somebody was being playful with
him, but he had not heard her and he did not look at
her. Not only were his eyes fixed on the door but his
whole body was concentrated on it.

Introduced in his turn, Mr. Wilkins was most hospitable and called Frederick 'sir.'

'Well, sir,' said Mr. Wilkins heartily, 'here we are, here
we are '—and having gripped his hand with an understanding that only wasn't mutual because Arbuthnot

did not yet know what he was in for in the way of trouble, he looked at him as a man should, squarely in the eyes, and allowed his look to convey as plainly as a look can that in him would be found staunchness, integrity, reliability,—in fact a friend in need. Mrs. Arbuthnot was very much flushed, Mr. Wilkins noticed. He had not seen her flushed like that before. 'Well, I'm their man,' he thought.

Lotty's greeting was effusive. It was done with both hands. 'Didn't I tell you ? ' she laughed to Rose over her shoulder while Frederick was shaking her hands in both his.

' What did you tell her ? ' asked Frederick, in order to say something. The way they were all welcoming him was confusing. They had evidently all expected him, not only Rose.

The sandy but agreeable young woman didn't answer his question, but looked extraordinarily pleased to see him. Why should she be extraordinarily pleased to see him ?

' What a delightful place this is,' said Frederick, confused, and making the first remark that occurred to him.

' It's a tub of love,' said the sandy young woman earnestly ; which confused him more than ever.

And his confusion became excessive at the next words he heard,—spoken, these, by the old lady, who said :

' We won't wait. Lady Caroline is always late,'—for
he only then, on hearing her name, really and properly
remembered Lady Caroline, and the thought of her
confused him to excess.

He went into the dining-room like a man in a dream.
He had come out to this place to see Lady Caroline,
and had told her so. He had even told her in his
fatuousness—it was true, but how fatuous—that he
hadn't been able to help coming. She didn't know he
was married. She thought his name was Arundel.
Everybody in London thought his name was Arundel.
He had used it and written under it so long that he
almost thought it was himself. In the short time since
she had left him on the seat in the garden, where he
told her he had come because he couldn't help it, he had
found Rose again, had passionately embraced and been
embraced, and had forgotten Lady Caroline. It would
be an extraordinary piece of good fortune if Lady
Caroline's being late meant she was tired or bored
and would not come to dinner at all. Then he could
—no, he couldn't. He turned a deeper red even than
usual, he being a man of full habit and red anyhow,
at the thought of such cowardice. No, he couldn't go
away after dinner and catch his train and disappear
to Rome; not unless, that is, Rose came with him.
But even so, what a running away. No, he couldn't.

When they got to the dining-room Mrs. Fisher went to the head of the table—was this Mrs. Fisher's house ? he asked himself. He didn't know; he didn't know anything—and Rose, who in her earlier days of defying Mrs. Fisher had taken the other end as her place, for after all no one could say by looking at a table which was its top and which its bottom, led Frederick to the seat next to her. If only, he thought, he could have been alone with Rose ; just five minutes more alone with Rose, so that he could have asked her——

But probably he wouldn't have asked her anything, and only gone on kissing her.

He looked round. The sandy young woman was telling the man they called Briggs to go and sit beside Mrs. Fisher—was the house, then, the sandy young woman's and not Mrs. Fisher's ? He didn't know; he didn't know anything—and she herself sat down on Rose's other side, so that she was opposite him, Frederick, and next to the genial man who had said ' Here we are,' when it was only too evident that there they were indeed.

Next to Frederick, and between him and Briggs, was an empty chair : Lady Caroline's. No more than Lady Caroline knew of the presence in Frederick's life of Rose was Rose aware of the presence in Frederick's life of Lady Caroline. What would each think ? He

didn't know; he didn't know anything. Yes, he did
know something, and that was that his wife had made
it up with him,—suddenly, miraculously, unaccountably,
and divinely. Beyond that he knew nothing. The
situation was one with which he felt he could not cope.
It must lead him whither it would. He could only
drift.

In silence Frederick ate his soup, and the eyes, the
large expressive eyes of the young woman opposite,
were on him, he could feel, with a growing look in them
of inquiry. They were, he could see, very intelligent
and attractive eyes, and full, apart from the inquiry,
of goodwill. Probably she thought he ought to talk,—
but if she knew everything she wouldn't think so.
Briggs didn't talk either. Briggs seemed uneasy. What
was the matter with Briggs? And Rose too didn't
talk, but then that was natural. She never had been
a talker. She had the loveliest expression on her face.
How long would it be on it after Lady Caroline's entrance?
He didn't know; he didn't know anything.

But the genial man on Mr. Fisher's left was talking
enough for everybody. That fellow ought to have been
a parson. Pulpits were the place for a voice like his;
it would get him a bishopric in six months. He was
explaining to Briggs, who shuffled about in his seat—
why did Briggs shuffle about in his seat?—that he must

have come out by the same train as Arbuthnot, and when Briggs, who said nothing, wriggled in apparent dissent, he undertook to prove it to him, and did prove it to him in long clear sentences.

' Who's the man with the voice ? ' Frederick asked Rose in a whisper; and the young woman opposite, whose ears appeared to have the quickness of hearing of wild creatures, answered, ' He's my husband.'

' Then by all the rules,' said Frederick pleasantly, pulling himself together, ' you oughtn't to be sitting next to him.'

' But I want to. I like sitting next to him. I didn't before I came here.'

Frederick could think of nothing to say to this, so he only smiled generally.

' It's this place,' she said, nodding at him. ' It makes one understand. You've no idea what a lot you'll understand before you've done here.'

' I'm sure I hope so,' said Frederick with real fervour.

The soup was taken away, and the fish was brought. Briggs, on the other side of the empty chair, seemed more uneasy than ever. What was the matter with Briggs ? Didn't he like fish ?

Frederick wondered what Briggs would do in the way of fidgets if he were in his own situation. Frederick kept on wiping his moustache, and was not able to look up from his plate, but that was as much as he showed of what he was feeling.

Though he didn't look up he felt the eyes of the young woman opposite raking him like searchlights, and Rose's eyes were on him too, he knew, but they rested on him unquestioningly, beautifully, like a benediction. How long would they go on doing that once Lady Caroline was there? He didn't know; he didn't know anything.

He wiped his moustache for the twentieth unnecessary time, and could not quite keep his hand steady, and the young woman opposite saw his hand not being quite steady, and her eyes raked him persistently. Why did her eyes rake him persistently? He didn't know; he didn't know anything.

Then Briggs leapt to his feet. What was the matter with Briggs? Oh—yes—quite: she had come.

Frederick wiped his moustache and got up too. He was in for it now. Absurd, fantastic situation. Well, whatever happened he could only drift,—drift, and look like an ass to Lady Caroline, the most absolute as well as deceitful ass,—an ass who was also a reptile, for she might well think he had been mocking her out in the garden when he said, no doubt in a shaking voice— fool and ass—that he had come because he couldn't help it; while as for what he would look like to his

Rose—when Lady Caroline introduced him to her—
when Lady Caroline introduced him as her friend whom
she had invited in to dinner—well, God alone knew that.

He, therefore, as he got up wiped his moustache for
the last time before the catastrophe.

But he was reckoning without Scrap.

That accomplished and experienced young woman
slipped into the chair Briggs was holding for her, and
on Lotty's leaning across eagerly, and saying before
any one else could get a word in, ' Just fancy, Caroline,
how quickly Rose's husband has got here ! ' turned to
him without so much as the faintest shadow of surprise
on her face, and held out her hand, and smiled like a
young angel, and said, ' And me late your very first
evening.'

The daughter of the Droitwiches. . . .

THAT evening was the evening of the full moon. The garden was an enchanted place where all the flowers seemed white. The lilies, the daphnes, the orange-blossom, the white stocks, the white pinks, the white roses—you could see these as plainly as in the daytime ; but the coloured flowers existed only as fragrance.

The three younger women sat on the low wall at the end of the top garden after dinner, Rose a little apart from the others, and watched the enormous moon moving slowly over the place where Shelley had lived his last months just on a hundred years before. The sea quivered along the path of the moon. The stars winked and trembled. The mountains were misty blue out-lines, with little clusters of lights shining through from little clusters of homes. In the garden the plants stood quite still, straight and unstirred by the smallest ruffle of air. Through the glass doors the dining-room, with its candle-lit table and brilliant flowers—nasturtiums and marigolds that night—glowed like some magic cave

of colour, and the three men smoking round it looked
strangely animated figures seen from the silence, the
huge cool calm of outside.

Mrs. Fisher had gone to the drawing-room and the
fire. Scrap and Lotty, their faces upturned to the sky,
said very little and in whispers. Rose said nothing.
Her face too was upturned. She was looking at the
umbrella pine, which had been smitten into something
glorious, silhouetted against stars. Every now and
then Scrap's eyes lingered on Rose; so did Lotty's.
For Rose was lovely. Anywhere at that moment,
among all the well-known beauties, she would have been
lovely. Nobody could have put her in the shade, blown
out her light that evening; she was too evidently shining.

Lotty bent close to Scrap's ear, and whispered.
' Love,' she whispered.

Scrap nodded. ' Yes,' she said, under her breath.

She was obliged to admit it. You only had to look
at Rose to know that here was Love.

' There's nothing like it,' whispered Lotty.

Scrap was silent.

' It's a great thing,' whispered Lotty after a pause,
during which they both watched Rose's upturned face,
' to get on with one's loving. Perhaps you can tell me
of anything else in the world that works such wonders.'

But Scrap couldn't tell her; and if she could have,

what a night to begin arguing in. This was a night
for——

She pulled herself up. Love again. It was everywhere. There was no getting away from it. She had
come to this place to get away from it, and here was
everybody in its different stages. Even Mrs. Fisher
seemed to have been brushed by one of the many
feathers of Love's wing, and at dinner was different,—
full of concern because Mr. Briggs wouldn't eat, and her
face when she turned to him all soft with motherliness.

Scrap looked up at the pine-tree motionless among
stars. Beauty made you love, and love made you
beautiful. . . .

She pulled her wrap closer round her with a gesture
of defence, of keeping out and off. She didn't want to
grow sentimental. Difficult not to, here ; the marvellous night stole in through all one's chinks, and
brought in with it, whether one wanted them or not,
enormous feelings,—feelings one couldn't manage, great
things about death and time and waste ; glorious and
devastating things, magnificent and bleak, at once
rapture and terror and immense, heart-cleaving longing.
She felt small and dreadfully alone. She felt uncovered
and defenceless. Instinctively she pulled her wrap
closer. With this thing of chiffon she tried to protect
herself from the eternities.

' I suppose,' whispered Lotty, ' Rose's husband seems to you just an ordinary, good-natured, middle-aged man.'

Scrap brought her gaze down from the stars and looked at Lotty a moment while she focussed her mind again.

' Just a rather red, rather round man,' whispered Lotty.

Scrap bowed her head.

' He isn't,' whispered Lotty. ' Rose sees through all that. That's mere trimmings. She sees what we can't see, because she loves him.'

Always love.

Scrap got up, and winding herself very tightly in her wrap moved away to her day corner, and sat down there alone on the wall and looked out across the other sea, the sea where the sun had gone down, the sea with the far-away dim shadow stretching into it which was France.

Yes, love worked wonders, and Mr. Arundel—she couldn't at once get used to his other name—was to Rose Love itself; but it also worked inverted wonders, it didn't invariably, as she well knew, transfigure people into saints and angels. Grievously indeed did it sometimes do the opposite. She had had it in her life applied to her to excess. If it had let her alone, if it had at least been moderate and infrequent, she might, she thought, have turned out a quite decent, generous-minded, kindly, human being. And what was she, thanks to this love Lotty talked so much about ? Scrap searched for a just description. She was a spoilt, a sour, a suspicious, and a selfish spinster.

The glass doors of the dining-room opened, and the three men came out into the garden, Mr. Wilkins's voice flowing along in front of them. He appeared to be doing all the talking ; the other two were saying nothing.

Perhaps she had better go back to Lotty and Rose ; it would be tiresome to be discovered and hemmed into that *cul-de-sac* by Mr. Briggs.

She got up reluctantly, for she considered it unpardonable of Mr. Briggs to force her to move about like this, to force her out of any place she wished to sit in ; and she emerged from the daphne bushes feeling like some gaunt, stern figure of just resentment and wishing that she looked as gaunt and stern as she felt ; so would she have struck repugnance into the soul of Mr. Briggs, and been free of him. But she knew she didn't look like that, however hard she might try. At dinner his hand shook when he drank, and he couldn't speak to her without flushing scarlet and then going pale, and Mrs. Fisher's eyes had sought hers with the entreaty of one who asks that her only son may not be hurt.

How could a human being, thought Scrap, frowning as she issued forth from her corner, how could a man made in God's image behave so; and he fitted for better things she was sure, with his youth, his attractiveness, and his brains. He had brains. She had examined him cautiously whenever at dinner Mrs. Fisher forced him to turn away to answer her, and she was sure he had brains. Also he had character; there was something noble about his head, about the shape of his forehead,—noble and kind. All the more deplorable that he should allow himself to be infatuated by a mere outside, and waste any of his strength, any of his peace of mind, hanging round just a woman-thing. If only he could see right through her, see through all her skin and stuff, he would be cured, and she might go on sitting undisturbed on this wonderful night by herself.

Just beyond the daphne bushes she met Frederick, hurrying.

'I was determined to find you first,' he said, ' before I go to Rose.' And he added quickly, ' I want to kiss your shoes.'

'Do you?' said Scrap, smiling. 'Then I must go and put on my new ones. These aren't nearly good enough.'

She felt immensely well-disposed towards Frederick. He, at least, would grab no more. His grabbing days, so sudden and so brief, were done. Nice man ; agreeable man. She now definitely liked him. Clearly he had been getting into some sort of a tangle, and she was grateful to Lotty for stopping her in time at dinner from saying something hopelessly complicating. But whatever he had been getting into he was out of it now ; his face and Rose's face had the same light in them.

' I shall adore you for ever now,' said Frederick.

Scrap smiled. ' Shall you ? ' she said.

' I adored you before because of your beauty. Now I adore you because you're not only as beautiful as a dream but as decent as a man.'

Scrap laughed. ' Am I ? ' she said, amused.

' When the impetuous young woman,' Frederick went on, ' the blessedly impetuous young woman, blurted out in the nick of time that I am Rose's husband, you behaved exactly as a man would have behaved to his friend.'

' Did I ? ' said Scrap, her enchanting dimple very evident.

' It's the rarest, most precious of combinations,' said Frederick, ' to be a woman and have the loyalty of a man.'

' Is it ? ' smiled Scrap, a little wistfully. These were indeed handsome compliments. If only she were really like that. . . .

'And I want to kiss your shoes.'

'Won't this save trouble?' she asked, holding out her hand.

He took it and swiftly kissed it, and was hurrying away again. 'Bless you,' he said as he went.

'Where is your luggage?' Scrap called after him.

'Oh, Lord, yes——' said Frederick, pausing. 'It's at the station.'

'I'll send for it.'

He disappeared through the bushes. She went indoors to give the order; and this is how it happened that Domenico, for the second time that evening, found himself journeying into Mezzago and wondering as he went.

Then, having made the necessary arrangements for the perfect happiness of these two people, she came slowly out into the garden again, very much absorbed in thought. Love seemed to bring happiness to everybody but herself. It had certainly got hold of everybody there, in its different varieties, except herself. Poor Mr. Briggs had been got hold of by its least dignified variety. Poor Mr. Briggs. He was a disturbing problem, and his going away next day wouldn't, she was afraid, solve him.

When she reached the others Mr. Arundel—she kept on forgetting that he wasn't Mr. Arundel—was already, his arm through Rose's, going off with her, probably to the greater seclusion of the lower garden. No doubt they had a great deal to say to each other ; something had gone wrong between them, and had suddenly been put right. San Salvatore, Lotty would say, San Salvatore working its spell of happiness. She could quite believe in its spell. Even she was happier there than she had been for ages and ages. The only person who would go empty away would be Mr. Briggs.

Poor Mr. Briggs. When she came in sight of the group he looked much too nice and boyish not to be happy. It seemed out of the picture that the owner of the place, the person to whom they owed all this, should be the only one to go away from it unblessed.

Compunction seized Scrap. What very pleasant days she had spent in his house, lying in his garden, enjoying his flowers, loving his views, using his things, being comfortable, being rested,—recovering, in fact. She had had the most leisured, peaceful, and thoughtful time of her life ; and all really thanks to him. Oh, she knew she paid him some ridiculous small sum a week, out of all proportion to the benefits she got in exchange, but what was that in the balance ? And wasn't it entirely thanks to him that she had come across Lotty ? Never else would she and Lotty have met ; never else would she have known her.

Compunction laid its quick, warm hand on Scrap. Impulsive gratitude flooded her. She went straight up to Briggs.

'I owe you so *much*,' she said, overcome by the sudden realisation of all she did owe him, and ashamed of her churlishness in the afternoon and at dinner. Of course he hadn't known she was being churlish. Of course her disagreeable inside was camouflaged as usual by the chance arrangement of her outside ; but she knew it. She was churlish. She had been churlish to everybody for years. Any penetrating eye, thought Scrap, any really penetrating eye, would see her for what she was,—a spoilt, a sour, a suspicious and a selfish spinster.

'I owe you so *much*,' therefore said Scrap earnestly, walking straight up to Briggs, humbled by these thoughts.

He looked at her in wonder. '*You* owe *me* ? ' he said. 'But it's I who—I who——' he stammered. To see her there in his garden . . . nothing in it, no white flower, was whiter, more exquisite.

'Please,' said Scrap, still more earnestly, 'won't you clear your mind of everything except just truth ? You don't owe me anything. How should you ? '

'I don't owe you anything ? ' echoed Briggs. 'Why, I owe you my first sight of—of——'

'Oh, for goodness sake—for *goodness* sake,' said
Scrap entreatingly, 'do, please, be ordinary. Don't be
humble. Why should you be humble ? It's ridiculous
of you to be humble. You're worth fifty of me.'

'Unwise,' thought Mr. Wilkins, who was standing
there too, while Lotty sat on the wall. He was surprised, he was concerned, he was shocked that Lady
Caroline should thus encourage Briggs. 'Unwise—
very,' thought Mr. Wilkins, shaking his head.

Briggs's condition was so bad already that the only
course to take with him was to repel him utterly, Mr.
Wilkins considered. No half measures were the least
use with Briggs, and kindliness and familiar talk would
only be misunderstood by the unhappy youth. The
daughter of the Droitwiches could not really, it was
impossible to suppose it, desire to encourage him.
Briggs was all very well, but Briggs was Briggs ; his
name alone proved that. Probably Lady Caroline did
not quite appreciate the effect of her voice and face,
and how between them they made otherwise ordinary
words seem—well, encouraging. But these words were
not quite ordinary ; she had not, he feared, sufficiently
pondered them. Indeed and indeed she needed an
adviser,—some sagacious, objective counsellor like himself. There she was, standing before Briggs almost
holding out her hands to him. Briggs of course ought

to be thanked, for they were having a most delightful holiday in his house, but not thanked to excess and not by Lady Caroline alone. That very evening he had been considering the presentation to him next day of a round robin of collective gratitude on his departure ; but he should not be thanked like this, in the moonlight, in the garden, by the lady he was so manifestly infatuated with.

Mr. Wilkins therefore, desiring to assist Lady Caroline out of this situation by swiftly applied tact, said with much heartiness : ' It is most proper, Briggs, that you should be thanked. You will please allow me to add my expressions of indebtedness, and those of my wife, to Lady Caroline's. We ought to have proposed a vote of thanks to you at dinner. You should have been toasted. There certainly ought to have been some——'

But Briggs took no notice of him whatever ; he simply continued to look at Lady Caroline as though she were the first woman he had ever seen. Neither, Mr. Wilkins observed, did Lady Caroline take any notice of him ; she too continued to look at Briggs, and with that odd air of almost appeal. Most unwise. Most.

Lotty, on the other hand, took too much notice of him, choosing this moment when Lady Caroline needed

special support and protection, to get up off the wall
and put her arm through his and draw him away.

'I want to tell you something, Mellersh,' said Lotty
at this juncture, getting up.

'Presently,' said Mr. Wilkins, waving her aside.

'No—now,' said Lotty ; and she drew him away.

He went with extreme reluctance. Briggs should be
given no rope at all—not an inch.

'Well—what is it ? ' he asked impatiently, as she
led him towards the house. Lady Caroline ought not
to be left like that, exposed to annoyance.

'Oh, but she isn't,' Lotty assured him, just as if
he had said this aloud, which he certainly had not.
'Caroline is perfectly all right.'

'Not at all all right. That young Briggs is——'

'Of course he is. What did you expect ? Let's go
indoors to the fire and Mrs. Fisher. She's all by herself.'

'I cannot,' said Mr. Wilkins, trying to draw back,
'leave Lady Caroline alone in the garden.'

'Don't be silly, Mellersh—she isn't alone. Besides,
I want to tell you something.'

'Well tell me, then.'

'Indoors.'

With a reluctance that increased at every step
Mr. Wilkins was taken farther and farther away from
Lady Caroline. He believed in his wife now and trusted

her, but on this occasion he thought she was making a terrible mistake. In the drawing-room sat Mrs. Fisher by the fire, and it certainly was to Mr. Wilkins, who preferred rooms and fires after dark to gardens and moonlight, more agreeable to be in there than out-of-doors if he could have brought Lady Caroline safely in with him. As it was, he went in with extreme reluctance.

Mrs. Fisher, her hands folded on her lap, was doing nothing, merely gazing fixedly into the fire. The lamp was arranged conveniently for reading, but she was not reading. Her great dead friends did not seem worth reading that night. They always said the same things now,—over and over again they said the same things, and nothing new was to be got out of them any more for ever. No doubt they were greater than any one was now, but they had this immense disadvantage, that they were dead. Nothing further was to be expected of them ; while of the living, what might one not still expect ? She craved for the living, the developing,—the crystallised and finished wearied her. She was thinking that if only she had had a son—a son like Mr. Briggs, a dear boy like that, going on, unfolding, alive, affectionate, taking care of her and loving her. . . .

The look on her face gave Mrs. Wilkins's heart a little twist when she saw it. 'Poor old dear,' she thought, all the loneliness of age flashing upon her, the loneliness of having outstayed one's welcome in the world, of being in it only on sufferance, the complete loneliness of the old childless woman who has failed to make friends. It did seem that people could only be really happy in pairs—any sorts of pairs, not in the least necessarily lovers, but pairs of friends, pairs of mothers and children, of brothers and sisters—and where was the other half of Mrs. Fisher's pair going to be found ?

Mrs. Wilkins thought she had perhaps better kiss her again. The kissing in the afternoon had been a great success ; she knew it, she had instantly felt Mrs. Fisher's reaction to it. So she crossed over and bent down and kissed her and said cheerfully, ' We've come in——' which indeed was evident.

This time Mrs. Fisher actually put up her hand and held Mrs. Wilkins's cheek against her own,—this living thing, full of affection, of warm, racing blood ; and as she did this she felt safe with the strange creature, sure that she who herself did unusual things so naturally would take the action quite as a matter of course, and not embarrass her by being surprised.

Mrs. Wilkins was not at all surprised ; she was delighted. ' I believe *I'm* the other half of her pair,' flashed into her mind. ' I believe it's me, positively me, going to be fast friends with Mrs. Fisher ! '

Her face when she lifted her head was full of laughter. Too extraordinary, the developments produced by San Salvatore. She and Mrs. Fisher . . . but she *saw* them being fast friends.

' Where are the others ? ' asked Mrs. Fisher. ' Thank you—dear,' she added, as Mrs. Wilkins put a footstool under her feet, a footstool obviously needed, Mrs. Fisher's legs being short.

' I see myself throughout the years,' thought Mrs. Wilkins, her eyes dancing, ' bringing footstools to Mrs. Fisher. . . .'

' The Roses,' she said, straightening herself, ' have gone into the lower garden—I *think* love-making.'

' The Roses ? '

' The Fredericks, then, if you like. They're completely merged and indistinguishable.'

' Why not say the Arbuthnots, my dear ? ' said Mr. Wilkins.

' Very well, Mellersh—the Arbuthnots. And the Carolines——'

Both Mr. Wilkins and Mrs. Fisher started. Mr. Wilkins, usually in such complete control of himself, started even more than Mrs. Fisher, and for the first time since his arrival felt angry with his wife.

' Really——' he began indignantly.

' Very well, Mellersh—the Briggses, then.

'The Briggses!' cried Mr. Wilkins, now very angry indeed; for the implication was to him a most outrageous insult to the entire race of Desters,—dead Desters, living Desters, and Desters still harmless because they were yet unborn. 'Really——'

'I'm sorry, Mellersh,' said Mrs. Wilkins, pretending meekness, 'if you don't like it.'

'Like it! You've taken leave of your senses. Why, they've never set eyes on each other before to-day.'

'That's true. But that's why they're able now to go ahead.'

'Go ahead!' Mr. Wilkins could only echo the outrageous words.

'I'm sorry, Mellersh,' said Mrs. Wilkins again, 'if you don't like it, but——'

Her grey eyes shone, and her face rippled with the light and conviction that had so much surprised Rose the first time they met.

'It's useless minding,' she said. 'I shouldn't struggle if I were you. Because——'

She stopped, and looked first at one alarmed solemn face and then at the other, and laughter as well as light flickered and danced over her.

'I *see* them being the Briggses,' finished Mrs. Wilkins.

That last week the syringa came out at San Salvatore, and all the acacias flowered. No one had noticed how many acacias there were till one day the garden was full of a new scent, and there were the delicate trees, the lovely successors to the wistaria, hung all over among their trembling leaves with blossom. To lie under an acacia tree that last week and look up through the branches at its frail leaves and white flowers quivering against the blue of the sky, while the least movement of the air shook down their scent, was a great happiness. Indeed, the whole garden dressed itself gradually towards the end in white, and grew more and more scented. There were the lilies, as vigorous as ever, and the white stocks and white pinks and white banksia roses, and the syringa and the jessamine, and at last the crowning fragrance of the acacias. When, on the first of May, everybody went away, even after they had got to the bottom of the hill and passed through the iron gates out into the village they still could smell the acacias.

THE END